Kicking Asbestos
A Novel

Alan Devey is the Author of two previous novels: Wallfloweresque and The Spirit of Nagasaki, and the Co-Creator of satirical webzine Home Defence (www.homedefenceuk.com).

Published in 2010 via Lulu.com

ISBN: 978-1-4457-5736-0

Copyright © Alan Devey 2010

The right of Alan Devey to be identified as the author of this work has been asserted by him in accordance with the Copyright, Designs and Patents Act 1988.

All rights reserved. No part of this publication may be reproduced, stored in or introduced into a retrieval system, or transmitted, in any form, or by any means (electronic, mechanical, photocopying, recording or otherwise) without prior written permission.

This book is sold subject to the condition that it shall not, by way of trade or otherwise, be lent, re-sold, hired out, or otherwise circulated without prior consent in any form of binding other than that in which it is published and without a similar condition being imposed on the subsequent purchaser.

Cover design by Chris Perry.

Lyrics taken from 'The Factory' by Warren Zevon, from the album 'Sentimental Hygiene', published by Zevon Music Inc. (BMI), © 1987 Virgin Records America Inc.

To H

> Early in the morning I feel a chill
> The factory whistle blows loud and shrill
> I'd kill my wife or she'd kill me
> But we gotta go to work in the factory
> Six days a week in the factory
> Up early in the morning at the factory
> I've been working in the factory
> Johnny, I've been working in the factory
> Kicking asbestos in the factory
> Breathing that plastic in the factory
> Punching out Chryslers in the factory
> Making polyvinyl chloride in the factory
>
> — Warren Zevon, *The Factory*

Chapter One

We eventually got moving about ten that morning, after those who'd been delayed finally made it to Docklands. There were the usual glitches on the tube, a smattering of security alerts flashing red across the network, a join-the-dots pattern of false alarms. The double-decker I rode from the east had stuttered along in a manner too irregular to be described as a crawl, navigating a circuitous path through logjams that were finally revealed to be the result of roadworks, some kind of police diversion, then a motorcyclist knocked off his bike. The man was sprawled motionless by his collapsed machine, helmeted in the gutter, a kind of swatted weakling defeated by the more powerful carapaces honking nearby.

  Despite these hold ups I made it to our rendezvous point in good time, a positive consequence of that interrupted sleep I'd been experiencing for weeks. This morning I woke at five with the certainty I was up for the day, roused by thoughts that wouldn't be suppressed, however much I longed for further oblivion. Standing beside the minibus outside our office building, I sipped coffee and smoked cigarettes, listening to Derek talk of what he'd watched the night before on TV, prevaricating over whether to phone the others who were due to be *chauffeured* today. A bustling little fellow, as smooth-headed as an alopecia sufferer, Derek had a tendency to enter into uninterruptible monologues lasting several minutes or more, and it was because of this volubility I normally tried to avoid him at work. But this morning I'd been content to let Derek ramble on, segueing from his opinions on some new sit-com to the necessity of changing the oil in his wife's car several times a year. His fascination with motor vehicles, this identification of something sacred in the engine and bodywork, a holiness that saw him commune with the workings every Sunday while his wife went to church, was behind Derek volunteering to drive us this cloudy morning, the sky under which he manoeuvred now, the bleak grey of long-dead skin.

  The minibus paused again, halted by congestion at a pedestrian crossing. I watched people assemble by the kerbside under green lights. Although the 'Wait' sign would have been illuminated by now, five or six individuals still pressed the related button. It was a mechanical movement, as if their touch alone could make the figure flash up and allow crossing of this road. These men and women had the empty-eyed look of the deeply drugged, sleep-deprived and unthinking. They must have known repeated depressions wouldn't stop the traffic any faster, but still they tried to hurry the process along, jabbing fingers against the control as they arrived at the kerb.

    The system finally clicked in, those on foot shuffling across the lanes like somnambulists, vehicles accelerating as far as the next junction once they were gone, Derek fighting for our place in the stream of movement. This minibus was supposed to be full today, each spot reserved through recent email chains for those who had no vehicle of their own, didn't live close enough to a colleague with space in their car. Several people had dropped out over the last few days, citing some sudden illness or ongoing medical condition, and that left our group smaller than expected. We sat in two rows along the sides, facing each other in the same layout as a prison van, that set up which placed suspects in sight of arresting officers at all times. Here the atmosphere wasn't as beaten-down. Whatever experience lay in store for us it wouldn't involve interrogation. Those inside this bus were anticipating the very opposite of incarceration, expected to be freed from workplace routines for the next few days.

    The new temp called Lindsay had been persuaded to sit up front with Derek while the rest of us lurked behind, buckled into this cross between a fuselage and a school bus. We drank hot, caffeinated drinks from cardboard cups, sipping through the tiny holes in their plastic lids, all except Wallis who sat next to me. His constitution wasn't suited to coffee, it wired Wallis's brain and made his heartbeat rapid, affecting him as a much stronger drink might influence me, to the extent that a cup in the afternoon could prevent sleep eight hours later, that buzz remaining in his nervous system an inordinately long time.

    Not that Wallis needed the caffeine, he was a naturally upbeat person, deep into his thirties and with the soft fleshiness of the kidult in his face and body. I'd come to know Wallis pretty well over the years, respecting the lack of qualms he had about still living with his parents. The man remained proud of his interests, formed in the teenage years and staying constant ever since; comic books and overwhelmingly heavy music, science-fiction sagas and making-of documentaries. Right now Wallis was engrossed in one of those film magazines he subscribed to, a glossy piece of work whipping up excitement for the autumn blockbusters that were currently arriving from Hollywood.

    Sometimes I envied Wallis, the way he seemed content to live out his existence on simple terms. However bad my mood in the office might be, it was impossible not to be engaged by Wallis's happy conversation, that enthusiastic interest in any aspect of my life I deigned to reveal. If he had any angst or dissatisfaction around his days, about being stuck in a role with scarce opportunities for promotion, about the extra weight he carried or the fact that good-looking women paid him little attention, Wallis didn't show it. I couldn't claim to be somehow deeper than him, in most of the ways that counted at work Wallis was more intelligent than me, but I needed to be in a stable relationship, or at the very least having regular sex, in order to radiate contentment toward my colleagues. Apart from Wallis, who I'd come to consider a friend, I saw people around the office as all of a type, individuals I'd rather walk away from than get talking to. If I hadn't been trapped in the same environment as them, needing to always be on guard against making the wrong type of impression, I wouldn't have made any effort.

We passed a tube station, a police officer in a bulletproof vest holding a gun to his chest, on guard at the entrance. As always the routes out of inner London were clogged, fume-pumping cars bumper to bumper as far as the eye could see. Derek had taken to uttering the occasional imprecation under his breath now, exhorting drivers to "come on!" or "make your mind up!" and I found myself watching Wallis flick through the pages of his magazine and wondering when he'd last made love, if ever. Once I might have laughed at somebody who stayed a virgin his whole life, but today I wondered if, over the course of a lifetime weighing up the pleasure and pain of relationships, his way of maintaining an emotional equilibrium wasn't preferable to the more typical experience. That feeling of being repeatedly kicked in the chest.

Grace and I split up a few weeks ago, and I'd felt like a fool ever since. After it happened I couldn't look for anyone to replace her in my bed, hadn't even considered it. I must have been hoping she would see her decision as a mistake, come back to Jay and everything he had to offer, a misguided fancy as it turned out. When I called Grace last Tuesday, to find out how she was and if she wanted to do anything over the weekend (*of course as friends*), the girl mentioned someone else, as if moving on so swiftly was the most natural thing in the world. At which point I found myself walking in circles around my flat, gesticulating wildly at nothing, the only sound I could force down the phone, the strange staccato breath of someone hyperventilating. At last I managed to blurt out; *yes, yes I'm okay*. Get through all the automatic pleasantries before putting the receiver down, unable to do anything for hours, nothing but sit and attempt to get some kind of handle on this horrible news.

    We'd been together for around a year when it disintegrated, a relaxed item, casual because Grace wanted it that way. She had just come out of a five-year thing when we met and was tired of what she called *serial monogamy*. Throughout our eleven months together I never revealed how close I was to falling in love with her, how much I wanted more time than she was willing to give. Sometimes I felt ignored, entitled only to the crumbs that were left once her family and job and network of old friends around London took its toll on her leisure hours. Grace was almost a decade younger than me, barely a quarter-century old, and she didn't want to be tied down, saying we should enjoy what we had. This was *fun* she said, and fun was good. But co-habitation? The long countdown to lift-off that was marriage and kids? Not for Grace. She might take off next year, disappear to another city or remote outpost on the other side of the world. There was no point getting serious, she hoped I would understand that.

    I tried, really I did, but we had such a rapport, clicked like interlocking parts in some larger purpose, liked and enjoyed the same things. Grace endured the stand-up comedians of variable quality I would drag her along to, shouted up for her team while watching football on a Sunday, spent all evening in a proper pub buying me beer, talking and listening. We could talk and listen for hours, as recently as weeks ago, even as those differences in worldview and personality became more divisive. She believed these signs meant we weren't truly compatible and so Grace ended it, swiftly and unambiguously. Even then I found myself opening up to her, exploring my past and feelings in a way I couldn't with anyone else. Now I'd lost that, Grace had found someone else to absorb her innermost thoughts, and I had nothing to replace her with.

    Wallis caught me staring, gaping down at whatever article on threequels and pyrotechnics he'd been engrossed in, asking me if I'd seen some action movie yet, a film that had been cleaning up at the box office. This was the third time Wallis had posed the same question in recent days, pushing his thick-lensed glasses up his nose and looking away from me when he spoke. He really loved this flick, and I wondered if my lack of contribution to its takings was some kind of personal affront. Movies were like causes Wallis adopted, acting as an unpaid marketing man for the film studios, and I always felt guilty letting him down. Luckily Anthea interjected from her position opposite, asked if that was the one starring the guy who'd been in her favourite television series a while back. Wallis said yes, yes it was, and began to fill her in on his upcoming projects, to which Anthea, a bony woman with skin the colour of milk chocolate, nodded in polite encouragement.

Our minibus traversed a multi-lane roundabout, Derek settling on the right-hand exit, an A-road less popular with those others circumnavigating Greater London this Thursday. Soon progress became swifter and unimpeded, the built-up square miles of the city left behind for sparer terrain. The encroachment of populous suburbs was replaced with turnings to out-of-town business parks, blue on road signs heralding motorways ahead.

Through the window I saw a flock of black birds ape our journey before suddenly veering off to the side, as if confronted with something implacable and threatening. From the driver's seat Derek explained to Lindsay why he wouldn't take the motorway, an implied level of insider knowledge causing her red hair to shake in agreement, the experienced motorist giving his passenger insights into this unfamiliar route.

"There aren't many main roads where we're going are there?" I heard her say, a feminine voice above the low burble of Wallis nearby. Derek agreed with her observation, launching into an anecdote about trying to find something better than a dirt track while driving through a particularly unspoilt area of North Devon, a place he described as akin to undiscovered wilderness. I thought about asking Lindsay to turn the radio on, thinking she might enjoy some music during our journey. Then I considered the news updates we'd be subjected to and was overwhelmed by a wave of exhaustion. There was also the likelihood of having to endure song after chirpy song, vapid pop stars telling members of the opposite sex how in love they were, would never have believed they could feel this way, wanted to be like this forever. Maybe Lindsay was still young enough to believe in it, I put her at around twenty-three, but she would realise one day, after divorce and broken hearts and depression and a series of screaming rows, so would all those mindless singers.

I yawned twice, remembering Grace when we were together. Few arguments there, just laughter and our like minds. She instinctively knew what I wanted in bed and would always move to satisfy my desires, a talent she treated with an offhand ambivalence, never realising the value of her gift.

Grace had occasionally responded to my recent emails, those cries in the electronic darkness I'd been sending out ever since she started seeing someone else. Her replies contained a few facts about this new partner who was even older than me, some kind of high-up in the advertising firm where she worked. I hadn't thought of myself as the kind of man to be afflicted by jealousy, had never suffered from feelings of inferiority before, but as I found out more of the background to their togetherness the tone of my responses became fraught. How long had he been there in her workplace, hanging around this young PA who was seeing *me*, worming his way into her life like the slimiest kind of invertebrate, just waiting for the right moment to make his move. I was desperate to win her back, but looking at what I had to offer in comparison with Grace's new dalliance, I found myself horribly wanting. In my head her new partner was the man of Grace's dreams, better for her than I could ever be, more wonderful in every way. He was exciting, moneyed, romantic, intelligent, attentive, better at sex, better for her career, just *better*. I could feel myself paling by comparison, drifting into the background of her life.

In my more lucid moments, between the drunken evenings and long nights of brooding, I could see I wasn't thinking logically anymore. After a year or two he'd prove as disappointing a boyfriend as me, and my friends were saying the fifteen-year gap between them would ultimately prove insurmountable. Still youthful, she would succumb to restlessness, give in to that occasional hankering for adventure, fly off to some other climate that promised unprecedented experience, their union coming to a similar end as her past relationships. The prospect held little consolation for me now, this vision of the future a long way off when she'd been hinting at moving in with him. In response I became even more self-flagellating, desperately invoking that question none of the dumped really wants answered; *what does he have I don't?*

Across the bus from me the lanky figure of James Bailey folded his laptop shut and looked around, as if to get his bearings. A young, well-spoken man, partway into our company's fast track after coming up through the graduate programme, James' customary pinstripe suit looked incongruous against the vehicle's Spartan interior. He'd been checking messages ever since we set off, was now forced back into the world by some physical necessity, a realisation flickering across his bland features.

"Excuse me Derek." James called to the front. "Are we going to stop for lunch at all?"

In response the driver made a ruminative noise, some cross between a hummed expletive and a sigh of distress, eventually verbalising the concern that we were already behind schedule.

I kept my glance averted, saw empty fields and a verdant wood pass by, some country pub with a car park full of muddied vehicles, their owners probably tucking in to the kind of lunch James desired, the man growing twitchy and restless before me. I couldn't remember the last time I'd felt hungry, food was a part of the routine I'd tried to stick with in recent weeks but eating remained one of many activities that somehow lacked relevance these days. Meals were just a habit, along with shopping and working and going to bed at an appropriate hour, in spite of my knowledge that sleep wouldn't come.

Maybe Grace was right, maybe she and I didn't suit each other, maybe we never would, but I couldn't change my heart. It pounded desperately, wanting to be with her once again. At first I tried to arrange a meeting, believing my presence would resolve the situation, let Grace realise what she'd been missing and then our life together could resume, everything I'd lost slotting back into its rightful place. But she was too busy with the usual time-consuming activities, commitments including that new man she was so enthralled by. Maybe the girl suspected what would happen had we met in person, how my company wasn't going to be a pleasant experience for her anymore. If not, she got an insight soon enough. When I failed to persuade Grace back into my life the communication became more anxious and melodramatic. I was terrified of her slipping away, wanting to know how she could just skip out on everything we had when, in reality, she was already gone. This realisation only dawned on me recently and, when it did, I wanted to know what I'd done wrong. Needed to take apart and analyse every painful detail so that I might change, begin the impossible task of finding another girl like Grace and keep my next girlfriend. If that involved altering my behaviour, my lifestyle, my entire personality, then so be it. We were all just works in progress, and if I wanted it hard enough I could reinvent myself, create a new Jay some girl like Grace might fall in love with. When I read back my most recent messages to her before pressing send, the words sounded like the kind of testament someone composes between sobs.

I rubbed my eyes, caught the sound of Lindsay adding her voice to those passengers lobbying for a *comfort break*. We were deep into country lanes now, passing hills and wooden signposts indicating villages called things like *Muckbeggar* or *West Curry*. At a particular point our surroundings opened out, revealing ploughed fields to the right and a ramshackle garage on the left. Derek turned in and we clambered out of the back door, the women heading for the brick toilet block adjoining this shop while Wallis and James went in to browse the food. I found myself before newspapers in plastic cases outside the shop-front, tabloids covering celebrity addiction and misbehaviour, broadsheets reporting on growing Middle East unrest, the violent suppression of dissent in Asia or, at home, yesterday's upping of the terror threat level for no discernable reason.

These headlines were bringing on a headache so I walked past Derek, our driver talking about horsepower to the attendant who silently filled the fuel tank, and crossed the deserted road for a cigarette. I struggled with my lighter for a while, cupping both hands against a wind that whipped up this afternoon at September's end, staring out at the monochrome shapes I took to be cows, laid down in a distant field off to the east.

All summer the weather had been intense and unpredictable, a suffocatingly muggy heat that left commuters sweaty and oppressed, combined with the fear everyone felt but never mentioned to make journeys into work a damp trial. Weariness became the default setting, a population told by the government to remain alert, yet unable to engage enervated senses for long as they stumbled through a haze of sluggishness. What little energy we accrued during our restless nights soon became dissipated in the sultriness of day. The heat could only be broken by storms or downpours, torrential rain cascading onto this country, floods which left low-lying towns and whole counties deluged, until the next heatwave came along to dry out wrecked homes and businesses. For once scientists and religious types were in assent, man was being punished for his misdeeds, this freakish or Biblical weather was down to the human race's abuse of the planet. That or moving too far from Jesus' teachings, it depended on your point of view.

The wind chilled me as I exhaled smoke one last time, stubbed the butt against a fence post before returning to the shelter of the bus.

The rest of our journey began convivially enough, colleagues refreshed by their break, the consumption of an improvised lunch. Then the sky above darkened to the extent that headlights became necessary, the wind gusting harder as it slammed the side of our vehicle like a wall-sized fist. Jitteriness crept into Derek's movements while Lindsay apologised for the inadequacy of her guidance.

"I can't see any roads on this part." She blurted.

"There are roads, plenty of them." Derek spoke under his breath. "They're too small to show up on a national map, that's all."

Leaning forward, James chose this moment to try and be helpful. "Why don't we just head for the sea? Once we get to the ocean you can navigate from there."

"That's all very well," Derek struggled to be polite. "But if we hit the wrong point I won't be able to join the coast road, we'd have to turn around and go back."

The minibus skirted the edge of a village as Anthea added her voice to the debate, everyone squinting to make out road signs in the descending gloom, trying to pick out the best route in time to turn. We crossed a burbling stream, water rushing over the rocks, drove onto a winding road between two grass expanses dotted with sheep, animals that appeared washed-out and straggly against the landscape. Derek had to slow to navigate increasingly sharp turns while to my left Wallis burped loudly. He looked increasingly pale, either from indigestion or the bickering.

Soon the green of our surroundings gave way to the briny scent of sea and a series of shed-like constructions, reminiscent of some long abandoned shanty town. The hills to our right morphed into sand dunes, a sight that caused Anthea to clap her hands together, announce that *now* we were on the right track, to which no one replied, the tension lingering. Grace came into my head then, as she always did when I needed to forget my present circumstances, think of something good in this life, a habit that seemed to be dying hard. I thought of the girl in the red dress she'd worn last New Year's Eve. How she would sidle into my arms at the end of a long day and tell me how comfy I was. The way she squeezed my thigh, gradually moving her hand up, higher and higher, until my heart raced and my body was flooded with sensation.

Wallis nudged me then and I looked down to see I'd been digging into the flesh of my wrist, fingernails leaving red marks as I came close to breaking the skin. My friend hadn't noticed this involuntary self-harm, he was drawing my attention to the miniature conurbation coming up ahead, a garish sign on that wire fence separating the enclosed hamlet from surrounding expanses of nothing. The atmosphere inside our minibus had lifted during my reverie, and now Derek grinned as he slowed the vehicle before turning left, into the *Sunlit Holiday Centre.*

Chapter Two

A man in an orange jacket gestured for Derek to turn right, into the main car park. We sidled into the first available space, surrounded by a score of cars used to transport staff here. Several people I recognised from the office must have just arrived, they hung around outside their vehicles, smoking and talking, discussing the vagaries of the journey down.

James reached over and allowed us to spill out the doors, hit by a blast of gale that made Wallis stagger to the side, even as his face showed relief at release from that confined and jolting bus. The man in orange approached, red-faced and shaped vaguely like a bell, pointing down the road to where we should check in. Everyone followed his directions, all except Wallis who stayed with me while I had a cigarette, exchanging pleasantries with the other smokers nearby, men who laughed about being transported to a Gulag, some kind of work camp designed to increase company profits.

I saw what they meant as we headed up that pavement running alongside the accommodation. A dozen rows of chalets came into view on our right, each oblong, flat-roofed and identical, battered from decades exposed to the elements and the colour of a worn-down cliff face. The few elements of greenery, those lawns and shrubs dotted around the concrete walkways and industrial bins, looked unnatural in these surroundings, like a window box on a tower block. Wallis asked if I could imagine this place filled with laughing kids on holiday, as it was a few weeks ago, and I admitted it was difficult. So much easier to picture this camp resounding with the noisy arguments of screaming families.

Within a few hundred yards we had reached the main building, a large dome set back from the road. It was fronted by a sign showing a map of the complex, different *zones* and attractions, illustrations bearing little resemblance to the reality, pointed out by a variety of cartoon animals. A few people milled around outside and, through the dome's glass front, I saw a line of employees snaking back to the entrance. Wandering up the steps, we joined the queue without a word, no one turning to look except Alice who gave a wave from further up the line. Everyone else was too engrossed in that scene unfolding near the check-in desk, a female camp employee trying to reason with Theresa Barnes.

Theresa was a prematurely wizened woman from a neighbouring section to mine who had built up quite a reputation for truculence during her years with the company. She continued to remonstrate with the girl, demanding to be put in the same chalet as her middle-aged friend Julie, the only person I knew who could abide her. At this point Norman Dobbs stepped in, one of the organising supervisors from our workplace. He explained that a great deal of thought had gone into the chalet allocations, because one of the essential ideas underpinning this trip was to encourage employees to mingle with those they didn't yet know, so it wouldn't be a good idea for Theresa to refuse the hand she'd been dealt.

I could tell Dobbs hadn't dealt with Theresa before, those of us closer to her low level at the company knew this line of argument wouldn't work. Theresa was stubborn as an autocrat, willing to ignore any reasoned argument in order to get her own way. Now Barnes jabbed a finger at Norman, reiterating the desire to stay with her friend as Julie Newman stood at the front of the line shame-facedly, the rest of us waiting in vain for them to move up.

Dobbs glanced back at us with some anxiety, maybe fifteen men and women craning their necks, tapping feet, or, in my case, making a show of studying my watch. Soon he caved in, told the girl behind her desk to room these two women together, swiftly moving away as if summoned elsewhere on important business.

The queue shuffled up, closer to that enormous spider dominating the reception area, a purple creation lurking ten feet up and occupying much of the dome's ceiling, surrounded by a thick web with nothing caught in it. This arachnid was made more menacing somehow by its wide, fang-toothed smile, meant to welcome guests into a period of holiday fun.

Our company had been mooting this experience for months, a process begun back in Spring when a directive came down from the top. The Chief Executives had fallen for some kind of presentation conducted by a corporate events organiser, gleaning statistics they quoted in the relevant emails. The high-ups believed an upturn in loyalty and positive thinking could arise from outings such as this, a rise in inter-departmental camaraderie. The initial idea had been for a whole week of activities somewhere picturesque and tranquil, camping in the Lake District or staying in a Scottish castle, but the feedback on these suggestions was wholeheartedly negative. Workers told bosses that seven days out of their lives was too much, they couldn't leave behind children and spouses, miss a raft of responsibilities on a whim of their employers. I heard a few second-hand mutterings about financial limitations too, how the utopian vision of these planners wasn't matched by budget allocations, that this subsequent scaling down was, in actuality, more to keep the bean counters happy than the result of employee feedback.

Whatever the reason, a compromise was eventually reached. A long weekend here, the company making up for this infringement on our leisure time by covering all costs, providing extra days leave *in lieu* for those who attended. The organisation as a whole had well over a hundred staff, but consultants weren't welcome because of other allegiances, while contractors had been told they wouldn't get paid for this time, so it was up to them whether they wished to accompany us or not. The only exceptions were some of the more popular temps like Lindsay, youngsters who saw the potential for a career at our corporation, or just felt like an adventure beyond the dreariness of the working day. In these instances they came to some kind of arrangement with their section heads, because everyone wanted the young and vibrant to accompany them.

Once you factored in these considerations, adding the no-shows, people who couldn't make it because of holidays, medical concerns, or just didn't care how adversely their prospects were affected by absence, the number of colleagues checking in today came to somewhere near the sixty-five mark. Not many holidaymakers to rattle around these surroundings, particularly since this camp could hold a couple of thousand during peak season. Whether it ever filled up nowadays was open to question, the look of debilitation about this place didn't suggest the resort was thriving. If the best offer to rent this complex on a late-September weekend came from my bosses, it suggested the place was available to pretty much anyone. That said, I had no idea how much our jaunt was costing the company. Even with such a thin intake, I might have been part of the last really profitable weekend at the *Sunlit Holiday Centre* this year.

We moved up the line, music from video games audible in the background. Above it a couple of guys with shirts tucked into their jeans discussed phone reception while peering at each other's mobiles. I'd left mine in my rucksack, currently languishing in the boot of the minibus. Not that it mattered, the only person I wanted to talk to was Grace, and she wasn't about to call me. According to these men it was impossible anyway, they were only getting one bar out of five on their signals, occasionally rising to two when they stepped outside, this reception still too momentary to make a call.

They were interrupted by Dobbs, returning from wherever he'd disappeared to after the incident with Theresa to usher the men in the direction of that open window, leaving me with Wallis at the front of the queue. The close proximity of Norman Dobbs unsettled me, this organiser who watched over us as if we were errant schoolchildren, capable of misbehaviour at any moment. He was the head of my section back in the office, although there were too many managers in the way for me to experience much direct contact with the man. Even so, Dobbs' presence on the seventeenth floor made me wary. He had a reputation for officiousness, for playing by the book, then suggesting improvements to said tome if he felt the detail was lacking. A good generation older than me, and with a full head of grey hair I'd often caught him combing in the office toilets, Dobbs made no sartorial concessions to our new environment. He was clad in the usual boiled-white shirt and dark trousers that left a good half-inch of sock showing, even when he was standing up. They weren't short particularly, it was more the way Dobbs kept his belt so high, some of my colleagues would speculate, only half-jokingly, he was at risk of catching his nipples in the buckle.

My aversion to this man was less about his dress sense than the ways he reminded me of my father, dead two years from an illness as brief as it was unexpected. Inexplicable to the doctors, those reassuring yet ultimately useless men who were still conducting tests and proposing innovative new treatments when he upped and passed away one distressing hospital evening, a night I spent somewhere else. Back then I'd come to terms with the worst of what psychiatrists would call my *unresolved issues* with the man, by the time my father died I was all but unrecognisable from that angry adolescent who had once made a list of his failings and carried it at all times, vowing not to succumb to the flaws that so infuriated him in the old man, as if I could somehow avoid the destiny imprinted in my genes through a cognitive trick.

That hand-scrawled piece of paper had been something to hold onto back then, a way of reminding myself that he wasn't entitled to express disapproval, my father less qualified than he thought to criticise my actions, tell me I would never measure up to his achievements, whatever they might have been. The contents burned their way into my brain over several bitter months, and I can still remember every word vividly. That list of flaws always came to mind when I encountered Dobbs.

Like my father he had a rigid routine, unalterable habits that saw Dobbs arrive in the office at the same time every day, often down to the second. He was a control freak with a tendency to meddle in the work of his staff, obsessing over tasks that didn't concern him, while outside the office Dobbs seemed to regard his wife as some kind of adjunct to himself, a personality-free woman, to be instructed in a way that would give Victorians pause. Willing to argue the toss over the tiniest of expenditures, Norman was quick to anger and had little regard for the sensitivities of others. When female underlings left his one-on-one sessions in tears, he would blame it on the *girls* for being thin-skinned, while Dobbs saw every ailment that afflicted people in his team, from asthma to diabetes to chronic back pain, as a manifestation of some weakness of character, impossible to sympathise with if he didn't suffer himself. Like my father before that final illness, Dobbs kept in shape, and so he remained healthy and unsympathetic, for now.

    I flinched as Norman put a hand on my waist and guided me forward, towards the hatch. This part of the dome was themed after piracy, rigging on the walls and sacks of what looked like booty piled by my feet, treasure chests and piles of fake gold to the side. Looking out of her porthole, the camp worker greeted me with a smile, asking for my name and staff pass.

    I confirmed I was Jay Hall, indicating Wallis who had dawdled up alongside to fiddle with his spectacles in an offhand manner. "I should be in the same chalet as Wallis Browne." I said.

    She checked her list. "I have you here sir, you were due to be sharing with two other gentleman but unfortunately they haven't been able to make it. I don't have a record of a Wallis Browne in with you."

    "A very recent change, the organiser over there authorised it." I pointed at Dobbs while Wallis offered his employee identification card. "The accommodation list has already been shifted to let Julie stay with Theresa, Norman told me there'd be no problem arranging another switch."

    "Okay…" She made a few amendments to her paperwork and passed two poorly photocopied maps over the counter with our keys. "You're both in number 364, enjoy your stay."

    The chalets formed a rectangular arrangement, four blocks of accommodation spread over two floors, facing each other across a patch of rough grass where seagulls landed every so often, massive birds the likes of which I'd never seen. Their wingspan must have been a metre and a half, feet and beaks bright yellow against grey and white feathers, the creatures hollering in a high-pitched squawk that suggested hostility toward other living things. We carried our bags along the balcony as they soared and threatened nearby, Wallis keeping up an excited jabber behind me. At the end of our block some others were settling in, a girl I didn't recognise leaning against the rail, as if there was something to look at beyond the close grey of the clouds, pushed across the horizon by the wind.

I unlocked the door to number 364 and dumped my rucksack on the scratchy carpet. Inside a musty smell hung in the air, like an old room in some grandparent's house, shut up and uninhabited for years. Underlying it there was a tincture of detergent and something similar to burnt meat, or maybe toast.

Wallis went to the toilet, returning to inform me there was a bath but no shower and he'd forgotten to bring any towels, would have to use one of our spare blankets instead. The front room of this four-berth chalet doubled as a sleeping area for two of the incumbents with a kitchen adjoining it and this was where I wandered, to boil the kettle and check our cupboards. I found a few complimentary sachets of hot drinks and an electricity meter with a small amount of credit left on it.

"You want a hot chocolate?" I asked Wallis.

"Yes please Jay." He switched the television on, our set located about five feet up on a specially designed bracket. Wallis occupied himself flicking through the channels on this push-button set, a veritable antique, about thirty years old at a guess.

I set his drink down on the oblong dining table and fished out my mobile, taking it and my pack of cigarettes out onto the balcony, mindful of that grimy fire alarm installed above the main door. Outside I positioned my back to the wind and turned on the phone, drawing deeply as I read a text message received many hours before from my operator about some amazing offer, exclusive to users of my network. I tried to put in a call as an experiment, find out how much credit I had left, but those men in the queue had been correct, there was precious little signal here.

I was still fiddling with my phone when a door opened two chalets down and Alice Mahoney came out, swaddled in an overcoat and knitted scarf. On seeing me she smiled and wandered down the balcony while across the way three males from another department unlocked their ground floor chalet and went inside, laughing about something as they hauled a crate of lager with their luggage.

"Hey Jay." Alice brushed a few strands of hair back from face, the jet black mane accosted by a harsh breeze. "How you finding it?"

"Fine. It's true though." I lifted my mobile to show her. "No way of contacting the outside world. We're on our own."

She smiled. "Yeah, one of the girls in my chalet was saying that. There's hardly any masts in this part of the country, it's so remote."

"Who you sharing with?"

"Natasha and Suzie, they're in legal or policy or something. Me and Nat got lifts up but Suzie came here by train."

"Train? Where the hell's the station?"

"About eighteen miles away, she didn't do her research." Alice grinned. "Now she's worried work won't pick up the cost of her cab. Best part of fifty pounds apparently."

"Christ."

"The taxi driver told her about the masts, said something like…" Alice changed her voice, attempting to impersonate a yokel. *"Ooh no missy, you won't be able to call anyone on that thing, not round here. Residents campaigned to stop those mast things, cause cancer they do."*

"Ever thought of giving up the day job, maybe becoming an impressionist?"

She pushed more hair behind an ear and pulled a face, as if I didn't appreciate good mimicry when it came my way. *"Come all the way from London you say? Wouldn't know any of them terrorist types I keep 'earing about would you?"*

I looked at Alice sceptically and she dissolved into a fit of giggles.

"Shouldn't laugh, Suzie's a bit upset, she keeps going on about it. How she couldn't convince the driver there wasn't an immediate threat of death in London, the way he kept patronising her and didn't listen."

I took a long drag on my cigarette. "People are less sophisticated down here, she's needs to understand that."

"That's what I tried to tell her, but it's difficult to get a word in edgeways, what with Natasha freaking out because she can't call her boyfriend, so *obviously* he'll think she's cheating. And she got the latest model phone last week, and it does everything except teleportation, so why won't the damn thing just work already?"

"Your chalet's shaping up to be fun."

Alice sighed, her dark brown eyes looking at me like I didn't know the half of it. "That's why I came out." She indicated the window behind us. "Who you sharing with?"

"Just Wallis."

"Lucky bastard." We glanced through the glass, inside my

chaletmate was fiddling with the TV. "I might have to come down and share with you guys."

"At your own risk." I stubbed the butt out. "Smells bad enough in there already, I can't imagine it getting any better."

Alice watched me flick the remnants of my cigarette over the balcony and shivered. "You know that's not good for you."

"No! Really?"

She pouted. "I'm going back to my roomies now Jay, catch you later."

I watched her go then, returning to that chalet where Wallis had finally settled on some satellite channel that showed music videos. On the screen a skimpily dressed R&B singer thrust her baby oil covered body toward the camera, in time with some hectic music.

"We've only got three channels." Wallis opined, settling into the sofa with his drink. "There's this one or the camp's own which is all just kiddie shows. Then there's one of the terrestrial ones, Channel Five I think."

"This is fine."

"I was looking at that thing." Wallis gestured to a small plastic box perched on top of the TV. "But it's not like any digital receiver I've ever seen."

"Don't worry about it." I gathered up my rucksack. "Do you want to sleep in here or the bedroom?"

"Here's fine."

I was packing some clothes into the drawers between our two tiny beds when there came a knock at the door. Wallis had gone into the bathroom several minutes earlier so I answered to find Norman Dobbs out on the balcony, laden down with bags of groceries. Doing my best to hide my distaste, I listened as Dobbs launched into his spiel, shirt speckled with sweat under his suit jacket. Each chalet was being supplied with provisions by the company; milk and bread, margarine and cheese, enough ingredients to make dinner this evening and a few electricity tokens for slotting into the meter. Wallis appeared behind me and I handed him the groceries while Dobbs continued, the occasional fleck of spittle disappearing above my right shoulder as his eyes concentrated on a point inside the chalet. There was an expectation we would meet beside the main gate tomorrow at 8.30am sharp to begin the day's team building activities. Everyone was expected to get an early night, so none of the facilities or on-site pub would be open this evening. Rest assured, the company had plenty of fun lined up over the next few days, but the organisers thought it wisest to keep everything low-key tonight.

Nodding and responding with affirmative noises at the appropriate junctures, I began to close the door as Dobbs finished talking, leaving the section head to pick up the other bags, move along to the next chalet and say his piece all over again. In the kitchen Wallis had pans of water humming on the stove and was already chopping vegetables, ready to add to that bolognaise our employers dictated we should eat with the spaghetti. With a hungry man's enthusiasm, Wallis listed the foodstuffs supplied; high-quality mince and expensive chocolate, free-range eggs and Polish sausage. Despite being nonplussed by the food itself, I was as surprised at its quality. I was the kind of man to subsist on simple, army-style rations if left to cater for myself, tending to keep my wages reserved for other purposes. But apparently the company wanted us sated and full-bellied this weekend, had blown its budget on gourmet food in the short-term rather than promising pay rises after our next appraisals.

The organisation had issued its first ever profit warning to the city back in the summer, and although the current climate meant this was nothing out of the ordinary for a business like ours, it still sent shockwaves reverberating through my office, prompting speculation and worry among those employees who derived an obscure gratification from gossip and fret. People were losing sleep over the possibility of a takeover or job cuts, some new management regime who would overhaul long-established ways of operating. None of this concerned me, and I tried to make Wallis understand it was best not to be too credulous about such possibilities. Don't believe anything negative unless it comes via an official communication I said, because there's no point casting around for jobs elsewhere unless you're actively unhappy, not when the facts around the precariousness of our circumstances were so opaque.

Most of my colleagues weren't so logical about the situation, fell for rumours and hearsay, horoscopes that warned of upheavals to come in their work zone. People placed great store in the lack of reassurance from managers who knew as little as they. Despite the inconvenience, I was amused when confirmation came through that the team-building event would be happening after all, a weekend that seemed to contradict such doomsaying. If this generosity was isolated, the funding one last flamboyant gesture in the face of the inevitable, at least those workers who'd given years of their lives to the company were getting some decent food out of it.

Wallis refused my offer of help with the preparations so I left him to it, took a bath in the uneven plastic tub that had seen better days, having to cling desperately to the handrail as I clambered out to prevent myself slipping on the smooth floor. When I re-emerged dinner was ready and, between mouthfuls, Wallis told me about a girl in Japan he was having an online flirtation with, the sky outside darkening and that wind continuing to whistle past our block.

For the rest of the evening we played cards with a vampire-themed pack Wallis had brought with him, soundtracked by the music channel on TV. I retired early, leaving my chaletmate to flick through those channels again in search of something compelling to watch, unable to accept the limited entertainment on offer. In my quarters I laid out on one of the beds, the mattress beneath me about six feet by three, so narrow that rolling over was fraught with danger. Trying desperately not to think of Grace, her cascade of hair and heart-melting smile, I lay awake for a while, listening to the occasional screech of a seabird and far-off calls from people in the camp. Eventually my mind shut itself down and I dreamt I was living with Grace in a cramped hovel, far from civilization. She would be leaving me soon, going away forever to serve in some overseas conflict, the kind of war, I knew instinctively, no one ever came back from.

My sad valedictions to the girl in my sleep were interrupted by Wallis banging on my bedroom door, saying it was after eight and we had to meet the others in half an hour.

Chapter Three

Wallis hurried alongside me toward the camp's entrance, both of us knowing we were late, only to discover a dozen or more employees hadn't materialised either and the organisers, so reminiscent of officials with their clipboards and lists, were growing twitchy and irritable. The sensible approach might have been to rethink this morning's activities, someone nearby was muttering darkly in phrases quoted from a weather report; *eighty mile an hour gusts* and *torrential rain later*, but there was no sign of a change in the plans. My colleagues huddled behind the gates and that shut-up hire shop while I smoked a cigarette, waiting to see what the powers-that-be would do next, those people around me disoriented and exhaustion showing on their faces. No one looked fresh or well rested after a night in the tiny beds, and in some cases bloodshot eyes evinced a late night drinking session. When the gale subsided I occasionally caught a whiff of alcohol on the breath of some of the men, a sweetly unpleasant tang.

At about ten to nine those in charge gave up waiting, left Dobbs at the gate to direct any latecomers, led us over the empty coast road and down a path to the shore. We passed a couple of boarded up huts and shuttered shops that sold ice cream or beach toys during the summer months, and there were a few bungalows in the distance, desirable retirement properties minutes from the coast, none showing signs of life.

The progression of our group, fifty-strong and led from the front, must have looked like a battalion to anyone in the distance, troops out on manoeuvres across some deserted land, a foreign legion marching in isolation. Up ahead the sand dunes were pockmarked by grassy hillocks, particles of grit whipped up by the wind to sting our faces. The organisers stepped in to help stragglers reach the summit, overweight colleagues or individuals approaching retirement age, all struggling to get their footing as I strode onward, holding my pace steady so as not to overtake those before me. Nearby Wallis slipped and slid in the dunes, panting audibly even as the wind howled around us, a hand down to steady himself while others managed to stayed upright.

Then we were at the top, greeted by panoramic views of the sandy beach becoming flat and detritus strewn as it stretched close to the ocean, seaweed and shells and pools of foam the tide left behind. Beyond the shoreline were other stretches of land, detail obscured by the mist but looming, dark shapes many miles out to sea. Far-off to the west the coast curved around on itself, while looking to our left I saw someone braving the elements to exercise their dog, a black outline chasing some thrown object across the sand. Ahead of us, down at the bottom of the dunes, a dozen piles of colour-coded equipment waited. The four remaining organisers, all dressed in fluorescent orange jackets today, beckoned those standing above them towards it.

 I slid down to the designated area where Giles Fairbrass, a middle-aged, ruddy-complexioned section head whose resonant voice made him the obvious choice for announcements, yelled our names above the wind. Everyone was placed into groups of six, some last-minute improvisation required to make up for those employees who hadn't appeared, then we were instructed to go and stand beside a pile of equipment. The paraphernalia was arranged on a designated section of beach, each heap including spades, wooden poles and planks, twine and a portable barbecue kit under canvas.

 "This morning's task is to work together and prepare brunch." Intoned Fairbrass, keeping his back to the swirling gale. "You'll need to dig a hole of the appropriate size to cook the sausages we have here for you." He indicated a cool-box positioned between two of the other organisers. "This involves first constructing some kind of shelter to keep the sand out. All the necessary equipment has been supplied in order to make this happen."

 My group stood beside a black flag and, like most of those around us, consisted of equal parts men and women. As Fairbrass spoke I was assigning tasks to them in my mind, ascertaining how to get this over and done with as soon as possible and get back to the relative warmth of the camp, even as my colleagues gazed at their materials with scepticism.

 "This isn't a race, and you won't win a prize for being first. It's all about cooking the food we've laid on for you. If you end up with full stomachs at the end of this challenge, then you'll have succeeded. Whoever we decide has been the most successful will be rewarded, and they'll be the ones who cooperate most effectively with each other. Everyone should use his or her unique skill-set to provide a bespoke and holistic solution. Myself, Nigel, Malcolm and John will be on hand if you get stuck, but remember – more haste, less speed! Alright everyone, off you go!"

 One of the organisers, Malcolm I think, blew a whistle unnecessarily, and everyone descended on their equipment, sorting through the objects or watching colleagues delve in with trepidation. I slid two of the wooden rods into the sides of the canvas sheet and directed the two youngest girls on our team, Catherine and Cheryl, to position this rudimentary windbreak where it would give the rest of us maximum protection from the elements. Of the others on my team, Dave I knew vaguely from our floor and I passed him a spade now, giving the other shovel to Alfred whose thick grey beard provided some insulation this morning. I pointed to the sand beneath our feet then, telling them the dimensions of those five holes that needed to be dug.

That just left Silvia, a stocky and resourceful woman of Mediterranean extraction in her late thirties I knew from the regular meetings we attended. Prevailing upon her to assist me, hoping Silvia was as strong and perceptive as she appeared, I asked her to pass me the required items, hold pieces of wood tight as I fastened them together with twine, feeling like a surgeon with the head nurse at his side.

Behind us I could hear the two girls squeal with displeasure every time the sandstorm hit their well-wrapped bodies. Yet they managed to keep the windbreak steady enough to allow me to work and with swift movements I constructed a secure, cage-like structure out of the available materials, Alfred and Dave digging steadily into the moist sand nearby.

The other groups examined their poles and planks, suggested possibilities and complained to the organisers about the circumstances surrounding this first activity of the weekend. By contrast, Silvia and I worked in near silence, the woman pre-empting my need for a steadying hand or another piece of twine from the bundle. I'd somehow managed to shut out much of the chatter, those people beginning to despair of ever succeeding, the painful sensation of squall on my exposed skin. I was working purely from instinct now, binding and tightening, breaking one of the planks over my knee without much fuss when I discovered it was the wrong size.

This was the type of work I'd done every day once, after ending two years of college with poor results, the legacy of my late-teenage discoveries; the girls and pills and booze, too much hedonism at an age when friends were pushing themselves onward, into the academic environs of university life. After failing my exams at the age of eighteen I drifted into physical work instead, removals or painting and decorating, even becoming a trainee handyman at one stage. Working with my hands to pursue cash in hand, it wasn't much of a career path (as my parents never tired of reminding me when I got home at night). Still I didn't feel as dissatisfied as perhaps I should have, although I wanted my own place desperately, needed to get out from under disappointed family eyes. But there weren't the earning opportunities for men like me anymore, those most suited to satisfying, physical work.

In years gone by I might have found employment in a steelyard, unloaded imports with other burly stevedores around the country's largest ports, fought my way through the dust of a coal mine or passed my years working as a machinist. None of these options were available anymore, the jobs had all become automated or disappeared, relocated to other countries where business was increasingly viable. When I did find opportunities, in the building trade or working on an oil rig for six months of the year, either the job paid too little to make my switch worthwhile, or it meant leaving the town I knew for some place unfamiliar and potentially grim. So I drifted along, well into my twenties and with no ambition to speak of, depending on my parents for their hospitality, the welcome in their modest home growing more strained with each passing year as I wished my weekdays away, killing time until I could hit the clubs on Friday night and forget about everything.

The shelter was complete now, a three foot-high construction with an opening on one side and four poles extending nine inches above it. With Dave's help Silvia and I positioned the box above that quartet of smaller holes we'd dug and slid the supports into the sand, packing it tightly around the foundations while Alfred sat nearby, talking to the girls who held the windbreak, Catherine and Cheryl shielding him between giggles.

It was a chance encounter in a pub one weeknight that saw me swap one rut for another. Martin had been one of those pupils at my school who excelled at sport and winding people up and not much else. If he'd left with any qualifications I would have been very surprised. Yet there he was at the bar, coming over to greet me like an old friend, wearing a shirt and tie as if respectable. Martin was eager to tell me what he'd been up to during the previous half-decade and over several bottled lagers I learned about that employment agency starting him in an office job, doing the kind of data entry that doesn't take long to master, no matter how inexperienced you are. Everyone knows how to use a keyboard after all, and although Martin started off on the minimum wage, he stuck around long enough for several pay rises, acting as if he thrived on the monotony and repetition, learning who to suck up to and which co-workers liked it if he moaned about the bosses. Within six months Martin was making a decent wage, enough to pay his rent and fund plenty of extra-curricular activities, if I knew what he meant.

At the end of that night, as I thought about getting up again in six hours to spend the day stripping wallpaper in a draughty room near Barking, my former schoolmate passed across the business card of his employment agent and told me to give her a call. That was how I ended up at the company all those years ago, trying to acclimatise to the conventions of an office environment with none of the camaraderie or banter of my previous workplaces, environments where men relied on each other to get a job done, to put in the sweat and elbow grease. Instead I found silence and partitioned cubicles and a screen to stare at for hour upon hour. I felt out of place for weeks, having more affinity with those men who arrived to water the plants or clean the windows than my immediate colleagues, unlike most of the starters my age who seemed instantly comfortable in their situation and were naturally higher in the pecking order than me. These graduates seemed either vocal and focussed, aimed at getting where they wanted to be straight away, or terminally bored. Many had fallen into the work after completing higher education and remained there due to the lack of more lucrative alternatives. Despite my initial feelings of inferiority, none of them treated me any differently because of my mediocre qualifications. Soon, terrifyingly fast as I look back on it now, I began to adapt to that gleaming seventeenth floor workspace where I spent forty hours every week.

Relieving the girls of the windbreak which would serve as a flysheet for our den-like construction, I made the rest of the black group hold our creation steady while I slid the canvas into place, securing it with half a dozen wooden pegs forced into the flat sand. This was the kind of task that came naturally to me, more so than those spreadsheets and databases I had forced myself to master, progressing onward and upwards over the past twelve years. My deskbound profession had never felt right, but it was what I'd ended up with, and now the only time I used that natural ability, to build or remake, was on modest DIY around my flat.

My body's potential to master the physical aspects of this world, to earn a living through its strength and taut muscles, had become even more limited with the recent influx of Eastern Europeans, a migratory wave of artisans that made casual labour almost impossible to find for someone like me. In the absence of other options I stayed on at the company, that way I was able to afford the rent on my place, the boxy flat I called home, a home I'd have invited Grace to cohabit if I thought for a moment she would move in. For the sake of my current lifestyle I went on spending the days in meetings, gulping coffee and manipulating information. What chance I had to exert my body came in those five-weekly trips to the gym, bouts where long-suppressed energy came out, sessions releasing all the salt and frustration and anger of being stuck at a desk, teeth clenching as I pounded the weights and running machine.

    I kept myself in shape this way, feeling the blood pump through my heart, reminding myself I was alive and wanted to remain healthy for as long as possible. More than that, I enjoyed the endorphins strenuous exercise released, hoped to reap the rewards in later life, even though staying in shape wasn't important for a man to go on earning his living, not anymore. The weakest and most indulgent of individuals could feel as good as me and live just as long, thanks to luck or the latest developments in medical science. Most of those other men at the gym seemed to stay toned for aesthetic reasons but vanity wasn't a trait I admired. Tight t-shirts and stripping to the waist each summer was all very well, fine if you thrived on the admiring glances of bimbos, went for the kind of girls who liked defined pectorals above all else, but I'd known enough of these sunbathing women to understand they were all superficial inside, talking of little except clothes and shoes and make up, celebrities and the trappings of materialism they sought out so single-mindedly. That kind of girl became tedious very quickly, however much the lust might rise in me at first.

    Shielded by our roofless tent, Silvia and Dave concentrated on lighting the barbecue set and getting the coals heated up while I scrambled inside to finish the remaining hole, digging out nooks in the side with my fingers so the metal grate would stay secure. Cheryl grabbed at the sleeve of some passing organiser and I heard his positive comments from my prone position, Malcolm saying he would get us some bangers from the cool box so our team could begin roasting them.

    I borrowed a pair of gloves from Alfred and gingerly took the fired-up hotbox from Silvia, placing it in the sand with the grate inserted above. Then I delegated the remaining preparation to others, Catherine and Cheryl particularly eager to get started on the cooking, turning sausages over the heat in a bubble of exultation.

    I left them to it, went off to find a discreet spot where I could have a cigarette in private. None of the other groups seemed to have made it as far as ours, those making any kind of progress were the ones that included a couple of capable people. The rest sat around and talked, only showing an interest when an organiser came around. Representing the supervisors I saw Giles and John, the latter resembling the aging football hooligan he was, with that thick neck and shaven head. They were stuck helping the useless, trying to give teams an indication of what they should be doing without offering overt help, fighting desperately against the wind and regular blasts of sand whistling down the shore. Behind these men a sheet of canvas was blown across the beach at twice the speed of that figure chasing. It was Derek I think, running after the flapping square in desperate pursuit.

There was a kind of recess up in the dunes, the nearby hillocks offering protection to the north and east where the gale came from. This spot also had the advantage of stopping me from being seen, so I lowered myself onto a flat patch of sand and relaxed, my cigarette barely lit when Alice appeared, so maybe I was visible after all. She was smiling in spite of the elements, as if we were out on some leisurely coastal expedition, wore a woolly hat and crimson fleece with black gloves, plonked herself next to me uninvited.

"Saw you working down there. I have to say I'm impressed, you've hidden talents Mr. Hall."

"Yeah, well, not much call for that sort of thing around the office." I blew a cloud of smoke upwards where it was blasted away by the wind.

"I could never put up something like that, make food and shelter from whatever's lying around."

"You don't have to." I looked at her. "All you need is a man on standby to do it for you."

She laughed, revealed small white teeth behind slightly chapped lips. Alice had mentioned her itinerant childhood once when we were making coffee in the office kitchen, how she'd spent her formative years shuttling between embassies across Asia and Europe, the legacy of a US diplomat father and Vietnamese mother. From the latter the girl inherited her fine features, impressive cheekbones, and that lustrous, black hair. Meanwhile the genes of *the old patriarch* (as she called him), provided her with an unusually tall and curvaceous body, along with a tendency to drop the occasional Americanism into her speech. I think she was around thirty, although I'd never asked.

"None of the guys in my *purple group* measure up." She said with disdain. "They're the kind of men who have to like, get someone in just to put a shelf up." She paused. "My last boyfriend was like that…"

My soul had been raw for weeks now, and the subject was probably best avoided. Still I had to ask. "When did you split up?"

"Two months ago, we were together eight years." From somewhere down on the beach came a barked shout of instruction. Alice wrapped both arms tightly around her midriff. "Feels both wrong and right, to be on my own after all that time. You know what I mean Jay?"

"Totally." I tapped some ash away and took two swift hits. "What is it about relationships? Why are there so many nasty side-effects?"

Alice looked out at the ocean. "I don't know."

"One day the person you're with is the most important human being in the world, at least to you, and you are to them…"

"You'd hope, you'd totally hope."

"Then you break up, and from that instant on you're not allowed to think of them in the same light any more. You can't be any more dependent on them than you would any other acquaintance."

"I know, it's crazy." With fumbling hands Alice extracted a tissue from her pocket, dabbed at her watery brown eyes. "I hate that. However nice you are about it, one of you always moves on sooner."

"Just happened to me." I flicked my dead cigarette into the distance.

"And you end up having to steer clear anyway, otherwise you come across as weird, obsessive."

"I guess that must be what Grace thinks of me."

"Grace huh?" Alice blew her nose. "Goddamn weather, making me all bunged up."

"Sure."

She looked at me. "I don't want to be like this Jay, you know? Thinking how I've been discarded and forgotten all the time, some pained, angry, tearful mess."

I thought of my ex-girlfriend, wondering how long she'd put off telling me that what we had was over. It's a natural inclination, this failure to tell those close to you what they don't want to hear. Had she been seeing her new man while we were still together?

"You're not a mess." I told Alice.

She smiled sadly. "I hide it pretty well most of the time, but when I think how I can't even be friends with him now, how he doesn't want to see me. I've said I'll never cause him any hassle…"

"He doesn't want to be reminded of what he's done, what he's capable of." I knew what it was like, being part of that human wreckage when a relationship ends, and I knew I was no better than her ex-boyfriend, capable of the same hurtful elisions. "If you were to hang out together again, like in the old days, it would prick at his conscience, remind him he's not a good person. Everyone wants to believe they're a good person."

"So I get punished for that?" Her voice ululated under the darkening sky, rain was in the air. "Everything we had together can just go? Eight years, cast adrift and forgotten?"

I didn't know what to say, I'm not good at reassuring platitudes, so I put my arm around her. The girl yielded, resting her head against my chest.

With impeccable timing, Wallis chose that moment to appear, huffing into view just as the first heavy drops began to plash down on the dunes. My friend had been scanning the area and now he hurried over, a sudden distraction pushing at the bridge of his spectacles, causing me to relinquish my grip on Alice before I'd fully registered how right it felt, having her in my arms.

Wallis garbled something about food and problems and we rose to follow, descending to the beach where a few groups were generating smoke from their cook-outs, the majority even more frustrated than before, struggling with their equipment. Theresa Barnes ranted at the red group, hunchbacked and uninterruptible as her stream of invective condemned team-mates' failings. The three of us were better off than them, handed sausages in buns by the rest of the black group which Alice was welcomed into, Alfred down near the barbecue attending to a vegetarian option, falling prey to the sudden rain. It was really coming down now and, as the drops fell and Wallis munched greedily on a hot dog beside me, I saw some of the lighter equipment strewn hundreds of yards away, blown across the beach by this squall.

A messy and pathetic scene all in all, despite the ongoing efforts of the organisers who'd been joined now by Norman Dobbs, desperately trying to keep the yellow team's rickety construction upright while Anthea and Lindsay strengthened the supports. This image, the slapstick nature of it, Dobbs' grimacing expression and the concerned faces of those others standing round to watch, it's seared into my memory because of what happened next.

The best way I can describe is that the whole planet suddenly shook. I've no experience of earthquakes, but it felt like a tremor and was accompanied by a huge bang. The sound resembled a thunderclap only louder, maybe twice as loud, at least I think it was. Certainly I remember my ears being engulfed by the noise and I was thrown to the sand then, cast down by the shock or the impact or whatever it was, shaken and churned inside and consumed by fear.

Chapter Four

The noise lasted less than a second and then came the ringing in my ears. I lifted my face from the beach, wiping wet sand off a cheek. The echo in my head came to be replaced by screaming, cries of fear from female colleagues and the hollering of men.

    I was on my feet quickly, rising to a bout of dizziness and the sight of everyone scattered on the sand, like corpses after some coastal battle. A few were moaning or shaking while others clasped hands over their heads, protecting themselves from more sudden noise. For some reason I didn't expect the moment to repeat itself, that violent shudder had the feel of a one-off event. Beside me Alice came up on her knees and I took her hand, lifting the girl to her feet as I asked if she was alright. Alice nodded and brushed the sand from her clothes, fat drops of rain falling on us both. Nearby Wallis was utterly still so I bent down to reassure him and after a few moments he rose groggily. There were grains of sand on his spectacles and Wallis' eyes had that same blank look as a child, awoken from some consciousness-enveloping nightmare.

    Unable to speak, but apparently responsive to basic instructions, I told Wallis to look out for the supervisors, make sure they were attending the worst hit and, if not, let me know. I was concerned for those men who hadn't moved since the shock, as well as vocal girls whose initial shrieks had been replaced with sobbing.

    I turned away from them and scrambled up the dunes, the rain soaking through my clothes, Alice following without a word. At the top we saw a thin plume of smoke, rising into the sky somewhere in the distance.

    "Where do you think that is?" She breathed.

    "I don't know." Our perspective made it difficult to assess how far inland the cloud originated. "Thirty miles? Maybe less."

    Alice leaned in to whisper above the wind, ask the only question on our minds. "Do you think its London?"

    We watched the white smoke spread outwards, gain in expanse and height, the legacy of some fire perhaps, once localised and now raging out of control. Colleagues joined us at our vantage point, Giles Fairbrass among them, his uneven features paler than I'd ever seen. Behind him people supported each other, like wounded refugees stumbling across some border, Malcolm with his hand around Theresa Barnes who whimpered forlornly, the kind of low plea a dog makes after neutering.

The stronger of these people wanted to go back to the camp immediately but Giles turned to halt them, imploring everyone to remain calm. He said this would all become clear very quickly, tried to sound reassuring and in control, even as the heavy rain soaked us and that smoke behind him came to dominate the skyline.

Coming out of the bedroom later, having changed out of my wet clothes, I found Alice ensconced on our sofa. Outside the wind continued to howl around the blocks while the rain looked like it was easing off, the cloud cover becoming lighter.

"You don't mind me hanging out do you?" She wore a functional black jumper now, sipped tea from one of the chalet's small china mugs. "There's a lot of freaking out going on in 368."

"Not at all. We're not panicking here. Panicking's no help to anyone."

I turned to Wallis, standing in what had come to be his regular spot, fiddling with the TV. "You found anything yet?"

"No. I swear this was Channel 5 yesterday, today it's just static." He pushed several black buttons on the set's front, finally arriving at the internal *Sunlit Holidays* channel. "This is about all I've found today. I don't think it'll tell us anything useful."

On the screen a boxy crocodile puppet, made from cardboard and felt, talked to a small child with a severe bowl-cut in a bare studio.

Alice looked at me over the steam emanating from her cup. "What do you think it was Jay?"

"Honestly? I've no idea."

Wallis took one of the seats by the table. "It felt like some kind of asteroid striking the earth, maybe a meteor."

"Do they make smoke?"

"Depends what they hit." Wallis didn't look at Alice when he talked to her, turning to me instead. "You ever see those old movies Jay? Something alien falls to earth bringing a deadly virus or new life-form with it and lots of strange stuff starts happening."

"Sounds a bit far-fetched Wallis." I'd been fiddling with my lighter without realising it, now I made a conscious effort to stop. "Surely they'd have told us if something was on collision course with the planet?"

"There's lots they don't tell us."

Alice said, "They're going to be talking about terrorism out there, at least until we know for sure. They are in my chalet."

"I'm just worried about my mum and dad." Wallis's normally cheery expression had disintegrated, his face hangdog.

"Everybody is sweety." Alice rubbed her forehead, looked out of the window. "I'm sure they're okay."

She didn't sound convinced.

The King Charles pub was situated at the side of the dome nearest our accommodation, accessible by stairs or a ramp. Inside the place was dimly lit and gave the impression of dustiness. There must have been twenty tables around the partitioned interior and at a third of them people from the company spoke in hushed voices. They drank wine or liquor this afternoon, their gestures nervous and skittish, anxiety written into distracted faces. I took a stool by the bar and ordered drinks from the teenager serving, a spotty youth with dyed blond hair who seemed entirely unaffected by whatever had happened earlier. He served us mechanically and begrudgingly, a *Sunlit* name badge on his chest revealing him to be Neil. Above the bar a television set, similar to the one in our chalet, flickered and jumped, shapes moving amid the distortion, impossible to pick out for long.

"What's up with the TV?"

"Main aerial's down, it's the wind. That'll be nine pound."

I paid the sullen kid, watching him stand on a stool to change channels, switch to the in-house station that showed children and their families skipping down a street utterly unlike any in the camp, some colourful and exciting and magical place. The youngsters held hands with what were meant to be members of staff in animal costume, prancing past stalls and amusements and sideshows, all promising different kinds of delight.

We sat at the other end of the pub, beside that back wall where a screen would show sporting events during the holiday season. Anthea and Lindsay from the bus were at the next table, along with Dave who'd been on my team earlier. The women wore the kind of masked expressions that reminded me of ambulance crews, workers who have finished a particularly bloody clean up, are forcing themselves to unwind without being quite able to forget.

Alice eschewed greetings. "Does anyone know anything yet?"

"Hi folks." Dave smiled woozily, stringy hair plastered to his patchy skull. "Not heard nothing me."

Lindsay gave him a look, equal parts pitying and irritated. "They say the land lines have gone down too. All the phones in the dome are dead."

"You've no idea either?" Anthea's voice sounded like a plea.

"I thought some kind of meteorite might have hit." Wallis said.

"Maybe it's finally happened, maybe they dropped the big one." Dave brought his fists up to his chin, exploded both hands outwards to signify an explosion, making a slurred *Pssssshhhh* sound as he did so.

"A nuclear bomb leaves a mushroom cloud, did you see a mushroom cloud?" Dave looked at Alice, not comprehending her. She turned to the other women and jabbed a finger in Dave's direction. "What's up with him anyway?"

"They're giving out treatment for shock in the first aid hut." Anthea glanced at Dave. "He accepted the sedative they offered, then he started on the scotch."

Dave swirled amber liquid around his glass while Wallis addressed me. "So that's what was going on."

Walking over we'd seen a group of people standing outside a raised square hut near the camp's rear fence. They were bracing themselves against the wind, so strong it was threatening to cause structural damage around the complex, and Wallis had been curious to find out what was going on. We hadn't investigated, it was hard enough to battle our way across the site as it was, but I did wonder about this apparently random gathering.

"The camp manager used to be a nurse." Lindsay told us. "She was really nice, checked me over and said there was no damage, to my hearing I mean. She gave me some pills in case I had trouble sleeping…"

"I didn't let her give me none of those pills." Anthea asserted. "I don't want to be drugged, I just want to get out of here…."

The pub's main door was flung open then and in burst James, a wild look in his eyes and hair still damp from the earlier drenching. He scanned the pub-goers, our table passing quickly under his vision, the man giving no sign of recognition. Eventually James alighted on a circular table in the centre of the King Charles, an area where a couple of middle-aged men conversed quietly over pints of bitter. Storming over to tower above them, lip quivering as his finger pointed shakily, James suffered from the directionless agitation and inchoate speech of a man unused to rage.

"Wha… What…. What have you done with it?"

"With what?" Asked the first seated man.

"Now, hang on…" Warned the other.

James reached in, taking two handfuls of the first man's jumper and lifting him off his stool. "MY LAPTOP YOU BLOODY, THIEVING…."

The other man stood while the one in James' grasp, a bloke who must have been a good foot shorter than him, shook and flinched and claimed to know nothing about any laptop. At this point I decided to go over and Alice came too.

The second middle-aged man was trying to pull James's arm away and reason with him at the same time, maintaining Roger had been in the pub the whole afternoon, but James was furious and too strong.

Nobody else seemed willing to do anything about this altercation, they were pretending not to watch as we approached the fracas. I grabbed the wrist connected to that fist James had drawn back, was about to use to strike the man called Roger. Wrenching this arm behind his back, James cried out in pain as Alice prised Roger from his grasp. James was taller than me but I had the weight advantage, managed to force him out the side door while, behind the bar, Neil looked on with an expression that came close to concern.

I kept a firm grip on the twisted arm, guiding James down the steps and toward one of those benches near the children's play area, advising him to *calm down* and *take it easy* all the way. The man was breathing heavily, snorting through his nostrils, and he had to be pulled down onto a bench, Alice placing her hand on his shoulder to encourage James to sit.

"What's going on?" She demanded of him. "What happened?"

James looked at the dirt between his feet, remaining motionless for long seconds. Satisfied that the potential for violence had passed, I took out my cigarettes and cupped a hand to light one. At last James spoke.

"When I heard there was a first aid point I went over and got checked out. I had some grit in my eyes and it was really irritating, so I got some eye drops from the nurse, she was really good."

Alice met my knowing glance over James' hunched back. "I went back to the chalet to apply them but Sid and Roger weren't there." He looked up at Alice. "I'm sharing with them."

"Right."

"I was about to go to the bathroom when I noticed stuff had been moved since I was last there. My laptop wasn't where I'd left it."

"You assumed one of them took it?" Above us a seagull circled, gliding through the dying squall.

"Who else? The chalet was locked." James flailed an arm toward the pub in front of us. "I've got one key, they've got the other. Roger even complimented me on it when I logged in last night, I let them check their emails…"

I thought of the two soft-faced men, having a quiet pint before they'd been so rudely interrupted. "They don't look like criminals to me." I said.

"All my work was on that laptop, everything." James sounded close to tears. "I was going to get on the internet after I sorted my eyes out, see if I could find out what was going on, what that noise was…"

"Good point." I nodded to Alice. "We wouldn't need TVs if we had the net." James was tapping a foot, still agitated. "Did anyone else bring laptops with them?"

Alice said, "They encouraged us to leave thoughts of the office behind, remember?"

James looked up. "Some of the organisers might have theirs, you could ask."

"We wouldn't need to if we found yours." Alice stroked James' arm. "Were any of the chalet windows open? Did it look like someone could have forced their way in?"

"It was all locked up. That's why I'm sure somebody in there with me took it. Maybe it's their idea of a joke?"

"I agree with Jay, I don't think Roger and Sid did anything." From our right a group of company workers appeared, walking past the swings and slides and complicated climbing frame to get to the pub. "We don't know who else has a spare key, anyone who works in this place might be able to let themselves in."

We looked at Alice, her pretty face thoughtful and sure. I marvelled at the girl's ability to restore trust, even if the possibility she'd mentioned wasn't reassuring. That teenager Neil, in there behind the bar, what did he get up to after finishing his shift? I imagined the kid creeping around this site - letting himself into empty chalets, rifling through my belongings - and felt like I'd been doused in itching powder.

Scratching my sides and rising to my feet, I decided to put such thoughts out of my mind.

"Let's go back in." I said. "I think we can sort this out now. Particularly if I buy everyone a drink."

Once the necessary apologies and restitutions had been made

everyone was content for James to join our group, add his intelligence to the theories we spent the next couple of hours mulling over. Perhaps because of the distance between us and the major cities, whatever had happened seemed far away, whether that proved to be the case or not. By now we were able to maintain a kind of detachment from the possible horrors, or there could just have been so many harrowing events in recent times, so much previously thought unimaginable, that we were inured to the terror, expected a continuation of such shocking acts somewhere at the back of our minds. Whatever the reason, and it could have been as simple as the alcohol, there felt like a tacit admission that we didn't know the dimensions of whatever we'd felt on the beach, it's scale and ferocity and consequences, and until we did, allowing ourselves to be paralysed with worry was a silly and weak way to behave. Not the manifestation of that indomitable British spirit everybody liked to think they embodied.

    Anthea wondered whether terrorists might have launched a dirty bomb, the type of attack she must have read about in the press but of which she had little understanding. Those who knew more explained it to her, how the point of a so-called *dirty bomb* was its subtlety, creeping up on an unsuspecting populace. Once detonated, such a device spread radiation over many days while remaining undetected, a gradual and underhand way of damaging living beings, not the kind of strike that threw fifty people to the ground many miles away.

    The idea of a missile attack was posited, but James didn't see how any home-grown terrorist could get hold of the materials to launch something with that kind of impact, not in the current climate. Everyone was suspicious of strangers this year, ready to report neighbours for the most minor of infractions, innocent residents who subsequently found their property stormed at dawn by armed response units wielding weaponry against the blameless. It was all-but inconceivable that some renegade cell, no matter how well funded, possessed the ability to launch such attacks on UK population centres. An international strike seemed unlikely, there had been no escalating tensions in recent days. Britain's relations remained strained with a dozen foreign nations, some known warmongers, but the idea of a sneak attack on these isles, hostilities begun by some country who had suddenly decided we were their primary enemy, it felt implausible.

    By now the pub was more than half-full, men and women drifting in, growing bored in their chalets and keen to connect with others during this uncertain time, join our tribe of the confused and the fraught. Behind the bar Neil had another camp worker helping him now, a borderline obese girl with acne on her chin and enormous hoop earrings, the pair serving a steady stream of vaguely intoxicated office workers, all thirsty for more.

At the other tables talk became louder, fuelled by alcohol and adrenalin, men failing to articulate their emotions as women asked where on earth the organisers had got to. People ate bar snacks, bags of nuts and crisps, appetites regained after the shock of late morning. A couple of blokes nearby talked about the staff, one was black and the other white. The pair worked in information management I think, and the latter was belittling the bar workers to his friend, saying he'd heard this kind of camp would employ anyone, no matter how long their criminal record. His chaletmate was incredulous until it was explained to him how, because of a lack of background checks, all kinds of ex-cons worked as security or behind the scenes in places like this, men with links to organised crime. The other one laughed, said that barman didn't look old enough to be *in* a pub, let alone have served time, although he would probably make a good stool pigeon one day.

They were interrupted by a theatrical voice from the other end of the bar, the supervisors putting in an appearance at last, Giles Fairbrass again the speaker. The general hubbub faded as everyone twisted in their chairs, positioned themselves to watch those five men in charge. Fairbrass seemed to have regained both his poise and the colour in his cheeks, that face the colour of rosé wine, a nose more crimson than flesh-coloured.

"Yes, yes, hello again. I see there's no need to call everyone together, you all naturally gravitate to the pub anyway." A couple of the organisers chuckled, nobody else made a noise. "I'm sure you're all keen to hear an update on what's happened." A low murmuring around the pub as Fairbrass scratched his bulbous nose before continuing.

"We've been investigating the situation this afternoon and all reports suggest a natural phenomena." Giles tugged at his nostril with a thumb and forefinger. "It seems we were unlucky enough to be caught in an earthquake, similar to the one that damaged parts of Liverpool last year. By a freak coincidence, it hit at the same moment as a very localised storm. That would have been thunder you heard." One of the other organisers, Malcolm I think, passed Giles a handkerchief.

"What about the smoke?" A female voice asked.

"Ah yes." Fairbrass shifted his weight. "That's entirely unconnected. The result of some agricultural incineration I believe."

More muttering from employees. I noticed Dave's head resting on his arms, the man made a kind of troubled lowing as he slept, like a distraught heifer.

"I know what you're thinking, with such unpredictable weather, how are we to continue the team-building activities?" I looked around the room, unable to believe anyone was thinking that. "Personally, I'm of the view we can still achieve unprecedented things this weekend. Certainly the latest forecasts predict that the worst is over." Behind him Dobbs nodded his agreement. "But it would be remiss of us to continue without taking into consideration the thoughts of our staff and, more importantly, the company's view." I sipped my pint and let myself relax for the first time since the incident on the beach. These men were on top of the situation, and it turned out not to be as bad as we feared. Worry I didn't even know existed had been coiled up inside me and now it oozed out of my pores, like fever sweat.

"In a few minutes we'll move to the dining area, where the staff of *Sunlit* have prepared a tremendous meal. During dinner, I would ask any of you with particular concerns to approach one of us." Fairbrass gestured at his group. "Later tonight Malcolm, John, Nigel and myself will head inland until we find an intact phone line on which we can contact our superiors. We will explain the situation to them and find out if their plans for you have changed, whether they would send you home or continue with the trip, as I am keen to do." I thought of my cramped flat, my *home*, and for once it was profoundly appealing. "We may not return until morning, so in the meantime Mr. Dobbs will be in charge." Norman ran a hand through his thick hair, gazing around the pub at us.

"Once you've finished your drinks, please come and join us in the restaurant area." Giles used the handkerchief to wipe his face. "This is clearly signposted at the front of the dome."

The supervisors disappeared and I drained my glass, aware from the moment he mentioned food that I was absolutely famished. At the other end of the table Lindsay was shaking a prostrate Dave, trying to wake him up. An unspoken agreement passed between myself and Wallis then, both of us standing, eager to eat. Alice abandoned her drink to keep up as we left the pub, encircling my arm with a hand to gain my attention.

"Did you notice it?" She whispered in my ear. "How bad Giles is at lying?"

Chapter Five

Word must have got round the chalets prior to our arrival, because several groups were already in the dining area, drinking red wine and buttering rolls, discussing domestic or family issues in a way that suggested they too had been reassured by the organisers' explanations.

I'd wanted Alice to extrapolate her suspicions, tell me why she thought our bosses weren't giving us the truth, what they hoped to achieve by misleading staff who would surely find out the facts soon enough. But as we walked in for dinner the girl *shushed* me, muttering *not here*, and she was unwilling to say any more within earshot of our colleagues.

Alice left me with misgivings, along with a vague sense she could be one of those people who saw a conspiracy in anything, the kind I sometimes heard about, paranoiacs who believed a government was capable of a major assault on its own citizens disguised as terrorism. Other kinds of skewed postulations would come out of the woodwork every time someone famous died, convincing salacious tabloid editors to give the theorists column space for their irrational speculations.

If Alice wasn't going to expand upon this mysterious logic I decided it was best to forget her words and sit down at a table with Wallis, opposite James and Lindsay who appeared to have hit it off in the pub and were now flirting wildly, eyes fixed on each other as the scent of roasting meat wafted in from the kitchen.

This room normally operated as a cafeteria for holidaymakers, summer visitors who would take their trays along the self-service area at one side of the light blue space. Mass reproductions of paintings with a nautical theme, fishing boats and yachts, hung on every wall, while today tables were moved to formalise the occasion, pushed together to make a banquet-style arrangement that stretched the length of this dining area, a right turn to accommodate the remaining guests. Staff hurried round this set-up, proffering water from jugs, filling and refilling wine glasses. Everyone present appeared to have rallied, put the events of this morning behind them, even if in places there was a sluggish edge to the bonhomie, perhaps the result of mixing alcohol with sedatives. One glass of red had already been knocked over by someone with less than the usual control over their limbs, causing service staff to scurry, fresh-faced girls who quickly absorbed the spillage with their cloths. Alice watched this scene from a few places away, a fixed smile on her face.

Across the way Dave had returned to coherence, talked with organisers John and Nigel toward the middle of the seated area, acting the extrovert after his impromptu nap. I watched Julie Newman rise from her seat beside Theresa, shuffle over to Giles who held court at the table's head, a few women in their forties providing him with an audience. Booming and expansive, Giles resembled some kind of medieval King, entertaining the servile courtiers.

A starter was deposited in front of us and Wallis tucked in eagerly, a few low slurps as my friend went at his asparagus soup. Julie stood behind Fairbrass' shoulder, waiting for a natural pause in his soliloquy to cut in. She was an undemonstrative woman who rarely spoke up, had to reach a level of injustice that would cause most people to snap with fury before making so much as a mild complaint. Even then Julie was more likely to turn it back on herself, imply it was her own fault you had trod on her foot, crashed into her car, botched her operation. That was why Julie's best friend was Theresa I supposed, a woman naturally outraged by most things, whose mind saw the world arrayed against her. Theresa needed a pliant witness to these unfair foibles, the vindictiveness of the fates.

Giles began to eat, dipping his rubicund head close to the bowl, failing to prevent flecks of soup from spattering his piebald tie. Julie took her chance and bent down to ask him something, the superior welcoming her interjection, offering up some kind of explanation with good humour. The woman listened intently, a hand fluttering to her mouth, the other tugging at that shapelessly prim skirt, body trembling as she nodded her assent.

One of the serving girls asked how the soup was and I remembered my food, got through the portion in a matter of seconds without really tasting it. Julie returned to her place alongside Theresa and I couldn't hear their exchange very well. Still, I managed to discern from Barnes' screeched replies that Giles had said it was unlikely attendees with mitigating circumstances, those like Julie who missed her son or Theresa who said she was worried about her sister, would be forced to remain in the camp beyond Saturday morning, not if they really wanted to go. Julie seemed satisfied with this response, empowered to request more wine the next time a waitress happened by, Theresa's grumbles continuing without the previous vehemence.

To my left Silvia was clad in a purple dress that accentuated her curves while doing its best to disguise the mannish aspects of her body. She asked me what they'd said and I told Silvia the supervisors would be back from their liaison with the bigwigs tomorrow, whenever anyone who could think up a reasonable excuse would get out of here. Silvia laughed and gulped her wine, pleased by the possibility of returning to London early, saying this weekend might not be a complete write off after all.

    The sense of relief and that free drink, our schedule falling apart and the sudden freedom in what had been a strict timetable, it gave this weekend the improvised, anything goes feel of a school trip gone horribly wrong. Men like Fairbrass and Dobbs reminded me of those schoolmasters back in my pre-pubescence, men who would take children into the woods or force us to circumnavigate ponds. Pompous and blustering, full of a sense of their own importance, these managers had the same harrying intensity as those teachers who sent us off with nothing more than a compass and ill-drawn map, expecting eleven year olds to find their way to an obscure point and back again. They talked of such challenges as if they were seminal events in our young lives, would lead to the manifestation of previously hidden survival skills. In fact most of the pupils simply ambled around aimlessly, kicked at trees and fungus until the signal summoned them back to camp.

    My classmates and I were very much the product of our environment back then, adept at dodging between moving cars or working out what confectionary we could afford with our remaining lunch money, but unconvinced by the countryside. The adults described this wilderness as some kind of Eden, a garden we would inevitably come back to one day, a return that would involve surviving on our wits, forging what we needed from the surroundings using long-dormant skills, like pioneers who built log cabins from scratch. Even back then I was more gifted than my peers at construction and creation, but I didn't buy this idea of taming the wilderness. Despite my abilities I conformed, fell in with the cynical posturing of other kids, knowing survival skills were of little use in modern society, as irrelevant as trigonometry or algebra, especially when the majority of us would go on to live deskbound lives, eventually understanding everything we needed could be learned from the computer's *Help* option.

    Those pointless outdoor activities of the primary and secondary years felt a long time ago now, efforts imbued with purpose by dint of our tutors' wide-eyed exuberance, their belief these experiences were vital to facilitate our move into adulthood. The people in charge were mendacious then, thinking they knew what was best, and they were lying to me again here, making me undertake team building tasks which had the reverse effect to that cited, led to disagreements and failure in most of the colour-coded groups this morning, before we were so drastically interrupted. I didn't know what it was that had intruded earlier, but I was positive now, certain somewhere inside it hadn't been thunder. There was rain but no storm, no lightning or clashing of weather fronts, and the chances of such a moment coinciding with a tremor in this part of the world was small enough to be non-existent. So the men of authority were lying to me still, those supervisors who roared with good humour as their main course arrived.

While everyone else was distracted by the arrival of the food, sliced roast beef and four vegetables under thick gravy, I slid from my seat and shuffled down the table, telling Wallis I'd *be back in a second*. I moved unnoticed, most of the diners approaching that stage of inebriation where a new personality emerges, louder and with less boundaries than the usual one, breaking free from that chrysalis of sobriety. Across the way Lindsay read James's palm, spoke of the intricacies in his lifeline, tracing her finger across the man's skin.

I knelt by Alice and the girl inclined her head, allowing me to speak into her black hair.

"What did you mean earlier?"

Seconds ago she'd been smiling at something one of the nearby women said, now she became serious. "Couldn't you see it?"

"See what?"

"Come on Jay, you don't have to be an expert in body language to notice how uncomfortable Fairbrass was. He's never that nervous speaking to us."

"Sure, but these are strange circumstances."

"If you want to believe everything's fine Jay, you go ahead and believe it." Alice turned fully, looking me in the eye. "Everyone else seems to be getting on with their day easily enough."

I glanced past her, seeing the people eat with gusto and gesture for more wine. "You're saying something *did* happen."

"Of course *something happened.* You were there, what did it feel like to you?"

I gazed at her sincere features, our faces were very close. "Not the weather, that's for sure."

"Sir?"

A voice from above, my legs were blocking the path of a girl trying to bring sauce to the centre tables. I gave Alice a glance and returned to my seat, eating my food slowly and methodically while refusing the offer of more drink. I wanted to fill my stomach and get out of there, smoke a cigarette and think everything through without being distracted by the growing raucousness all around. This place had the atmosphere of a work Christmas party, the usual conventions of decorum abandoned for one night only, social etiquette disregarded by drunks. The dining area felt like it was getting brighter, fluorescent lighting beating down on me in that windowless room to create the foundations of a migraine.

After forcing myself to swallow a final mouthful, I told Wallis I needed some air and I'd see him back at the chalet. I stumbled out then, past Silvia who watched me with concern, Theresa cackling hideously and pointing a wrinkled finger at someone, noticing Derek with his hand on the leg of some woman, a colleague who wore a wedding ring and so much make up she looked like a painted doll.

At the dome's front the air was relatively still, just a light breeze, although the night remained cold. I hurried to light my cigarette, what little wind there was coming off the sea now, brackish in my nostrils, a briny undercurrent replaced with the scent of something charred as it changed direction. A security guard appeared through the front entrance, beside that fenced off tennis court which was visible from the coast road. He hurried toward the smaller chalet blocks at the back of the dome, his stride a cross between a stroll and a waddle. Caught by an urge to walk off the heavy food, I followed this hefty figure at a distance, watching him scale the steps of a block as I stayed at the side of the dome, close to the wall.

The guard disappeared inside one of the first-floor chalets, the accommodation here comparatively well kept, given a lick of paint some time in the last thirty years. Perhaps these were the *luxury apartments*, that section where holidaying families would pay extra to stay. Continuing to circumvent the main building, I came upon a smaller structure positioned behind the dome, a path running between the two.

I walked along the alleyway, seeing a garish display up above, just visible through the murk. It announced this place as the *Splash Zone*, the name implying a complex of slides and other water-related entertainment, but when I peered in the long window all I could see was a swimming pool, indistinctly lit by far-up lamps, the place dimmed at night. There was nobody at poolside, no movement within, just the still surface of the water, dark and strange under my gaze, eager to trick the eye, make me believe this was some other element reflecting those strip lights above.

Staring at this pool for a long time, I finished my cigarette while shielded from the breeze on two sides, the air here odourless and mild. Alice was so certain we'd been misled by the organisers, fallen for lies they had spent the afternoon concocting, while we were getting drunk in the pub and swapping paranoid suggestions. The dinner lay awkwardly in my gut, causing bouts of discomfort and indigestion. If some major event had occurred in the outside world, another terrorist event with multiple casualties, some *senseless attack* from extremist religious groups or sudden national catastrophe, why would Giles and the others hide it from their employees? It didn't make sense.

I watched that water inside, so inaccessible and dark, like an underground lagoon or the soaking conclusion of a dank well. Truth or fiction, it didn't change our circumstances. The four of them would be out of camp soon to receive further instructions, Nigel having abstained from wine during the meal, and he would no doubt occupy the driver's seat. On their return we'd know if the company was willing to take the sensible way out, cancel what remained of this ill-fated weekend, a suspension that would allow our group to return to loved ones, those who had loved ones.

Lighting another cigarette, I turned my gaze away from the pool and that hypnotic light reflecting on its surface, moving down the pathway to emerge in the main area of chalets, those blocks where we were staying. I turned left, heading for the back of the camp, a narrow road with more parking spaces along the rear side, the tall fence separating this kidney-shaped centre from endless fields to the north. I didn't understand how it could be prudent for our supervisors to lie in the short-term. There was nothing to be gained from undermining trust in the company, not as far as I could see. That was the part which bothered me most, a nervous tic convulsing through my mind.

I passed the hut that served as a first aid post earlier in the day, all shut up and silent now. Cutting inside the grass was wet underfoot, ground boggy from the morning's downpours. I saw a shape between two blocks that looked like a bag of rubbish from a distance, thoughtlessly discarded. As I came closer I saw it was actually some kind of animal, lifeless and still, ears drooping in the mud and feet stretched out at unnatural angles. The corpse of a rabbit, recently dead. There had been an outbreak of myxomatosis earlier in the year, a disease which decimated the leporine population and led to endless stories of tearful children who had lost their pets, the story supplanting horrific world events in the papers and on TV. Closing in, I saw this creature hadn't expired from a virus, its last moments were frenzied and violent. The animal's guts hung out of it, pink and red viscera spooled on the earth. What might have killed this rabbit was unclear, as was the reason why a predator would refuse to eat the animal after mauling it, or where its killer could be now.

Shuddering a little, unnerved by the presence of death, I hurried on as the nausea rose in me, walking through the area where I stayed, some lights left on and thoughtlessly burning electricity. I wondered which block Dobbs and the other organisers were in, their whereabouts hadn't been mentioned to the wider group and perhaps that was deliberate. This was the problem when my confidence began to erode, I quickly became unwilling to believe those who had proved untrustworthy, even if it was only once. In recent times Londoners had been particularly afflicted, we could no longer rely on the authorities' ability to keep us safe. Instead we assessed every stranger encountered to discern the threat posed, fearing what lurked in luggage or strapped under clothes, obscured by that unseasonably heavy coat.

A few weeks ago, just before the problems between us grew too obvious to be ignored, I invited the person I still thought of as *my girlfriend* to the cinema. Typically, come the day, Grace forgot she'd agreed to meet me, had a family get-together that clashed. I found this out a few hours before I was due to meet the girl, when she answered my follow up text with an apologetic one. Maybe Grace never intended to come in the first place. Whatever her intentions, I hadn't been to the movies in a long time, and this was a flick Wallis wouldn't shut up about, a hyper-kinetic thriller about some guy whose identity had been wiped by mysterious powers in the intelligence services, so I went on my own.

About half an hour in, the audience were recovering from the adrenalin surge of an extended car chase through the city streets, when there was some kind of disturbance to the rear of the auditorium. I found out later that a man of indeterminate ethnic origin had disappeared, as if to the toilet, leaving behind a leather satchel under his seat. Five minutes later, when he still hadn't returned, people on either side began to confer, the communal worry growing until one young woman with a limp decided to take the initiative, leaving the movie theatre and scanning the foyer for someone who could help.

The woman returned with an usher who took one look at the

satchel and put into practice those long-memorised evacuation procedures, taught at his induction. He announced the cinema was to be emptied, raising his voice above the barked dialogue coming from the digital stereo system, asking everyone to head for the exits in an orderly manner. Unfortunately the screening was a busy one, and a single uniformed teenager was never going to exert sufficient control over a crowd who immediately moved from unrest to panic as they became aware of the danger. I was seated on the opposite side of the auditorium from the kid who was desperately trying to guide this rush of people, and I saw my aisle becoming packed as filmgoers hurried to escape, pushing each other out of the way as the fear gripped, envisaging their bodies blown to smithereens.

Unlike the frightened crowd I was able to keep my calm and see that, without intervention, the weaker individuals were going to get crushed, the slowest trampled in this rush. Something kicked into gear then, something I didn't know was coming, would never have claimed I possessed; I found my voice. Repeating the usher's instructions to *proceed towards the exit*, I called above the fraught hubbub of voices, steadying those overwhelmed with fright and about to lose their balance, using my strength to hold back men who tried to shove their way past the less than mobile. With my help scores moved freely toward the doors and out into the cinema's glass entrance. Even as the fire alarm began to sound, causing the other screens to empty, I found myself outside on the pavement with the rest of the clientele.

As it turned out, our efforts were misguided at best. When the police arrived to investigate the suspicious object they found that man who had temporarily abandoned his bag alone in the auditorium. A Sikh who was suffering from a hideously upset stomach, his illness had precipitated a fifteen-minute trip to the toilet that simply couldn't be postponed. With trembling hands he showed officers the innocuous contents of his satchel and was allowed to leave, those of us who hadn't yet wandered off invited to receive complimentary tickets for a later showing as recompense.

It was the usher, a young guy called Mahmood, who told me what happened while thanking me for my efforts. He believed there could have been injuries had I not intervened. In the end it might have been just another of the city's false alarms and I wouldn't be recognised for my *heroism*, but Mahmood wanted me to know I should be proud. It was almost as if he was disappointed for me, sad his workplace remained undamaged by some homemade explosive device.

I told the usher to think nothing of it, left without picking up my free pass and would never know how the movie ended. Such alarms were too commonplace to be remarked upon nowadays, dozens of evacuations every day from trains or nightclubs, anywhere groups of people gathered, places a bag might be left by some drunk or thoughtless individual. Football matches, concert venues, even entire city centres were regularly emptied because of these alerts, the British growing accustomed to interruptions in work and social schedules, being locked down inside a building or directed out onto the street. Our possessions were ransacked and bodies fondled by burly, unsmiling men at the front of any building we needed to get inside, security workers who body-searched their own gender and endeavoured to eye each race with equal suspicion.

The camp ended here, a go-kart area to my left with small-scale vehicles abandoned higgledy-piggledy on a tyre-bordered racetrack, while to the right sat that rectangle of chalet blocks furthest from the dome, eight in all, the paint peeling from their exteriors and cracks visible in flimsy walls. I moved onto the grass separating them, seeing the other side of this accommodation was just as ruined, metal steps encased in dirty-brown rust, numbers missing from the splintered chalet doors.

Lights gleamed in several of the ground floor apartments so I ambled towards them, walking the path that led past lounge windows. Curtains were drawn in the first chalet that showed signs of life, the booming yet sharp din of a surround-sound TV turned up loud. There was a small crack where the cheap grey material didn't quite meet and through it I saw part of an enormous television, a widescreen set taking up most of the wall. On it a documentary played, people running across a thoroughfare while being shot at by police. These running battles were followed by clips of buildings destroyed in some war zone, although I couldn't tell whether this was contemporary news or archived footage. A DVD machine sat near this massive television, but I wasn't able to see whether a disc was being played, or if the person inside had somehow managed to pick up a news channel.

Frustrated, I moved on to the next chalet where the synthetic curtains were a good six inches apart, everything revealed to such an extent I had to catch myself before walking in full view of its interior. Fortunately they weren't paying attention, that man and woman making out on a leather sofa directly below my sidelong gaze. Inclining my head, I looked around the chalet's interior, a place markedly different from the one I was staying in. Expensively furnished, with comfortable armchairs and a deep-pile carpet, this room was filled with gadgets. Alongside a TV and DVD player, on a par with the ones I'd seen next door, there was a laptop open on the table next to a digital camera and, in the bedroom, a video camera on its tripod, set up to face a sumptuous double bed that filled much of the space.

I moved my head further to see into the kitchenette, well stocked and full of appliances. That was when the couple beneath me relinquished their grip on each other and I shrank back, fearing one of them would spy my face in the dark above, spending a moment facing away from the chalet and listening to my heart beat. The brief glance had been enough to recognise this pair, Neil and that fat girl who had been serving us in the pub earlier.

So these were the staff chalets, housing camp workers for the season and perhaps at other times too. It made sense for casual employees to live on-site, this place was so remote they probably travelled twenty miles or more to work, didn't earn enough to cover the petrol for going back and forth between shifts, while for those who didn't drive commuting wasn't even an option. No doubt the camp owners factored in this roof above their heads, reduced their pay accordingly, down below the minimum wage. Yet if they earned so little, I didn't see how the likes of Neil could afford that cornucopia of gleaming innovations I saw in his temporary home.

Glancing back inside, I noticed Neil had gone to the bedroom while the girl below me removed her top, displaying a white bra above rolls of fat. She really was hideous, twenty stone at least, with spots and birthmarks dotting her pasty white flesh. Neil carried the camera and tripod into the living area before pointing it at the girl, having to adjust the viewfinder to get her entire bulk into shot. He removed his clothes, revealed an erection that protruded from a red, blotchy area on his crotch, then stepped into the kitchen. Neil's scrawny body was pink against the white paintwork as he went through cupboards and drawers, eventually finding what he wanted before returning to the lounge, applying chocolate spread to his genitals with a plastic knife.

The girl anticipated his approach, leaning forward and making a sound like some discriminating diner confronted by award-winning food. She used her drooling mouth to gobble up Neil's engorged member, the kid's face turning red and a trickle of gel or sweat running down his forehead. His blond hair was almost level with my horrified face but Neil's eyes remained shut and, within seconds, she'd licked him clean. The girl stood with some difficulty, pushed the boy down onto the sofa forcefully, struggling out of her huge skirt and stained underwear. I turned away and began to dry heave, the settee straining on its frame behind me, squeaks and moans as the girl straddled him, their noises covering the sound of me bringing up fluid onto the ground. Conscious of how isolated I was then, I took off, running out onto the main road and back towards chalet 364, drawing air into my lungs and willing myself not to be sick.

Chapter Six

The sky was an astonishingly lurid red this morning, as if the whole surface of the country had been inflamed. I watched cloud cover move in from the west to obscure this strange sight, a white bank rolling across to replace the hyperreal sunrise, the cumulus tinged by that pigmentation behind. This insulating cloudbank glowed at the edges above me, up early after a restless night. I'd been out on the balcony smoking and absorbing the dawn for a while, wondering if this meteorological display of fiery impressionism was a natural phenomenon or the result of some manmade catastrophe.

When I got back to number 364 last night Wallis was already asleep, snoring softly on the sofa bed he'd managed to partially unfold, passed out from too much wine and curled up like a hedgehog. I heard him rise several times in the night, staggering to the bathroom then kitchen, running the tap until the lukewarm water disappeared and he could take some cool refreshment. Wallis wasn't usually the type to over-indulge, would quickly move on to lime and soda whenever we went for pints after work, but he had fallen prey to the extra imbibition encouraged by that free wine, readily flowing and guzzled by all yesterday evening. Like many others around the camp, my chaletmate would be suffering the after-effects when he finally got up.

I'd heard others in the night too, after I'd got in and splashed my face for several minutes before laying down on my bed, gradually starting to feel better in the head and belly. Drunk men shouted at each other while women laughed, asking the way to chalet number whatever and expressing distaste at the muddy puddles which dotted the site. I overheard some of my colleagues inviting others to a party, perhaps the men across the way, since I definitely heard music at one point and it could only have emanated from their TV, rhythm and blues followed by hip-hop. Even as this revelry died away, come the small hours when bonhomie and supplies of alcohol were exhausted, I remained awake, turning over the day's events in my head, failing to lock them together. Lying there I speculated in circles, thoughts speeding up like a whirligig, disorientating me just as those spinning rides had, back when I was a kid. I might have nodded off once or twice, but deep sleep wasn't within my grasp and soon I heard the screech of seabirds as they began their morning reconnaissance, scavenging food amid the camp's detritus. Deciding to give up on rest then, treading softly near Wallis' unconscious form, I unlatched the door to be confronted by that all-enveloping phosphorescence, first light feeling like the ultimate daybreak on some other planet, a world prone to the most extreme meteorological events and doomed because of them.

There was an open bag of rubbish outside the chalet opposite and one of the huge seagulls pecked its way through the contents, casting aside beer cans with its beak, a frenetic attempt to find edibles. To my right the door of 368 opened and Alice stepped out, clad in a shapeless wool jumper that came down to her knees over black leggings. The girl stretched extravagantly and gazed around, coming to notice me ten yards down the balcony, stock-still and pretending not to watch. Alice flinched slightly, but her face resolved itself into a sleepy smile and she dawdled along the walkway.

"We're gonna have to stop meeting like this."

"You mean trapped in a shitty holiday camp?"

"Harumph!" She yawned. "Somebody got off the bed-bus at the wrong stop this morning."

I laughed. "You what?"

"Something the old patriarch used to say." She pulled at a loose thread on her sleeve. "Why so crabby Jay?"

"Didn't get much sleep last night."

"Me neither." Alice gestured to the other end of our block. "They both came in absolutely smashed. Then Natasha pukes in the sink and doesn't bother to clean it up, so Suzie accuses her of being bulimic, which is like, utterly ridiculous."

"Food didn't sit right with me either."

"This was more to do with the amount of wine she downed as far as I could tell. So then it really kicks off."

"Yeah?"

"Suzie accuses Nat of being selfish and self-obsessed and self-centred and all sorts of other stuff involving her self."

"Self-abusing?"

Alice looked at me witheringly. "Good to see my dramas can still put a smile on your face Jay."

"Sorry, go on."

"Natasha and Suzie are both claiming the other ate the food we had left, then Nat starts crying."

"Great."

"Just bawling her eyes out, saying she doesn't want to sleep in the lounge, so I offer her my bed to keep the peace." Below us the seagull had found a half-eaten sandwich among the rubbish, was attempting to swallow it in one gulp. "But Nat doesn't want to sleep in the same room as Suze and Suzie's still going at her…"

"One of them needs to get out today, if only for your sake."

Alice rubbed her eyes. "We finally reached a compromise, but everyone was shaken up. I thought there was going to be hair pulling at one point. Didn't expect to have to physically intervene between two silly girls this weekend."

"Silly *girls* huh?"

"For sure." Alice brushed some hair away from her forehead. "Sometimes I feel like a guy on the inside, especially compared to them."

"You're not male, just sane." I offered her my cigarettes. "Smoke?"

"It's times like these I wish I did, but no." She waved the offer away. "Must have got a grand total of three hours sleep last night."

"More than me." I shook my lighter and eventually a flame appeared. "I've been standing here for ages. Did you see the sky at dawn?"

Alice shook her head.

"It was amazing." Drawing on the cigarette, I stared up at the clouds, conventionally tedious now and darkening from the west. "An incredible sight, kind of eerie."

The girl looked at her watch. "Do you think Giles and the others will be back by now?"

"Could be." From behind us came the sound of Wallis coughing. "There's only one way to find out."

The girl span away from me, talking as she moved. "Let me put a face on, then we'll go see."

Alice didn't look any different when she reappeared, not to me anyway, but I wasn't at my most perceptive after that sleepless night. We took the quickest route back to the camp road and followed it round to the car park, Alice describing the neuroses she'd witnessed in her chaletmates all the way, Suzie's domineering control freakery and the insecurities of Nat. The shop by the entranceway was open so we entered and inside Alfred browsed the poky interior, scratching at his beard and muttering as he surveyed sparse shelves.

There wasn't a great deal of choice but I picked up a few essentials, stuff Alice wanted but couldn't buy because she'd left her purse behind, restricting my own purchases to bread, teabags and cigarettes since I planned to leave the camp later today. The girl behind the counter, her hair in bunches and both arms dotted with fresh-looking bruises, watched us with insolence before ringing up the sale, chewing noisily on some gum as she chucked our food into a flimsy carrier bag. I thanked her sarcastically before we went over to the vehicles, Alice checking the spaces for Nigel's beamer, a luxury car she'd ridden in before, said it was impossible to forget that kind of status symbol. We wandered between electric cars and family saloons, drew a blank and conceded defeat after two circuits of the car park.

Sitting on a bench that overlooked the entrance, we waited for the managers to drive back in while consuming the yoghurt drinks Alice had chosen for breakfast. A security guard stood by the barrier across the way, a red and white horizontal bar that prevented unauthorised cars from gaining access. I glanced behind me and realised we were close to the staff chalets, something I pointed out to Alice who asked me how I knew, so I told her what I'd witnessed the night before.

"Well, like my brother always says, ugly people got to have sex too."

"You didn't see it. How either of them could get aroused was a mystery to me." A couple of our colleagues appeared from the right and went into the shop. "Surely no sex is better than doing it with somebody repulsive?"

"I don't know, it's a powerful urge."

"But screwing someone I didn't even *like*, I'd just regret it straight after. How do people get that lustful?" I remembered the scene in the restaurant that previous evening. "Like Derek last night, all over that woman. What's her name?"

"Who, Sandy? They've been having an affair for ages."

"See, that's what I don't understand." I took a sip of the raspberry flavoured yoghurt. "What's the point? People are only going to get hurt. Does Derek need nookie that badly?"

Alice laughed. "*Nookie?*"

"And if they're *in love* why doesn't he just leave his wife?"

"I don't believe they're *in love* as such." The men came out with bags of shopping, both looked as if they'd slept in their clothes. "They're just bored, something like that puts a bit of excitement back into life."

"The wrong kind of excitement. It's always the wrong kind these days."

"Philosopher too huh?"

Dave appeared, walking towards his car to retrieve something from the boot. He raised a hand to us in acknowledgment and seemed well, although his hair was all over the place. Dave's head looking like someone had glued wire wool there for a joke.

"Is boredom behind all of it?" I squinted at Alice, noticing her make up now, the subtle eye shadow and defined brows. "Is that why I see so many sites and web pages for *casual encounters*? You can access loads at work."

"I know."

"All those requests for *NSA fun*...."

"...with a *VWE guy*."

"That's it, and I always wonder, who are these people? Do they actually exist?"

"Oh, they exist."

"Now I think, are they all cheating on someone? Nobody seems to want strings anymore, but strings are what you get when something meaningful happens. When you embark on a relationship with someone strings are the best thing that can happen, surely?"

There was silence for a while. A car traversed the coast road outside the camp, its exhaust made a grinding sound. After the vehicle passed Alice responded.

"My take on it Jay, is that there are a lot of people out there still looking for love, whatever you define love as. But they're outnumbered by people who want something quick and gratifying." She put the yoghurt down and laced her hands together. "Maybe that's to do with the times we live in, how we can't be sure what's going to happen from one day to the next. I don't think I'd want to bring a child into the world at the moment, not even if I had the chance. Not with things the way they are."

"I won't be doing that anytime soon either."

"So we take what we can, while we can. More than that, when you're with someone, when you start dating, and stop me if I'm rambling here..."

"Not a chance."

She smiled. "No one knows how to make a person fall in love with them, and that means you're taking a huge risk, if you happen to be the one falling in love."

"It's not something you can help."

"Well, you can. You can run away from it, that's the point. People are scared of so much these days, and getting your heart broken is right up there with the worst. For girls it's relatively simple, to attract a guy and make him want to share your bed, that game we understand. That's a situation where you can protect yourself and exert a certain amount of control. When it comes to lust I can call the tune to my satisfaction. Try that when you're head over heels in love with someone, see what happens."

"You're saying love would ruin your life?"

"It doesn't have to." Alice sighed. "Although I guess it hasn't treated me too well lately." The girl turned to face me, folding a knee up under her body. "Put it this way Jay. It's taken a long time for women to feel free enough to do what they want in this world. If they've got it all planned out, their best years travelling around or moving abroad or pursuing a career they really enjoy, then falling in love with some guy, all the compromises you have to make, it can totally mess up your plans."

"Not like a night of *fun*."

"Nope, and love's sometimes the opposite of fun." She began to pick at her sleeve again. "Love's too overwhelming. It's work and it's pain and sometimes it's a prison you can't escape."

I finished the drink, only noticing now the expiry date had passed. "Okay, I see. Not sure I agree with you, but I understand."

"Doesn't matter whether you *agree with me* babe, reality isn't after your approval. Think differently if you want, but that's like denying the night or the sea, tide comes in anyway." Alice stood, collecting her shopping from the floor. "Come on, we could be sitting here forever."

I saw a scrawny figure coming out of the staff accommodation behind us then.

Alice said, "So Mr. Hall, what now?"

"Hang on a sec." The camp worker dragged his heels through the grass and I guessed he was on his way to work a shift, blond hair gelled into spikes this morning. Flashing back on the kid, naked in his chalet, I tried to suppress the disturbing image and called out.

"Hey, Neil! Is *Splash World* open?"

The kid looked surprised, glanced at his watch. "Yeah, will be."

I turned to Alice. "Fancy a swim?" I asked her.

Wallis had taken some persuading to come to the pool, unconvinced by my argument that a quick dip would alleviate his hangover.

He'd been sipping hot milk back at the chalet, watching some kung fu movie the internal channel was showing, the programmers having apparently realised that promotional films aimed at kids weren't likely to keep the present guests entertained for long. Wallis just wanted to lie on the sofa and vegetate, told me he wasn't a strong swimmer and didn't possess the kind of physique to show off in public. I assured him it would only be Alice and myself, that he was among friends and I would really appreciate his presence, and eventually he relented.

We undressed now, a cramped changing room that smelt faintly of bodies and bleach, bare feet reacting to the cold floor. For some reason Wallis had brought a pair of Bermuda shorts with him this weekend, perhaps a legacy of that recently departed seasonal mindset, summer having only ended a few weeks ago, chronologically at least. The shorts came down beyond his knees while Wallis' upper body was smooth, the flesh of his torso sagging below the waistband.

I wasn't as prepared as Wallis, would have to wear my boxer shorts and make sure they were buttoned up tight, flexing my biceps now as I waited for him to finish dithering, surreptitiously admiring my physique. Usually I only noticed the imperfections; my stomach that could have been flatter; the hair growing in the wrong places; the calf muscles out of proportion to the rest of me, no matter how much time I spent strengthening them at the gym. Today was different, today I looked pretty good.

At last he was ready.

"You keeping your glasses on then?"

"Yes." Said Wallis, and that was the end of our conversation.

We padded out of the male changing room and into the main chamber, that great pool which had felt so unearthly yesterday evening, viewed from outside on a darkened night. Today it was just like any swimming facility in a provincial leisure centre, the water clear and cool and rich with chlorine. Being there this morning was only strange because we were the sole occupants of that high-ceilinged room, an unoccupied lifeguard's post halfway along the side, the seat positioned about eight feet up to give someone a panoramic overview of everything that went on in the water.

Energised by the realisation we had this place to ourselves, Wallis jogged to the steps leading to the shallow end, a pale man whose feet made a slapping noise on the tiles, every inch the big kid.

Wallis clambered down and tested the surface with a toe, slowly submerging himself up to the neck, cheeks puffing as his body acclimatised to the water's chill. I watched his tentative approach, then took a run up and dived in, the shock of impact feeling good as it cleared my mind. I swam underwater for a few strokes before returning to the air, shaking my head as I resurfaced, the room still echoing from the sound of my body hitting the water.

I swam a few lengths at a leisurely pace as Wallis moved halfway along the pool's length, holding onto a rail all the way, feet stretched out in front of him. When I paused at the side he called across, said I'd been right, this *was* a good idea, he felt better already. Then Wallis went silent and I followed his stunned gaze. Alice strolled out of the changing room, wearing an orange bikini that complemented her bronze skin. The girl stood a couple of inches below six foot and was perfectly proportioned, shapely legs and curves and a glint of metal where her belly button had been pierced. Only now did I realise quite how Amazonian this girl was, in the office she tended to wear clothes that underplayed her physique. Seeing her full breasts, accentuated by that bikini top, I realised why. If she had revealed any cleavage during work hours, Alice would have found herself surrounded by lecherous managers and horny young men staring at her, annoying other women as she unwittingly disrupted the frustratedly priapic, destroying their ability to put in a full day's work.

"Hi guys." Alice walked to the steps, her back adorned with tattoos, some kind of oriental phrase between her shoulder blades, an immaculate calligraph of black letters. There was another at the base of her spine, some kind of dragon I think, and a third began on her left hip before being obscured by her bikini. The girl eased her way into the water, then pushed off from the side of the pool, swimming over to me gracefully, like some amphibian most at ease in the depths.

We trod water and I saw that Alice had her hair tied up, some strands escaping to lay moist against her face.

"Want to do a length?" She asked and I nodded my response. "Race you."

The girl set off without warning, getting a head start that infuriated me, but I swam purposefully and was soon gaining on that lithe figure ahead, my crawl stronger and more competitive than Alice's stroke. By the time we hit the end I'd caught up with her, and in smoothly touching the side, then pushing myself off from the wall, I overtook the girl. Then I really cut loose, arms eager for the next section of pool, feet kicking in time, a length before the girl had made it two-thirds of the way. I relaxed at the edge, watching her splash towards me while Wallis floated on his back nearby, paddling with both hands as he bobbed near the surface, still wearing his spectacles.

"Had enough?" I asked.

Alice dug a finger in my ribs, causing me to buckle at the middle, my grin disappearing in an instant. "I let you off the hook just then Jay, I know how important it is for you males to win."

"Okay, fine." I rubbed my side, splashing her as revenge, a fountain to fend off further assaults. Alice cried out and covered her face until I stopped.

"Again." I said. "There and back. And don't worry about going easy on me this time."

I set off at a leisurely pace, feeling the presence of another body over my shoulder, maintaining my speed to keep her just behind. As we came into the home straight I slowed, as if tiring, allowing Alice to overtake. The girl finished seconds before me.

We rested at the side, the winner out of breath while I barely showed any effects from my exertion. In the distance Wallis climbed out of the pool, evidently he'd had enough.

"You want to go one more time?" The girl demanded between gasps. "Or do you know when you're beaten?"

I laughed and placed a hand on top of her head. Alice's eyes rose questioningly as I brought all the power of my upper body to bear, pushing her down under the water, I held the girl there for a few seconds, bubbling and squeals rising from her mouth, before just as suddenly relinquishing my grip on her and kicking out of reach.

"Bastard!" Alice spat water, tried to smash a tsunami in my direction, but I'd swum away. "Get back here!"

"Not a chance." Continuing to evade the livid girl, I remained just beyond the reach of her arms, that vengeful face changing to a sly smile as she gave up the chase and sank underwater instead. An instant later I felt the momentum of her body strike me, Alice's arms locking round my waist, taking us to the pool's end as we hit the wall, my back taking most of the impact.

"Ow!"

She came up for air, a hand against the tiles either side of me.

"Serves you right."

"You letting me go?"

Alice wrapped her legs around my thorax, I could feel her heels pushing into my buttocks. "Not a chance."

My hands went to her sides, Alice's skin soft, her body close. "Nice bikini by the way."

"Thanks." The girl's voice was husky. "Didn't know whether to bring it or not."

"I'm glad you did."

"Guess I'm an optimist."

I looked at Alice, her face inches from mine, those eyes wanting something. Our limbs were entwined now and we gripped each other tightly, her lips moving closer. I was profoundly turned on, equal to everything that might have been waiting outside the pool. None of it held any fear and nothing was hanging over me, there wasn't any reason to be worried or disillusioned. There was only this girl and the water and my belief in the immanence of a kiss.

The sound of a throat being cleared came from close by and the two of us separated, a pair of embarrassed children caught petting away from the group. By the time I'd registered that attendant standing over us, a slack-jawed man in his twenties with a beaky nose prominent on his cranium, Alice was already out of the pool.

We listened to Wallis buzz on leaving the *Splash Zone*, talk of how much better he felt, that dip revivifying his mind, my friend having worked up a healthy appetite. The three of us were walking down the side of the dome when we came upon a commotion outside the King Charles, about twenty-five of our colleagues sitting on benches or stood nearby, a sense of outrage in the air as they confronted Dobbs to express their suspicions. Norman encapsulated my idea of harassed, attempting to bat away their accusations and insults, biting his bottom lip as subordinates demanded the section head elucidate, voices raised and fingers jabbing allegations of incompetence and betrayal. Dobbs fussed and evaded, swaying a little under the barrage, tugging at his hair with a hand as he tried to explain why the other managers hadn't returned.

Chapter Seven

Inevitably Theresa Barnes was at the forefront of these hostilities towards Dobbs, her scoliotic body bent like a question mark, demanding answers he wasn't able to give.

"Where are they then?" She squawked. "It's gone noon."

Dobbs looked ashen-faced. "They'll be back soon. Giles must have been delayed."

Alice spotted one of her chaletmates watching the scene unfold, that pale-skinned redhead called Natasha. We sat down on the bench beside her.

I saw Theresa gesture to Julie Newman, her friend sitting at the edge of this disturbance, a sad smile adorning her face. "Julie has to get back and check on her son. We were told we'd be able to leave this morning."

"I can't let anyone go without authorisation."

"So get *authorisation*! Call them!"

Dobbs sighed, tired of placating this mob that simply didn't understand his position. "The phones are still down."

Theresa Barnes made a *pfftt* noise and went to comfort Julie, curving an arm around the woman as she sat. Even without her the unrest continued, more unsettled colleagues Dobbs was powerless to reassure. He reminded me of some deluded Minister of Information, addressing the world's press to deny his country was being invaded, even as they saw it happening behind him.

Beside me Natasha whispered to Alice, the girl skinny and nervous, bowing her head as she spoke of missing her boyfriend, being unable to take much more of this place.

"I'm sure my fellow managers will return any minute now." Norman was visibly wilting, if anyone had seen Dobbs like this in the office they'd have got him a glass of water, whatever their opinion of the man. "In the meantime, everyone is free to use the camp facilities, or perhaps you could go for a walk on the beach, now the weather's cleared up."

Emerging from the throng, Roger didn't look as if he was in any mood to enjoy *Sunlit's* entertainment possibilities.

"I don't think you realise quite how serious this is becoming." Roger had maybe half a decade over Dobbs and used all the authority of his age to patronise the younger man. "Sid can't find his medication. He needs to get somewhere they give out emergency prescriptions."

Norman Dobbs pulled at the collar of his white shirt. "There's nothing else I can tell you Roger."

I craned my neck to see Roger's middle-aged friend. Sid didn't look well, great black circles around his eyes and the demeanour of a man who's recently lost the use of a limb. Near me Wallis had been watching proceedings and now he turned my way expectantly while Alice had finished listening to Natasha and leaned across, her mouth close to my ear.

"Nat's distraught." Her hot breath made me shiver. "Cabin fever maybe, she's going to drive herself crazy if she stays here."

"People are sick, Sid needs a doctor."

"We have to do something Jay." I glanced at those people, all assembled outside the King Charles. Apart from the ones who were desperate to leave like Theresa and Roger, there appeared to be a grumbling acceptance of Dobbs' stubborn stance, everyone acknowledging they would just have to wait it out. Nobody looked like volunteering to help Sid, they preferred not to get involved, stick with what we'd been told was the company line. As head jobsworth, Dobbs embodied this attitude. A wave of contempt came over me then, and although it went against my natural inclinations, that tendency to stay in the background, my unwillingness to draw attention to myself unless absolutely necessary, I considered stepping in. Trying to put conflicting impulses to the back of my mind, alongside the potential risk to my career, I took a decision, feeling the pressure of Alice at my side, her presence urging me to intervene.

I turned to the girl. "Do you think you'd be okay driving a minibus?"

"I can try."

Moving to Roger and Sid then, a hand on each of their shoulders, I told the men that help was available and attracted the attention of Dobbs. Norman regarded me like I was some kind of nuisance he should have recognised as I walked across, waiting until all eyes were on me.

"Everyone, hello." People gradually ceased their talking. My legs felt numb, as if I'd been sitting in the same position for hours. "Most of you know me, I'm Jay Hall. Unless there are any objections, I intend to take those with valid health or personal reasons to the station, from there they can get a train home."

I knew Dobbs was trying to interrupt but I wasn't about to accede to him.

"We've got Julie, Theresa and Sid so far. Is there anyone else who needs to leave but doesn't have a car?"

Near the back Natasha raised her arm.

Roger said, "I'm going to travel with Sid, at least to the station."

"Okay, good." There was muttering from a few people before me. "I'll get the key to the minibus and we can meet beside it." I nodded to my colleagues while naming them. "Nat, Sid, Theresa, Julie – pack your stuff. We leave at two."

"If the others aren't back by then." Norman's voice was more fractured than adversarial, a weak radio signal.

"Yes, as long as Giles and the others don't return with some other plan before then." It felt like I was in charge now, and while it was gratifying to be listened to by this score of people, I wasn't enjoying it much. "If you do run into anybody else, or become aware of anyone with legitimate reasons for wanting to get back to London, please let them know."

I went over to Alice while Dobbs got the last word in. He must have realised that to contradict my plan would further weaken his authority so instead Norman chose to issue a veiled threat.

"But remember, we've the big party scheduled for this evening and request everyone's presence. There's a free bar all night that Giles and myself have arranged…"

The group dissipated now, some returning to their chalets or heading for the front of the dome, others spotting the pub had opened and moving inside. Dobbs continued to speak, even as those he addressed disappeared out of earshot. Alice was thoughtful, while beside her Natasha looked up at me with the kind of admiration a daughter has for her supposedly heroic daddy. Seeing Nat like that pleased me, but I also felt horribly foolish for some reason. I told the girls to go back to chalet 368 and pack up Natasha's belongings while I retrieved the minibus key, inviting Wallis, who I felt guilty about leaving out of the upcoming journey, to accompany me towards reception.

The hatches were all shut, I suppose the camp hadn't anticipated anyone checking out today, but Wallis found the manager's office round the corner, near the arcade. Tracy Ashborne was at her desk dealing with paperwork, two large cabinets on either side of her office which overflowed with pharmaceutical equipment, ampoules of medicine, bandages and salves, supplies for her sometime role as first-aider. I asked whether she'd been approached by a man in his fifties who had misplaced his pills and the female manager said yes. Tracy was very sorry, but she would have to tell me what she'd told Sid and Roger, this place wasn't as well stocked as a high street pharmacy, there was simply nothing here for them.

Although her name badge informed me Tracy's title was camp *General Manager*, the woman retained the bustling, competent manner of a professional nurse, sending out unspoken signals that there was a line here you didn't cross. I wouldn't have wanted to feel Tracy's wrath, the woman was sturdy and ample, probably taller than me, and with the kind of face that feels like it's on a different scale from most, a prominent nose and mouth which wouldn't have looked out of place on a man. Thankfully she received my request for information with good grace, noting only that all five organisers had the same list, so it was strange I should solicit the information from her.

I mumbled something about being unable to find them at the moment, not wanting to get into the specifics of how four of them were missing, and I'd rather have knocked on every chalet door than approach Dobbs after bypassing his ineffectuality earlier. Norman might well have refused to impart the details to me anyway, but it took Tracy a matter of seconds to find the only Derek in our party, Derek Cattermole who was staying in chalet 680. She leaned across the desk to prove it, revealing some kind of major scar just above the wrist as her sleeve drew up. What little I saw of the wound looked horrible, a patch of skin burnt or seared by some chemical, a leathery brown colour against the pink of her unblemished flesh. I was still wondering about the full extent of this scar, how Tracy could have sustained it, after I'd left her office, walking over to Derek's chalet with Wallis. My friend had evidently been mulling things over too, since he chose this moment to verbalise his concerns.

"Are you sure this is a good idea Jay?"

"Somebody has to do it." We cut between blocks that felt oddly familiar. This looked like the place I'd seen that dead rabbit yesterday. If so, the remains had been removed. "I'll only be gone a couple of hours, do you want me to pick you up anything?"

Wallis went quiet, I assumed he was considering the possibilities, a magazine or comic he might want, but instead my friend said, "What if you don't come back either?"

I fumbled for my cigarettes. This was the issue I'd been trying to avoid even though it had occurred to me and, I'm sure, Alice as well. The managers had told everyone they'd be returning as soon as possible, but only Dobbs was still convinced, waiting for his familiars like some faithful hound, hopeful but mistaken. What Wallis didn't realise was that Giles had already lied to us once, saying they knew exactly what had struck while we were on the beach. Perhaps he hadn't been telling the truth yesterday either, maybe the other section heads never intended to reappear.

"I'll be back mate, don't you worry." My cigarette tasted unusual, as if I'd been hypnotised into finding it repulsive. "You don't think I'd abandon you?"

Wallis smiled. "No, it's just…"

"Besides, all my stuff's here." We reached the block that included chalet 680, I threw away my cigarette before it was even halfway done. "I want you to keep your eyes open while I'm gone, let me know what's been happening when I get back, can you do that?"

"Sure."

Derek took a long time to answer the door, I had to bang and call out for several minutes before he realised I wasn't going to give up and came to meet us, warily allowing me to step inside. At first he was reluctant to hand over the keys, the man full of questions, asking if those in charge had given their approval and pointing out he was the one who'd signed for this vehicle. If someone else crashed it, he'd be liable. The chalet around Derek was a mess, clothes and food wrappers strewn across the surfaces, and the man himself looked like he'd just thrown on a t-shirt, was agitated as a parolee who has been roused to form part of something dubious. He regarded me sceptically, Derek rubbing at the dome of his smooth head, while I assured him there was nothing to worry about, anxious at how close we were getting to two o'clock. That was when the source of Derek's awkwardness became apparent, Sandy emerging from the bedroom in a nightgown, the woman looking older without her make-up, greeting her lover's guests as if we were old friends paying a social call.

Sandy disappeared into the shower and I resolved the issue swiftly, informing Derek that, if I remembered rightly, I had his wife's email address and I was sure she'd be interested to learn of his mistress, even if I couldn't care less. After that there was no need for further discussion.

I tried to have another cigarette while waiting by the minibus and jingling the keys in my pocket but it remained off somehow, as if the tobacco had been mixed with something unsavoury, a substance leaving a bad aftertaste. Giving up, I discarded it and watched Natasha approach, Alice carrying her chaletmate's baggage, the belongings of a girl who looked frail and ill. I opened the back door and let Nat in while Alice stored her stuff in the luggage compartment. The time was a few minutes before two and those clouds above us were gradually changing, moving from a benign grey to the kind of night-evoking shade that brings with it heavy rain.

Our male passengers were right on time, Roger shambling over in good humour, helping a wheezy Sid up the steps and into the rear of our bus, leaving myself and Alice outside to await the final pair.

"We're really going out then." There was apprehension in Alice's voice.

"Yeah." I resisted the urge to put an arm around her. "We'll find out exactly what's been happening."

Alice looked at me. "What if we end up in the middle of it, have to confront something terrible?"

"Nothing's out there. Anyway, we're not going far." Some kind of entreaty was buried in her dark eyes. I tried to think what someone heroic might say in these circumstances. "Even if it is dangerous, I wouldn't let anyone harm us."

"Some things are too big for one guy." The girl glanced away, at Julie and Theresa approaching slowly, the latter more interested in talking to her friend than being on time. "I guess speculation doesn't get us anywhere."

"Leave the worrying to me, you focus on driving us out."

Theresa Barnes jabbered away, thought she'd left something behind but was unable to remember what, wondered where they should hand their keys in, what her sister would be doing now, God willing. We guided her and a silent Julie inside and I raised my voice above her stream, asked if any of our passengers knew whether this was it, or if we should wait for others. Nobody responded so I supposed everyone else was obeying Dobbs' directive, either that or they'd been tempted by the promise of that gratis catering later on.

I slammed the back door and climbed in next to Alice who was familiarising herself with the controls, reversed us out of the parking spot and onto the road leading out of the camp. The security man at the exit was huddled up in a great jacket with his collar up and he responded to our approach by raising the barrier, nodding as we passed through and I gave him a wave of thanks.

We came out onto the coast road, Alice leaning forward to ask if there was anything coming from the left. Once she had confirmed both lanes were empty we accelerated out, overshooting as Alice took us onto the grass verge opposite, inches away from a ditch that was several feet deep. Correcting our trajectory just in time, she wrenched at the steering wheel in desperation, a jolt from the uneven surface under our wheels making my heart palpitate, quieting Theresa and the others.

I spoke under my breath, told Alice everything was fine, that she should relax and drive at her own pace, there was no hurry. Then I turned to reassure those in the back, Natasha gazing at me with worried eyes, her skin almost translucent, Sid having a coughing fit beside her.

"It's okay, just a ramp in the road."

Roger passed Sid a bottle of water and eventually the hacking ceased. Theresa resumed her narrative about some person she'd entrusted with watering her plants this weekend. Meanwhile Alice looked out at the road with a new intensity, concentrating on every twist and declivity of our route, those surroundings that looked so different from up here, the rolling hills and flat fields stretching inland. We passed a golf course near the coast, deserted now but well cared for, greens and bunkers forming another island of artificiality in this landscape. The road veered sharply to the right then, arrows indicating this curve was almost a right angle, Alice having to brake and shift through the gears, and soon we were heading away from the shoreline, deracinated fields on both sides. I was sure some of them had been populated with sheep on the way down, but perhaps that was another section of countryside. It all looked similar to someone like me, a city type unused to this topography, the demarcations of rural land.

Rain began to fall, a few heavy drops at first, Alice coolly flicking on the windscreen wipers in response, but soon it became the kind of downpour that floods uneven roads. I focussed on picking out road signs at junctions and roundabouts through the spray, informing Alice which exit was appropriate for the small town we were heading towards, a place with a train station and working phone lines, Theresa Barnes' voice was just background noise now, like the rain or our engine's hum.

As we progressed the water kicked up from the bus wheels and visibility grew worse, the murk and dark clouds overhead giving our surroundings a dusky aspect. We traversed a single-lane bridge over a swelling brook, Alice asking me to turn on the headlights. I scanned the dashboard, feeling the minibus slow as I searched for the switch, wondering if she was aware of the risk we might aquaplane, the vehicle unable to stop in time because of surface water.

I pushed the button to activate the lights and rose quickly to make sure I'd got the setting right.

"What's that?" Alice demanded.

In the distance some arrangement of vehicles blocked our route. Human shapes moved around structures, and there was some kind of tent erected to the side of the thoroughfare. Alice slowed our approach, stopping the bus about fifty metres from the obstruction. These were military vehicles, two jeeps facing each other across the roadway, one truck to the right with canvas stretching over it, a semi-circular roof that troops would sit underneath for journeys.

"Army."

A figure wearing a camouflage poncho peeled away and came towards us. In the back Theresa asked why we had stopped. The man stared at Alice through the windscreen, then moved to the passenger side. In his right hand he held a rifle by the barrel. A tap at the window made me bring it down, allowed droplets of water to blast my face.

"Hi." Alice spoke across me but the soldier didn't respond. His face, partially obscured by the hood, was unreadable. The man looked about sixteen, but he must have been older. He looked at me as if I'd automatically know which question to answer, as if he shouldn't need to ask.

"We've got some sick people in the back." I explained. "We're taking them to see a doctor."

The soldier glanced into the closest rear window but I didn't think he'd have seen much, not through the rain-spattered glass. I checked on our passengers, all wearing the expressions of the watchful and powerless, like patients in an Accident and Emergency ward. I told them we'd be moving again very soon while the soldier spoke into some kind of two-way radio, held the portable device up to his ear, his back to the wind. By the time he returned I'd grown weary of this taciturnity and closed my window, trying to keep out that rain which had soaked my left side. He tapped on the glass again and I rolled it down angrily.

"Look, can we speak to whoever's in charge?"

The soldier gestured with the end of his gun and set off toward the roadblock. I told our occupants I'd be back in a minute but Alice shook her head.

"I'm coming with you."

We went out into the soaking rain and it occurred to me that traffic might be lined up behind. I glanced back, at the road stretching away from our parked bus which was entirely empty, a sight that made me aware I hadn't seen a single car since leaving the holiday complex. Alice was waiting for me so I moved to catch up, striding towards the encampment, this whole set-up feeling like the kind of improvised checkpoint that bars the main route in some paranoid dictatorship. More men in ponchos carried rifles back and forth between the troop carrier and canvas tent as we passed their vehicles, none of them looking our way. The soldier leading us gestured to the entrance of a tent which was reminiscent of a small marquee, something it must have been hellishly difficult to construct, out here in the middle of nowhere.

Inside this tent was partitioned into three areas, Alice and I invited to occupy the folding chairs in a kind of reception. We were left to listen to the rain, splattering on the canvas above. The wordlessness of these people had infected us, although Alice did move her arm closer, eventually putting a hand in mine, a gesture of solidarity or the need for reassurance.

A swoosh of material indicated the arrival of the man in charge from behind a canvas flap as Alice relinquished her grip.

"Come in won't you?" The officer said, before disappearing again. We followed him into his quarters, seating ourselves opposite him at a metal table. The man in charge was about my age I would have said, but with the upright bearing and rhetorical certainty of somebody trained to command subordinates. There was very little space here in his improvised office for military appurtenances, just some Ordnance Survey maps strewn across the table along with his radio.

"Tell me, why were you out on this filthy day?"

My tongue felt wet and heavy in my mouth. Alice said, "I'd like to know why you've blocked the road."

The officer looked at Alice with interest, as if studying an alien substance under a microscope. "I have my orders." He said at last.

The girl turned her face away. There was something professorial about this man, despite his uniform. A budding pomposity that enabled me to imagine him half a century down the line, a retired colonel boring dinner party guests with endless burbling about combat zones. The vision destroyed some of his power and I spoke up then, gave a brief summary of the events which led us here, that ill-fated team-building weekend and our stay at the holiday camp. I kept it simple, leaving out the incident on the beach and the disappearance of our managers, was just beginning to detail reasons for this afternoon's trip when there came shouts from outside.

The officer rose and made for the exit without a word. I followed him with Alice behind. Outside the young soldier who led us here was standing with his back to a jeep, one of four servicemen who observed Roger stumbling down the road towards them, barely noticing as his feet splashed at puddles, soaking his legs.

"Stop! Stop there!" The soldier yelled, but Roger didn't seem to hear him. He was calling out something about Sid, about needing to know what was happening. Roger advanced further, he was about fifteen yards from the roadblock now, at which point the quartet of armed men raised their rifles as one and aimed them at him.

Chapter Eight

The sound of guns being cocked must have forced some awareness into Roger, because at last he obeyed those calls to *stop*, halting his unsteady stride to peer through the rain and mist as if short-sighted, trying to make out what the blurred shapes were doing with those objects they pointed at him.

I looked back and forth between the confused middle-aged man, sopping wet and with the rain beating down on him, and those four soldiers treating him as their target, none of them much older than kids. Somebody needed to intervene, but if I were to distract anyone, generate the slightest movement in Roger or the flinch of a single trigger finger, any attempt would end in disaster.

The officer came to Roger's rescue just in time, from his post at the roadside where he studied the scene dispassionately. Able to ascertain that this shambling, unarmed figure wasn't the enemy, the commander ordered his men to lower their rifles.

"Go back!" He barked to Roger, the man wavering uncertainly.

"Go on," I called to him. "I'll be there in a moment." Then to Alice, "I'll get him on the bus and come straight back."

"Stand down!" Was the order as I tried to ignore the troops, armed and jittery behind my back, jogging to catch up with the departing Roger and escort him to our vehicle. I claimed to be on top of the situation when he asked, saying he should remain patient and all this would be resolved.

The back door opened and I shepherded Roger inside, squelching as he moved to a seat, Theresa fussing over him and Julie taking off her woollen scarf, encouraging the man to dry himself with her garment. Natasha and Sid looked on, the pair of them meek and blank-eyed, like beaten-down prisoners. I explained we were delayed at an army checkpoint, that the military had claimed control of this area and I was speaking with the man in charge to let us drive on. Theresa began asking something but I pretended not to hear, slamming the door shut and splashing my way back to the encampment, hands above my head to avoid more false alarms. I must have looked ridiculous in this pose, placatory and terrified.

Advised to return to the marquee tent while the officer spoke with his men, Alice and I went back inside, damp and silent now. The girl looked shell-shocked, matted hair sticking to Alice's face and her breathing audible, heavy and irregular. I couldn't think of anything to say, feeling that water ooze through my shoes and into my socks, peered across at the maps instead, at a couple of areas marked by hand. They covered this county, the plans mainly showing featureless terrain, the same as that landscape we'd driven through.

The officer appeared, grunting to himself as if dissatisfied, long seconds while he checked the two-way radio before acknowledging us.

"That's what happens these days when people blunder in."

"Roger's worried about his friend." My trousers felt clammy and unpleasant on my legs. "We need to get him treatment."

"I hope you can understand, the requirements of one man must be weighed against the overall picture."

"Its not just *one man*." Alice's voice was low, her face looking down. "We've got others in there."

The officer looked at her with curiosity, an irritatingly blasé figure. I wondered how justified his self-importance was, whether these men really had much of a purpose, out here in the wilds.

"These are civilians, they need your assistance." The words sounded more confrontational that I'd intended. "Are you going to help them?"

The men eyed me now and I noticed at least a day's growth of stubble on his face. "I can talk to my superiors." He said.

We were asked to leave while he contacted the ranking officer on his walkie-talkie. I sat outside, straining to hear his side of the conversation from my seat while, back at the holiday complex, Wallis was becoming embroiled in preparations for the evening.

As Wallis would tell me later, after I'd disappeared without him, my friend went back to chalet 364 and endeavoured to cook the frozen pizza he'd bought from the site shop, choking as a cloud of black smoke emanated from the cooker when he looked in on the food. A layer of crusted sediment had formed at the bottom of the oven and it burned afresh each time the power was turned on. The acrid fumes set off the fire alarm above our door and Wallis waved a towel at the device impotently in a bid to halt the noise, a harsh bleep that didn't seem to rouse anyone else in the vicinity but annoyed my friend to such an extent he stood on a chair to disable it. Opening every available widow in an attempt to ease the smell of burning, in the end Wallis' lunch didn't come out so much cooked as incinerated. Still, he had never much worried about the niceties of his meals, crunching that hard crust while slumped on the sofa to watch *Sunlit*'s internal channel, now showing some kind of art house film without the subtitles. The movie starred Japanese actors and quickly became both explicit and distasteful, sequences involving torture or perversion, causing Wallis to flick through the channels once more, an automatic exercise for him which bore no results, pointless fiddling with that box on top of the set bringing up nothing but static.

 A sense of boredom was encroaching like the tide, so Wallis wandered out onto the balcony, watching the rain as it began to fall. It was then a strong draught caught our door and slammed it shut behind him. Discombobulated, Wallis fumbled in his pockets for the chalet key, a key, he came to understand with a sinking feeling, he'd left on the kitchen table. Gazing up at the lounge window, Wallis wondered whether he might fit through the narrow gap, realising he was too bulky to get inside that way, would become stuck at the shoulders or stomach even if there had been someone present to give him a bunk up.

 Uncertain of what to do next, Wallis checked his watch and saw the time was after three, I was expected back in less than an hour. Somewhat heartened, Wallis walked down the balcony to number 398, aware of an ache in his loins that signalled the need for relief. Nobody answered his knock, if Suzie was inside the girl wasn't responding to visitors, so Wallis took himself down the stairs and out into the rain-battered centre.

 The rubbish outside number 327, that ground floor chalet opposite us, had expanded exponentially. Litter covered the outside pathway as well as the grass, dragged here by gulls and blown about in the wind. Picking his way through the cartons and cans, Wallis found the chalet door unlatched and pushed at it gently, the sound of wrappers and paper sliding away as a result of his pressure.

 Inside there came the pungent smell of burning marijuana, Dale Packer laid out on the sofa smoking a joint, his rugby player's bulk stretched across the furniture, one foot dangling above a floor covered with food that had been trodden into the carpet, discarded men's magazines showing naked girls pawing each other for the camera. I'd never met Dale before but Wallis was familiar with him, my friend worked closely with some girl who had fancied Packer, and when Dale finally took the hint, starting to visit twice a day and pay her attention under a variety of unconvincing pretexts, Wallis had to put up with the awkward and embarrassing seduction, played out at an adjacent desk.

 Uninterested in people unless they could do something for him, help with his career or supply useful contacts, Dale was an unsubtle ex-public schoolboy with a tendency to rub colleagues up the wrong way. But like everyone at the company, Dale found no cause to dislike Wallis, my friend viewed as unthreatening and inconsequential, incapable of causing anybody problems. Dale invited him in, barely averting his gaze from the television, a naked Japanese man anointing a corpse in a series of languorous, soft focus shots, erotic and disturbing. Wallis was introduced to the other occupants of 327, Ejiro and Rob at the table surrounded by a pungent haze, the latter apparently rolling another joint. Their guest asked if he could use the toilet, to which Dale grunted a monosyllabic reply.

From his description it sounded like the chalet's drugged torpor was all but unbearable. Even Wallis, who tended to confront everything life threw at him with the same accepting state of mind, was growing perturbed. This uneasiness came less from the knowledge these men were committing a sackable offence than the state of their accommodation, the rooms having degenerated into what his mother would call *a pigsty* in less than two days.

Worse was to come, Ejiro's voice warning Wallis as he walked down the hallway, a stoned drawl with a hint of African informing their visitor the toilet was broken. When Wallis opened the bathroom door the odour of cannabis came to be replaced by something earthier and more repellent. His first instinct was to flush, consign that floating faeces and stained paper to oblivion, but a few yanks at the handle revealed that Ejiro was correct, the metal lever flopping in response to his touch. There was no pressure here, and apparently someone had already dismantled the cistern with the intention of fixing it, failing miserably before abandoning the cracked lid on the floor.

The sight of that overflowing toilet left Wallis unable to go, as if he'd been caught attempting to urinate somewhere public, that dull throb in his bladder impossible to ease and the burnt pizza threatening to resurface. Wallis hurried out then, told Dale and the others he would see them later, rushing to the camp's centre and assaulted by that rain cascading down.

Wet and bursting, Wallis made it inside the dome and turned right at that massive purple spider overhead, into the area opposite reception where he found the gents, urinated then washed both hands thoroughly, drying his hair and neck under the hot air blast of a single working machine.

Having got his breath back, feeling fresh and warm and much better, Wallis came out to the sound of arcade machines in the amusement area, deciding with a flush of liberation to exchange a note for coins at the change machine, spend the rest of the afternoon playing video games until I returned. In the arcade Catherine and Cheryl were operating a metal claw with a spectacularly flaccid grip, trying to grasp a soft toy and manoeuvre it to the exit chute, one of the girls clapping her hands when it looked like the other might succeed. Heading for the pair, people who were happy and pretty and normal, Wallis saw the camp manager collect coins from a wall-mounted machine that dispensed electricity tokens, talking with someone as she did so. Wallis looked over, automatically meeting Dobbs' eye and instantly regretting it.

"Aha! Now here's a likely candidate!" Norman announced, unaware of Wallis's name and trying to hide his ignorance. "You'd be willing to lend a hand and help us prepare wouldn't you?" Wallis stopped in his tracks, confused as to why his plan to play games had suddenly fallen apart and unsure of how to respond. Dobbs didn't wait for an answer. "Come with me then."

The manager led him up the main flight of stairs toward the dome's first floor. Wallis following begrudgingly, wishing he was with me and upset at the unfairness of it all. When they got to the hall that would host this evening's revelry his fears were confirmed, Dobbs had picked Wallis out to be his lackey, replacing one of those *Sunlit* workers who hadn't appeared this Saturday. The supervisor must have seen Wallis as the type to assist in fetching and carrying, the kind of tasks usually undertaken by ill-paid porters.

Half a dozen teenagers wearing the red polo shirts and name badges of the camp ambled around this main space, a place where shows would be hosted during the summer season, when entertainers performed up on the stage that was currently obscured by velvet curtains. Employees carried paper plates and disposable cutlery, unfolding tables beside the bar in an area earmarked for the buffet, a couple of staff ensuring the fridges behind were full of beer, bottles overhead ready to dispense their liquor.

Wallis was directed to help where required, finding himself reduced to the level of those pimply boys and girls, paid by the hour to scurry back and forth between storerooms and kitchen. Joining them, he overheard the unaffected conversation of teenagers, helping himself to crisps that were emptied into bowls now Dobbs had hurried off somewhere else, a single perk during this unasked for shift-work. Two girls with bleached blonde hair discussed what they were going to do with upcoming days off, bemoaning the need to work on a Saturday night, the only time when it was *buzzing* in their home town. An extremely camp male came over and talked about a fancy dress party he was holding while his parents were away, teasing the girls verbally as he touched their bodies, squeezing breasts and behinds while they giggled at his nerve, flirtatiously telling the effete kid to *go away*.

Trays of appetisers under cling film were brought out, causing Wallis to salivate further, making him wonder if he could slip the cover off for a second and help himself, deciding against it when Tracy appeared and began to call out orders at those workers who were slacking off. As one of the weekend's customers, Wallis expected the camp manager to go easy on him, perhaps even allow my friend to leave, but Tracy didn't treat Wallis any differently to her other charges. He'd been reclassified, was just another minion now, told to go join a gangly youth on the steps at the hall's rear, stick decorations and inflatables high up on the wall.

Wallis and another male went over to this darkened area and began blowing up balloons, tugging at the rubber with their hands and expelling air into the coloured sacs. The employee managed to inflate his share easily enough but Wallis was soon out of breath, struggling to exhale with the required force and wishing there was a canister of helium he could use instead.

Sitting on the stairs to rest, Wallis surveyed the scene, seeing someone move in the DJ booth next to the stage and Tracy marching across the lacquered floor to check the disco lights were functioning. Wallis wondered, as he sometimes did, if he ought to stand up for himself more often. People like Dobbs used his amiability against him, and occasionally it made Wallis feel the way he did now, like a doormat. But deep inside my friend knew he could never change, didn't want to be the sort of person who caused conflict and hassle for others. Besides, Norman was evidently struggling. The other organisers hadn't returned, leaving Dobbs to coordinate tonight as best he could. Wallis decided not to be too outraged about being made to muck in, it was just degrading to be enlisted in such a menial capacity, unpleasant for a man in his thirties to discover he was no good at the most basic of tasks, unlike those two lads behind who talked as they inflated more balloons.

"Yeah, we just leave them to it."

"I'll be glad of the lie in."

"Not our problem anymore, thank fuck."

"Girlfriend'll want me to take her shopping, now I've got my wheels."

"Fun." The squeak of a balloon being blown up. "I've gotta see the owner before I go."

"Never met the geezer. What's he like?"

"Yeah, okay. Bit weird, but so's everyone ain't they?"

"Tell me about it."

"If you get on well with him you can earn extra. Perks, if you know what I mean."

"I've heard that."

"Yeah, it's alright…"

Dobbs arrived then, strutting across the hall to liase with Tracy, pinning down the timings and final details. Wallis moved further into the shadows at the back, hoping no one would see him slack off, feeling like a naughty schoolboy as he pondered the possibility of reaching the exit without Norman noticing. The section head looked fraught, Dobbs' movements twitchy and agitated, as if he wasn't coping well with all that was going on, everything he'd suddenly become responsible for.

The stage's great speakers were tested then, crackling with power as they emitted a few seconds of some song Wallis didn't recognise, a dark instrumental piece, gloomy and slow. Wallis saw that his chance to slip away had gone when Dobbs came over, once again he'd been too meek to sneak off. Frustrated with himself, Wallis wished he had left the camp with me, little did he know that my excursion into the world had gone desperately wrong.

After what seemed like an age the officer called through the canvas partition to us. We found him straight-backed like before, hands obscuring his mouth while the fingers rubbed at a knuckle.

We sat and waited for him to speak, anticipation in the air.

"Well?" Alice said at last.

He would only look at me. "I've spoken to my superiors, relayed what you told me."

I nodded, we'd been privy to some of the early part of this conversation, talk littered with phrases like *they say* and *according to them*. The logic behind his questioning of our account was a mystery and, as the exchange went on, this officer had been reduced to noises of agreement, finding himself unable to get a word in, receiving chapter and verse from whoever was at the other end.

"Those in charge are of the opinion you would be safer back at the holiday centre. I have to say, I agree with them."

It took a moment for the words to sink in. The officer drew his chair back as if ready to bid us farewell. I didn't know how to come back to that, felt tongue-tied and useless, it was left to Alice to provide a dissenting voice.

"Safer? Safer from *what*?"

He stood. "I'll take a summary of today's events and record your vehicle's number plate so we know who you are in future…"

"No. No, that's not good enough." Alice's voice wavered, the girl on the verge of hysteria. I'd never heard her like this. "What's happening out there? You have to tell us!"

The officer sounded weary. "I'm sorry Miss, even if I understood the full picture anything I said would only raise more questions than I could answer. I remain under strict instructions…"

"Right, sure." Alice rose, I still couldn't think of anything to say. "Thanks for your time."

Outside the afternoon had grown lighter, the rain reduced to a drizzle. A couple of soldiers watched as I quickened my pace to keep up with Alice, the girl's eyes obscured by tears.

She fell against the minibus and slid down into a heap, head in her hands. Natasha's quizzical face stared out at me from the nearest window.

I crouched down to Alice's level. "Let me have the keys." I said.

I'd never driven a vehicle this size, hadn't even handled a car in years, but Alice was in no fit state, curled up in the passenger seat without a seatbelt. She didn't move as I instigated a three-point turn across the roadway, taking us back towards the *Sunlit Holiday Centre*. Fully aware of my shortcomings I kept the vehicle's speed at twenty miles an hour all the way, electing to drive in the centre of the road rather than risk my wheels near the edge, telling myself there was no other traffic here, nothing that might result in a collision. In fact, the only car we passed on our return was some kind of sports utility vehicle, parked off in a lay-by, and I was too concerned with anticipating the next turn to see if anyone was inside.

When I'd started up the engine I told our passengers we were going back, trying to block out Theresa's demands for an explanation, the woman saying this wasn't fair on any of them. Her insistence eventually petered out when I didn't respond, Alice silent beside me in the front, and I wondered if I'd destroyed any faith the girl might have had in me, taking over this drive the least I could do after my failure to back her up.

When I first started at the company I'd often find myself copied in on emails whose authors were verbose and intimidating, used words of four syllables or more, terms I'd never encountered before. Over the past few years I'd been slowly rectifying this weakness in myself, a conscious decision to strengthen my vocabulary, reading non-fiction or highbrow novels for half an hour most evenings, a dictionary on hand at all times.

It was a hard habit to get into at first, this regular exercising of my mind, a similar flexing to that workout my body enjoyed on trips to the gym. Still I knew the better I expressed myself in the presence of my bosses, the more likely I was to be promoted. Nowadays I occasionally dropped a long word of my own into an email, *pejorative* perhaps, or *concatenation*, and I knew I could have debated that army officer on the wisdom of his decision; it wasn't as if he overawed me intellectually. I might even have pressured him into rethinking, tricked that man into revealing a little of the purpose behind his temporary barracks, but I didn't. It wasn't his intelligence or innate sense of authority that won out and left me smaller in Alice's eyes. No, it was the knowledge he held all the cards, knew so much more than me. That gave the army man his power, and taking on the powerful still felt unnatural. Maybe I was a coward after all.

We were back on the coast road now and Theresa was complaining again, asking what we were going to do now, how much longer she would have to stay in the holiday camp coming up on our left, that complex which looked even more like a blot on the landscape this afternoon. The ersatz hospitality of the place was lit against the dusk that had begun to descend and I swerved the bus slightly to get everyone's attention, shouting that we would find the nurse and see out the rest of the weekend then leave, just like the company wanted us to. I wasn't happy at withholding everything Alice and I had learned from those soldiers, whatever that was, but telling these people the full story, letting everyone know what had happened out there, that wouldn't help anybody. It could only cause more panic and anxiety and fear of what was to come, that same fear which sat heavy in the minds of myself and Alice, dark and pulsating and as inseparable from my being as a malignant tumour.

Chapter Nine

My colleagues queued for the buffet, heads angled forward like buzzards, using spoons and tongs and fingers to heap great piles of food onto their plates, chicken legs and sandwiches, potato salad beside sausage rolls. I watched them from the side while leaning against the bar, seeing no need for this eager jostling, a hustling line the legacy of too many work dos where the catering never matched the hunger, left copious bellies unfilled.

Despite this free-for-all I knew the food prepared would be ample, leave plenty for latecomers thanks to numerous absentees as the party began. There were the four managers who hadn't reappeared today, must have got out of the camp before the roadblock was assembled and been unable to re-enter, if they'd ever intended to return. Added to this quartet were those I'd driven back in the minibus an hour ago, men and women who were now in their chalets, resting or asleep.

Dale Packer and his two chaletmates were the only ones beside me at the bar, the trio glaze-eyed and more interested in drinking than the buffet. The one called Rob ordered three pints of lager, struggling to focus on the barmaid's badge as he stretched over the partition to ask *Hayley* what she was doing later when the girl returned with his drinks. Hayley smiled at this rumpled man with the furry sideburns and yellow film across his teeth, telling Rob something non-committal I didn't quite catch.

After parking the bus I'd jogged straight to the dome, found the camp manager's office empty so began my search of the rest of the building, frantically sprinting between unfamiliar rooms, into a games area full of sporting equipment that had seen better days, grimy pool tables and ping-pong paraphernalia. Then I was standing in a dusty and deserted cinema, rows of shabby crimson seats flipped up before me, finally bursting into that hall where Wallis saw me arrive and attracted Tracy's attention. The camp manager wasn't easily persuaded, those mannish features etched with scepticism as I asked her to abandon administration of the upcoming festivities. I explained our failure to help those sick people, some even worse after that journey into the outside world, and the former nurse eventually relented, agreeing to open the first aid point, take a look at Sid and Natasha.

Both of them were sedated now, being looked after by colleagues while Julie Newman had also been given something for her nerves, medicine which would knock the woman out for a while. Theresa was the only one from our ill-fated trip who had made it into the hall apart from me, that woman inside the melee gathering quiche and lettuce and chips onto her plate, her appetite unaffected by the stresses of the afternoon. Most of the others in line steered clear of her blabbering, Theresa verbally appraising the various foodstuffs as she picked her way through proprietorially. Only Alfred was willing to listen, standing next to the hunched woman he commented on her conclusions whenever a pause came in the observational stream, apparently able to tolerate this woman's personality, content to spend his time coddling her while everyone else steered clear.

While the others had been in the hut receiving treatment, Wallis told me what had happened while I was away, so pleased by my return he didn't think to ask why people destined for the train station had come back too. Wallis was back at the chalet now, having borrowed my key, less than fussed with getting his hands on the food, saying he'd eaten already. After she got off the bus Alice went straight to 368 without a word while Roger waited for Sid, both men looking like they needed a lie down. Roger was particularly shaky after his experience, how close he'd come to being gunned down. It had taken a while to sink in, but now the realisation seemed to linger at the forefront of his mind, making it difficult to focus on anything else, Roger's fingers trembling and his face the colour of sour milk.

Roger was in no fit state to join an evening of festivities, no matter how compulsory. This party had been envisaged as the culmination of two days team building, a means of getting everyone in the same room, those colleagues brought closer by interaction and co-operation, a celebration of our newly strengthened togetherness prior to tomorrow's departure. As it turned out the occasion was more like a diversion from reality, taking our minds off the situation around us. We were trapped now, cordoned off by those security forces I'd encountered earlier, and no one knew when we'd be allowed out of this place, none of those forty people eating at tables on the carpeted area before the bar. They were more in the dark than me about our current confinement, its impact and after-effects, although there remained a hum of uncertainty in the air, a sense that worrying about indulgence was no longer relevant. Some were going back for second helpings already, shovelling greasy, salt-speckled food into their mouths, like weightlifters desperate to make up their calorie intake for the day.

Catherine and Cheryl were two who bucked this trend, the girls picking at salad with the care of those who knew the impact of every mouthful on their figures. They scraped butter off bread and nibbled pastry in tiny bites, an obsessive observance of consumption, girls indoctrinated with the knowledge food isn't some benevolent sustenance but a potential enemy, ready to steal your looks if accepted too willingly, resulting in cellulite and spare skin and the kind of extra pounds a sunbather is ashamed to reveal on the beach.

Whatever your opinion of their mindset, it would have been churlish to argue with the results. The pair looked amazing this evening, hair straightened and nails painted to match their lipstick. Cheryl wore a black dress hugging her slim body while Catherine had on shorts over tights and knee-high boots, a white top ending above her belly button, revealing some kind of red and black tattoo at the base of her spine, the top of a purple thong each time she leaned forward to converse with her friend. They were both in their early twenties and had retained that teenage aptitude for talking endlessly about nothing, having spent most of their time chatting since our arrival at the *Sunlit* complex and were still finding subjects to talk about now, interesting each other so much, there was no need to seek out anyone else.

The contrast with that next table along was pronounced. Dobbs sat alone, using a fork to eat his coleslaw steadily, looked as if he didn't really taste the food, a glass of whisky beside his plate. In-between bites Norman scratched at his legs, then his side, then his shoulders. I didn't think I'd ever seen him drink before, Norman struck me as too repressed to let some other side of his personality seep out thanks to alcohol. Getting himself placed in charge by default, waiting in vain for those other managers to return, being confronted by the group then undermined by me, perhaps it had all taken a toll. Dobbs sipped the neat scotch, staring ahead with eyes that saw nothing, flicking his hand on the side of the chair as if to dislodge something, a gesture I found faintly disturbing.

I didn't have a drink, the thought hadn't occurred to me, so when Alfred came over and said he'd get me one it took me a while to interpret this offer, realise I had to make a decision, the generosity downgraded by that free bar but still welcome.

"Here you are!" He handed me the pint I'd asked for. There were flecks of some kind of sauce in Alfred's beard, crimson and green. "You couldn't get them back in the end?"

"No. There was a checkpoint, we got turned away."

"You did the best you could son." Alfred looked out at that part of the hall reserved for dancing, lit red then blue then yellow by lights above the stage. "There are worse places to be stuck."

"Sure."

"You're put out Jay, I know. I'm not happy about being here, of course I'm not. Did you know I served in Borneo?" Alfred raised the glass of wine to his lips, he wore grey trousers with a tightly ironed crease in them. "We got separated on a jungle recce once, don't remember how. It wasn't until the next day they found us. We went all night without shelter and God knows what climbing on us. Spiders as big as your fist…"

"Sounds nasty."

"The worst part was having no idea how long it would be before we were found, wondering whether it was right to stay where we were or keep moving, try and find our unit." His breath smelt of carbohydrates, like biscuits and starch. "When I think of that night, things like this don't seem so bad. We just need to prepare for whatever comes next."

A couple of people came in through the entrance and headed toward the food, Wallis was one of them. "What do you think is next?" I asked Alfred.

"I don't know, we need to make a few calls, find out…" The man's fingertips rose to his beard, rummaging through the hair as if he expected to find something there. "But one thing national service gives you, or it gave me anyway; you know when you're being fooled with."

"A gut feeling."

"I can sense it, and I'll tell you for nothing, I don't believe those phone lines went down from the wind."

"No?"

"No, and even if they did, someone could have got them up and running by now, don't you think?"

"I don't know." The DJ was playing novelty pop songs from the last few decades at a low volume, segueing one annoying but catchy track into the next. "You think it was sabotage? Somebody knocked out the connection?"

"All I know," Alfred lowered his voice as Hayley came close behind us. "Is that I'm not usually wrong, not when I think I'm being fooled with."

From opposite sides the barmaid and Theresa Barnes closed in then, halting our conversation and leaving Alfred to become Theresa's advisor once more, the woman musing long and loud over which of the bar's multiple delights she should try. I went over to Wallis who was plucking occasional morsels from the buffet, his plate a sparse mixture of foodstuffs, none of them touching each other. It was like the meal of a man suffering from some kind of psychological syndrome, and he seemed disconsolate in an obscure way. Soon I pried it out of him, Wallis describing the gruesome horror flick he'd seen on the in-house channel before coming out. Characters were being killed in horrific ways, ritual disembowellings and eyeballs gouged out, young actors meeting hideous ends before Wallis made the effort to turn it off, bewildered by what he'd seen and wondering if this was something long-banned, because normally he could recognise any horror movie within a few minutes. Wallis was a fan, a buff, but not when it came to films like that.

    I told him to forget it, those scenes were just warped entertainment for teenage boys, he should know that better than most. Wallis remained unconvinced while people finished their food, clustering at the bar to find out what was on offer for nothing, Sandy left Derek's table to order drinks, the woman heavily powdered and painted. Her body was that of a forty-something mother but Sandy's face had the artificial colour of some bodice-clad queen from the Restoration era.

    Finding the minibus keys in my pocket, I went over to Derek who sat watching his mistress at the bar, whistling to himself with legs crossed. The noise stopped when he saw me approaching and Derek became clenched and wary, a malevolent gnome glaring up suspiciously. I handed Derek the keys and thanked him, feeling a twinge of conscience for my earlier actions, that heat of the moment blackmail. Going against his usual garrulousness, the man barely acknowledged my words and any guilt dissipated when Sandy returned bearing two flutes of bubbling liquid. I thought of Derek's wife then, blissfully oblivious to her husband's infidelity, wondered which man had been cuckolded by the woman greeting me with her thin-lipped smile, Sandy's skin a mass of unnatural whites and reds.

    The volume was raised then, a DJ cranking up his music, continuing to play the kind of songs I would expect to hear at a wedding reception, universally recognised classics of naff. It was a signal for the party to begin in earnest, the records effectively drowning out all quiet conversation in the hall.

    Dobbs pushed past me with an empty glass, moving barwards while muttering something I couldn't hear. A few of my colleagues responded to the forceful music by carrying their drinks out to the middle, as if drawn by some unseen force. Only Dale had no hesitancy about him, sloshing a pint onto the lacquered flooring as he strutted towards the centre of attention, that bull-like body moving jerkily as Ejiro whooped behind him and Rob followed, the three of them apparently oblivious to their isolation, these colleagues watching their antics. This trio were coming up on some kind of controlled substance, Dale possessed by the conviction his compact body could dance in ways inspiring to others, the pair of chaletmates copying his moves.

Dobbs had been running fingers through his grey hair for what seemed like minutes, and now one hand tugged at the follicles while his arm made a kind of shivering motion, Norman draining the fluid from his whisky glass and gazing around at the dancers and stage, as if unable to work out how he'd ended up there. Then he put the glass back to his lips, a confused expression on Norman's face when he found it empty. I didn't know how much Dobbs had drunk, but it was at least two measures and they might well have been doubles. He certainly didn't look like he needed any more, a supposition proved when Dobbs tried to get up, caught a foot against the leg of his chair, then tumbled to the floor, landing heavily on an arm as the glass skittered from his grasp.

I was closest to Dobbs and had no qualms about stepping in, hearing the laughter of Dale and others across the way, Wallis helping me get the man to his feet, Norman blabbering something about *quarterlies* and *period ends* in my ear. I wanted to get him out of sight as soon as possible. Despite my distaste for this man, nothing good could come from people seeing their superior like this. He'd been left in charge after all, this was the manager with our immediate destinies under his control, it was vital he kept up the pretence.

We supported Norman across the hall and up to the back, hearing him claim he didn't need our help, could *walk fine thank you very much*. I set him down against the rear wall and sent Wallis to get a pint of water, staying to watch Norman display the considered pronunciation of a first-time drunk desperately pretending to be sober.

"Can you understand me Norman? Do you know where we are?"

"Ah Jay." At least he recognised me. "*Of course* I know where we are."

I felt myself bristle, that sense of superiority was returning in him. "Let me know if you feel sick."

"Sick? Ha! That's a good one."

Wallis arrived with iced water and I made Dobbs drink some of it, rallying him further. The man gazed out at the scene before us, more people on the fringes of the dance floor, girls holding cocktails and bottles of brightly coloured fluid, mouthing the lyrics to the song that played.

"What am I going to do?" It sounded as if Dobbs was talking to himself, I had to lean in to hear. "This is all mine now."

I turned to Wallis. "Go and find Tracy if you can." My friend scuttled off.

Dobbs was scratching his crotch absent-mindedly, as if no one could see. "...I think the company's trying to test me. I don't know what happens if I don't pass. I *will* pass."

"This isn't about you Dobbs." It was never pleasant to be confronted by the depths of Norman's egotism, I suppose I should have expected it by now. "You've been left holding the baby, that's all. Everyone's in this together."

Dobbs looked across at me, his eyes a watery, bloodshot blue. "You think you're so clever don't you Jay? *Jay Hall.*" A thin strand of saliva dangled from his lower lip. "Trying to put me down, trying to sideswipe me."

"Nobody's trying to *sideswipe* you."

"Didn't do you any good though did it, going over my head? Didn't get you anywhere."

"You're drunk Dobbs."

The lines of his face rearranged themselves into a smile. "Because you don't know what's going on. Nobody does."

"Including you."

"Oh, I know more than you think, a lot more."

I was tired of his manner and the circumstances, this babysitting of an adult I disliked. Like some disillusioned childminder, right now I just wanted to wipe Dobbs' mouth, put him to bed, and get on with my own life.

"So what *do* you know?" I asked.

But Dobbs had receded again, back into his own world, a place where he could mumble about being victimised, assert his own importance while tugging at his groin, as if unable to get the parts in a comfortable position, trousers drawing up above his shins as he did so.

Wallis returned with the camp manager and a security guard, hefty and squat, tiny features in a jowly face. Tracy bent down to take a look at Dobbs, shining a pencil torch in his eyes as she pulled the lids back without ceremony, the man flinching when her fingers made contact with his face.

"Alright, fine." With a nurse's lack of respect for personal boundaries, Tracy began to rummage through Dobbs' pockets, extracting a chalet key from the prone figure and bringing it up to the light. "Number 117. That's not far, get him up."

Dobbs recoiled from the security man's approach. "I can go myself." He said, rising unsteadily.

"That's fine Norman." She backed off a little, although the guard remained close to Dobbs, within catching distance should he fall. Tracy went ahead of them and held open the door, advised incoming guests to stay back as they guided Dobbs out of the venue.

I told Wallis to remember the number of Dobbs' chalet, his mouth moving as he repeated *one-one-seven* to himself. For the first time today I felt like a stiff drink but I'd left what remained of my pint on a table somewhere, and there was a constant presence at the bar now. People were getting through the measures quickly, going back for more inside minutes, working the two girls hard, Hayley and the other one who poured ale and cider over ice, vodka with fruit juice and creamy liqueurs.

Anthea had her handbag on the floor and was moving around it, fist pumping the air ironically, her stick-thin legs revealed by a short skirt, heels she threatened to topple from with each sudden movement, the woman synchronizing her body to the music. I sat at the back with Wallis who, like me, had no inclination to shout above the noise or reflect on what had happened with Dobbs, instead we just watched.

Lindsay and James came into the hall, dressed very casually, the girl's hand wandering to the back pocket of his jeans, that guy who stood taller than everyone else as they perused the buffet, unable to keep their hands off each other even then.

From my vantage point on the steps I noticed there was another exit, beyond the bar and to the right of the stage, a door partially obscured by the DJ booth. Inside that cubicle a shadow could be seen intermittently, some kind of headwear prominent as it crouched to operate the equipment. Wallis and I were a long way from the fun here, beneath drooping balloons and paper chains my friend had helped put up, a company banner prominently displaying our employer's logo above, an attempt to make us feel part of something bigger.

After a few minutes I wended my way between Cheryl and Catherine who smiled and waved, a couple of overweight men jiggling further across, Ejiro pretending to break-dance for the amusement of his chaletmates, the man's motions wild and chemically enhanced.

I ordered a pint and a soft drink for Wallis, found myself next to a waiting Silvia, so after being served I got the attention of the other barmaid.

"Thanks." Silvia shifted her square shoulders, occupying the space vacated by a fat man from the techie department who removed a tray of drinks. "How's it going Jay?"

"I've been better."

When our drinks arrived we walked beyond the buffet to talk as Wallis found some guy he knew. I noticed a couple of painful red blemishes on Lindsay's neck in passing, the girl at a table with James, eating slowly.

We reached a well-lit corner close to the entrance, beside a closed hatch that would have sold drinks to kids in the summer, milkshakes and flavoured slush, a vending machine on the other side with empty racks.

"Did you see that?" Silvia must have noticed me gawping at Lindsay's injuries. "Those marks?"

"Yeah, they love bites?"

Silvia laughed coldly. "Not sure I'd call it *love*, I'm lucky enough to share a chalet with Lindsay."

"Really?"

"And James, last night at least." Silvia swigged her beer straight from the bottle, had little time for the affectations of femininity. She wore loose clothes and no make up this evening, had always been this way when I saw her in the office, causing some to gossip about possible Sapphic tendencies, say *wasn't it a pity* Silvia didn't package herself more glamorously. With that naturally tanned skin and those strong features, Silvia could have been quite something. If she would simply wear clothes that disguised her stockiness, did something with that matted hair falling all over the place.

"You've heard them?"

Silvia rolled her eyes. "I'm in the next room, what do you think?" Under the table James groped one of Lindsay's buttocks, the girl closing her eyes in response to his touch. "They were at it for hours, all last night and today. The noise was horrendous. I don't know what he does to her, but nobody's ever done anything like that to me."

I smiled. "You sound disappointed."

"I'm not, I don't enjoy suffering." She glanced over. "Some of the noises Lindsay makes, it sounds like she's in agony. I've thought about going in and stopping it, but I don't want to see what they're doing."

"Maybe she likes a bit of pain with her pleasure."

"Or maybe she's just acting, doing what he wants, too young to know any better." There was the hint of an accent behind Silvia's impeccable English, possibly Spanish, or Portuguese. "This morning I saw her coming out of the shower with all these, *injuries*."

"They're just experimenting." We both had more than a decade on the pair and I think it sounded that way. I wouldn't have expected Silvia to be this prudish, but I guessed she had been raised in some kind of religious tradition. "I'm sure it's all consensual. They've got *safe words* or whatever."

"You haven't heard her." Silvia took a long draw of the beer. "Her cries, its what somebody sounds like when they're being tortured."

Before us the movement was becoming more complicated and widespread. Derek and Sandy joined the throng now, tentative and a little overawed, as if they hadn't done this sort of thing in years. Dale cast regular glances at Cheryl and Catherine, the girls shaking their lithe bodies in unison, facing each other as Cheryl stretched linked hands to the roof, her friend spinning, bouncing low on her heels, revealing that skimpy underwear each time her body lowered itself. I watched Dale stare at Catherine, the man draining his glass before going to the bar for another.

"Feels strange." I told Silvia. "It's like everyone here's been liberated from the normal rules. They've found some kind of freedom to take advantage of this situation, all except me."

"Funny kind of freedom."

"Oh absolutely." I drank my beer, pondering my plans for tomorrow, after everyone had slept this off. "You know what I mean though. The company's responsible for most of the rules I live by, now they've brought me here, a place where everything restricting me has been removed."

"It's ironic alright, when you put it that way."

Lindsay dragged James into the throng, grasping him close as the music changed to some salacious bump and grind, turning her back on the taller man and shaking red hair in his face, body gyrating into James' groin, hands behind her so he couldn't get away, not that he wanted to.

Somehow my glass was empty and I asked Silvia if she wanted another. The woman refused, giving me a look that made me think of all the understanding and sympathy my mother never had for me, back when I used to binge drink every weekend. I went to the end of the bar to be served quickly, standing in a section smelling strongly of child's vomit and looking more closely at the exit near the DJ booth, that door bearing a

RESTRICTED sign. When I moved away I caught sight of Alice coming in accompanied by Suzie. They ignored the buffet and went straight to the bar, Suzie muscling her way to the front, that tall girl with a loud voice and demeanour of utter certainty. Suzie wore heavy boots under an ankle-length flower-pattern dress, an outfit that felt at odds with her personality, ordering drinks as Alice moved towards me.

"Hi." She said.

"Hey." The girl looked incredible this evening, and I couldn't help wincing at my failures of the afternoon, wondering if I frittered away that intimacy we built up. "Listen, I wanted to apologise…"

"No need." Alice looked up at me, eye shadow and lipstick matching the pink of her low cut top. "There was nothing we could have done, they weren't allowing us out. I just couldn't accept it, stupid." Her black hair was tied in two bunches and a glittering necklace stopped just short of Alice's cleavage. "I only hope Sid's going to be alright."

"Yeah, me too." From our left Tracy strode across the hall and through the RESTRICTED door. "We've done all we can, Roger's looking after him now." Beyond the exit I caught a glimpse of stairs leading up. "How's Natasha?"

"Spark out." Alice fiddled with the hem of her skirt, summery and chequered and ending well above the knee. "I hope she stays that way."

Suzie brought Alice a rum and coke, giving me a disdainful look which made me realise I'd been staring at her chaletmate's legs, still as perfect and slender as they'd been this morning, wrapped around me in the pool. Alice didn't seem to notice my glances, held Suzie's drink while that taller girl went to the bathroom.

"We'll get out of here tomorrow." I said. "Even if I have to knock on every door in the county to find a working phone."

She smiled. "That'll be cool." We moved out of Rob and Ejiro's way as they hurtled to the bar. "I've been worried, you know. About what those soldiers thought they were protecting us from."

"Yeah." The disco lights changed colours before us. "I didn't expect you to come out tonight."

"Suzie convinced me, she didn't want me moping around the chalet on a Saturday night, told me to get all dolled up." Alice sipped her drink. "You don't disobey Suze."

"I'm glad you did." My nose itched, I scratched it. "You look amazing."

"Thanks. This is what us girls do when we're low." Suzie reappeared and Alice handed her the glass of wine. "Dress up, beautify ourselves. It's therapeutic."

"Feel any better?"

"I guess so."

I could feel my body losing its battle with intoxication. The lack of sleep had lowered my alcohol tolerance. Wallis was still talking with that man who looked like a larger version of himself, bespectacled and podgy but wider, bending down to listen to my friend. Alfred rose from his table, escorted Theresa out of the hall, the woman's expression making it clear she was upset about something. Dave was on the dance floor, doing what looked like some kind of jive with Anthea while Dale moved toward Cheryl and Catherine, his thickset frame obtrusive and the girls only interested in dancing with each other. A man I'd never seen before crossed the room followed by a security guard, moving quickly in a kind of uncomfortable lurch. He was small with a hairless head, the normal width at its crown but narrowing further down the face, finally tapering off into a terribly weak jaw. They both disappeared through the *RESTRICTED* door as Silvia came across, talking to Suzie nearby.

"Dance?" Alice asked.

We were both at the end of our drinks, those last mouthfuls of beer having brought with them a familiar loss of inhibition, the seeping away of self-consciousness that have led a sober Jay to refuse.

"Sure."

Avoiding the pools of spilled liquid we eased our way onto the increasingly sticky dance floor, Alice stopping near the overweight men who'd been out here a while and were now barely moving, sweat patches visible on their clothes.

The music changed to a guitar-based song from the nineties, an anthem I'd often played before going out, back in my clubbing days. Alice shimmied close to me as I shifted my feet uncertainly, her top slipping to reveal glimpses of a pure white bra, the girl attracting admiring glances from some of the men, the likes of Rob and Dave who had never seen her this way before, so much perfect brown skin on display, a comely form revealed by her seductive outfit.

I couldn't tell if she wanted me to hold her, the girl felt a little distant, preoccupied, and so I kept a subtle space between us, a gap ensuring our bodies only touched accidentally. Nearby Dale Packer had insinuated himself with the younger girls at last, leaving his chaletmates behind as he shouted above the music, first into Catherine's ear then Cheryl's, a meaty hand moving to each of their lower backs in turn.

Away from our group there was the sound of glass smashing to the floor. A slower number played as people edged away from the shards, closer to myself and Alice. Derek and Sandy had their bodies together, swaying in a clench, the woman's mouth finding his. I saw Derek's tongue move between Sandy's lips, red and pinguid as it explored her slimy orifice. Dave was attempting to grope Anthea, sweat glistening on his forehead as he pawed at her skinny behind, the woman pushing him away with some vigour. I felt the nausea and dizziness rise in me again, the legacy of that lack of rest and stresses of the day. James and Lindsay bumped into Alice, who was regarding me with some concern, then reeled back the other way, their bodies entwined like lustful contortionists, Lindsay's hand moving to the bulge in his trousers.

"Do you want to get out of here?" Alice asked. "You look like you could use some air."

I half walked, half staggered over to Wallis who was deep in discussion with his bigger lookalike, the pair talking about the latest album by some doom metal band they followed. I told my friend I was leaving while Alice excused herself for the bathroom. The bar was full of drunks now, people leaning on the counter to ask for more. My unsteadiness was a kind of conformity here.

Men were doing tequila shots while women stumbled on their heels. Somebody fell over on the dance floor. All around me colleagues carried on their flirtation and fondling and frottage. In a moment of lucidity I remember thinking this was like the last ever office party. With the world about to end, all manner of debauchery and licentiousness was permissible. What I was witnessing here amounted to the over-indulgence of the doomed.

I saw Dale try to encourage Cheryl and Catherine to sandwich him with their bodies, storming off when they refused. Silvia watched from the sidelines, nothing in her expression. Pushing to the centre, Suzie elicited woops from some of the women who would never have spoken to her at work. They encouraged the girl to dance in that awkward manner of the extremely tall, laughing at Suzie behind her back, one of the straps of her dress falling down to reveal a flat chest, pockmarked with moles. Dave became aware of her presence, this new sphere of oestrogen nearby, dancing over to Suzie while smoothing at his hair, urging her to press against him, apparently desperate to copulate with any available female. Ejiro moved toward Anthea in a similar manner, flattering the older woman with his attentions.

I felt like I was going to retch by the time Alice came to pull me away. Then we were outside, revived by the freezing air. She led me by the arm back to our chalet block, a glimpse of something on fire inland before I concentrated on the grunt and heft of placing one foot in front of the other. Deep down I was aware this wasn't how I wanted to appear, not to the attractive girl who remained silently focussed on getting me back, but I had little choice.

By the time we reached chalet 364 I had regained some of my composure and the need to be sick was subsiding. I could climb the metal steps unaided, although it took a while to fit my key in the lock. Once inside some part of me that needed to play the host kicked in and I turned the heating on, got a shivering Alice my jumper and relieved myself in the bathroom. By then I was back to my old self, splashing warm tap water on my face, the liquid so cloudy it looked like a preparation of soluble aspirin.

When I came back into the lounge Alice was stretched out on the sofa, bare legged still, her painted toenails extending in the direction of that warmth emanating from the radiator. I tried to ignore her legs and offered the girl a cup of tea, the pipes emitting a loud gurgle before spewing out a spray of murky water, making me hope any bacteria would be destroyed in the boiling.

We talked for a while about trivialities, tacitly avoiding mention of anything we'd just seen. Alice asked if I had deliberately given up smoking, said she wouldn't have thought this was the weekend to do it, and the thought of nicotine entering my bloodstream sparked a craving. I excused myself to the sound of Alice's laughter, wore my coat out onto the balcony and lit another of those horrid tasting cigarettes, smoking it down to the butt despite the unpleasant flavour, as if this were some kind of medicine I needed to take.

I stared out at the night. Being alone with Alice had left me feeling centred, and I wondered if I should think about what to do next, knowing the masculine mindset demanded I make a pass at the girl, this exotic beauty I'd somehow enticed back to my place without even trying.

There was movement at ground level, two figures returning to their chalet. I caught voices on the wind and realised it was Rob and Ejiro, the men probably going back for a smoke. They were joined in the shadows by an odd, lumbering shape that proceeded to follow them inside. I suppose it must have been Dale, carrying something heavy I couldn't quite make out.

I went back inside where Alice was washing our cups, thinking about what I'd seen, knowing in my fuddled brain that something was going on there, something I needed to comprehend.

Alice saw the confusion on my face. "What's wrong?"

I was about to respond, when we were interrupted by a frantic hammering at the door.

Chapter Ten

We recoiled with a start, it sounded as if someone was trying to pound their way in. I went to the door and found Wallis with a fist raised, about to bang again. Cheryl looked lost behind him.

"Don't you have a key?"

"I saw the light on." Wallis came inside, followed by that girl in her black dress. He was agitated, pacing the floor.

"What's wrong?" Alice asked. I could see now Cheryl had been crying, her hair wind-blown and face a mess, mascara smudged and a salty wetness shining on her cheeks.

"Catherine's disappeared." The words came out in a whimper.

"We think someone spiked their drinks."

A realisation burrowed to the surface of my brain.

Alice said, "Who do you think it was babe?"

"Who got those drinks for you Cheryl?"

"The big guy," She had both arms wrapped around her chest. "I don't know his name."

"Dale." Wallis looked at me. In our minds we were halfway out the door. "Let's go."

After Alice had left the hall with me Wallis finished his conversation and discovered he was peckish, pleased to discover enough food remained to make a decent plateful. Deciding not to eat at one of those tables between dance floor and bar, having already witnessed inebriated revellers stumble against the furniture as they made their way to the drink, Wallis chose instead to sit on the steps at the back.

He ate the food methodically, occasionally hearing noises from the darkened area behind as the DJ segued one song into another by the stage. Glancing over his shoulder on one occasion, Wallis caught a glimpse of ginger hair above a gyrating body, Lindsay straddling James, the pair of them fully clothed, but making the kind of moans that suggested they were having sex back there.

My friend turned his mind to other things, science-fiction storylines and the collectibles he would buy after payday next, eyes on the swirling bodies and erratic movement of the dancers. Cheryl emerged from the throng while he finished his meal having told Catherine she needed to sit for a while, and flopped down a couple of metres away. She leant back on her elbows and shut her eyes, a bottle of fizzing, yellow liquid in one hand, resting against her thigh.

Wallis watched the girl. Cheryl was good looking certainly, glamorous and attractive, but he was more concerned about that drink which was gradually slipping from her grasp. The bottle pointed at an acute angle now, was falling further as she descended into sleep. He wondered whether to intervene for a long time, aware Cheryl was about to spill drink over herself, sopping fluid over an expensive black dress. When it looked as if the drink couldn't slip any further without falling from her hand, Wallis got up and eased it away, making hand gestures as she woke, hoping to indicate he had only been trying to help. The girl didn't mind, smiled and said Catherine wasn't as much of a lightweight as her, had taken up some guy's offer of more drinks while she'd been away in the bathroom. Talking of which, she needed to speak to Catherine, would Wallis stay here while Cheryl went and found her friend?

Wallis was amenable as ever, watching this suddenly talkative girl go back into the centre of the hall as he tried to work out how many years it had been since he sampled an alcopop. My friend sniffed at the bottle's rim then, surprised to notice something unusual in the odour, mixed in with that alcohol and artificial fruit, something chemical and salty and entirely out of place.

A few minutes later Cheryl came back, perplexed and uneasy, told Wallis that Catherine had disappeared, wasn't in the hall or toilets, while nobody could recall seeing her leave. Cheryl felt certain her friend wouldn't have gone back to the chalet without saying anything, for the past couple of days they'd been inseparable, and at this point she was beginning to worry.

Wallis was the only person still at the party with a clear head, had an advantage over those others downing shots or dancing erratically before them, and this enabled him to put some suspicions together. He asked Cheryl to try her drink, just the tiniest sip, a few drops on her tongue to activate the taste buds and nothing more. The girl did as she was told and pulled a face, accepting a mouthful of Wallis's lemonade to take the flavour away, confirming the drink didn't taste right.

Increasingly worried, the pair left the dome, checking Cheryl's chalet on their way over. But Catherine wasn't in number 226, and it was this absence that led them to me, Wallis not thinking too clearly by the time he began to bang urgently on our chalet door.

I ran down the steps and across the swampy earth to 327, jumping over that rubbish surrounding the entrance, a swollen moon illuminating my way. The lights were on so I pummelled the door with my knuckles, yelling at those inside to *Open Up!* Wallis caught up with me as I took a step back, monitoring the chalet for movement, Alice and Cheryl picking their way through cartons in our wake. I waited about thirty seconds and, when there was no response, took a step back to kick at the door. Its flimsy lock gave instantly.

Inside Rob and Ejiro looked as if they didn't understand what was happening, so fucked up that even turning their heads from the TV screen was more than they could manage. The pair were watching footage of a beheading somewhere in the Middle East.

"Where's Dale?" I demanded.

They looked at me uncomprehendingly. Noises, like a bed being destroyed, came from one of the other rooms. I pushed my way in, seeing Catherine's shorts on the floor as I entered.

Dale was on top of her, the girl's tights shredded and her t-shirt pushed up around her neck. The man thrust his body into her, uninterested in the world outside this act. Catherine appeared to be unconscious, her head lolling to the side.

Putting a hand on Dale's shoulder, the man turned his head and I punched him in the face, hard. He fell off the girl, sprawling there naked from the waist down. In the doorway Cheryl screamed at the sight of her friend. Scrambling to his feet, Dale launched himself at me, knocking the wind from my body and taking us both into the lounge. Alice moved away and past us to cover Catherine with something. We landed on the floor amid newspapers and rubbish, Ejiro and Rob didn't move. Dale was grunting like a Neanderthal, had me pinned down with his bulk and punched me in the stomach. Wallis comforted Cheryl, helping Alice lift the unconscious girl off the bed.

I felt like I was going to be sick, it was a useful moment of clarity. Using Dale's weight against him, I rolled us over. The television showed amateur footage of a man being stoned to death. I brought a knee up into Dale's testicles, feeling him wince at the impact. Cheryl was crying and shaking as Wallis ushered her out. Dale thumped me in the kidneys with a fist and I brought up some bile onto his chest. He was heavier than me, but much of it was fat. Dale didn't work out regularly and it was beginning to tell.

The other men in the room didn't move a muscle, it was like they were watching from behind some impassable barrier. Dale shrugged me off and I crashed against the sofa, hand reaching for a china cup discarded there. Alice and Wallis carried Catherine outside, one flopping arm over each of their shoulders. A kick in the side almost lifted me off the floor. Dale sank to his knees to beat me. From the TV there came the sound of a bloodthirsty mob. The cup was in my hand and I gave it everything I had, breaking the china on Dale's forehead. He sank backwards and I struggled to my feet coughing, the adrenalin racing through my veins. Alice shouted *Come here Jay!* from somewhere out in the night.

Dale was still conscious, blood trickling down from the top of his head. I tried to say something but couldn't. Ejiro was staring at Dale with an expression of wonder. The man's body took up a large portion of floor, that cock Dale had forced into the drugged girl tiny and pale now, flaccid like the rest of him.

Alice called me again. Spasms of pain were shooting through my jaw and torso. Dale was making a sputtering noise. I crossed the carpet of rubbish, slipping on paper and magazines as I pitched myself toward the door.

Unsteady on my feet, I caught up with the others somehow. Cheryl had regained some of her composure, proved capable when Alice instructed her to take over from Wallis, sobbing quietly while supporting her unconscious friend. My head span, the world was growing unclear and I wondered absently if I was blacking out.

"Help Jay back to your chalet!" Alice ordered, and I remember admiring her then, that girl as shocked as the rest of us but keeping her voice level, giving Wallis instructions while carrying most of Cheryl's weight.

The next thing I knew I was on a bed in my chalet, given aspirin and a glass of opaque tap water. I swallowed three tablets and a little of the cloudy liquid, gradually becoming more *compos mentis* before touching the damaged parts of my face and body experimentally, flinching at the pain. There would be bruises, and it hurt to speak, but I didn't feel too debilitated, no permanent damage as far as I could tell.

One of my fingers had been cut by a shard of china and the blood seeped down to my palm, drying there. My mind was trying to process what had happened, racing as I focussed on the ceiling, that shabby white stucco and flaking paint. There came a soft knock on the chalet door.

Wallis went to meet Alice and I heard the girl ask if I was okay, my friend's reply inaudible. They talked for a while then Alice came in and perched on my bed.

"How are you?"

"It only hurts when I breathe."

She smiled, placing a slender hand on my forehead as if to take my temperature. "Wallis is going to find that nurse woman and get you a first aid kit."

I held up my hand, encrusted with crimson blood. "I could use a plaster."

She shook her head. "That bastard."

"How are the girls?"

Alice examined my injury. "Cheryl's shaken up, not surprising is it? I've told her to watch over Catherine, sleep in the same room as her and not answer the door unless its one of us. It'll get pretty bad when Catherine starts remembering."

"Everything's going to bubble up at some point."

"This is nasty." Alice said, examining my wound. She left the room then, returning with a bowl of water and some toilet paper. "Here, let me wash it."

Alice took my hand and cleaned the blood away, a tender gesture. Nevertheless, it localised my pain to a specific point.

"Ouch."

"Sorry."

"Don't worry." The gentleness of her touch nullified the agony, at least in part. "My own fault, I should have thought about it, picked something up in the first place." My mouth felt misshapen. "I could have clubbed him unconscious with one good hit."

"Such a fucking scumbag." Alice breathed.

"It's weird, you know." My finger was clean now, the gash smaller than I'd thought but deep. "You automatically think about going to the police, it's the obvious next step."

"Yeah, and then you remember. There are no police." She put the bowl down. "There's nobody."

I placed my other hand on her wrist, felt the warmth and pulse there. "We'll work out what to do." I coughed again, trying to prevent my words tailing off. "…just let me rest for a while…"

The effort of speaking had become too much. I released Alice and lay back, stomach aching, a steady throb in my side, waiting for the hurt to ease.

Meanwhile Wallis was moving toward the dome, all het up with thoughts of what Dale might do when he recovered from the fight and unnerved by the force of a new moon above, that light rendering him all too visible as he scuttled between chalet blocks. It was late, after midnight, and the security guard who usually stood by the dome's entrance had knocked off for the day, leaving the door itself unlocked. Inside there weren't many lights on, but enough patchy brightness to see by. As a matter of course Wallis checked the payphones by that out-of-order cashpoint inside the entranceway. They remained dead, no tone or crackle from the receivers. That was when Wallis heard banging further along and followed the noise to its source.

Roger was there, inserting coins into one of the vending machines on the wall, swearing when his change passed straight through and jangled down into the metal trough below. He would frown, curse, collect the money, then repeat his actions.

"Have you seen Tracy?" Wallis asked him.

"Who?" Roger looked at my friend as if he was speaking a foreign language. Part of Roger's shirt protruded from the zipper of his trousers.

"The camp manager. She's also the first aid woman, about this tall and…."

"No, no I haven't." Roger banged the side of the vending machine with the base of a hand. "We've run out of electricity and this thing won't give me any more. Sid's getting cold and I can't see what I'm doing in our chalet. Damn near bust my leg."

"I'm going to find someone."

Wallis left him smashing the dispenser pointlessly and walked to Tracy's office, finding it locked he ran upstairs, breathing heavily by the time Wallis reached the hall.

The room was empty of company employees now; they'd all been ushered out or drunkenly disappeared of their own accord. A couple of male teenagers were putting tables away and removing the decorations while barmaids patrolled what had been the dance floor, one with a mop and bucket the other wielding a broom, a dustpan at the end of a long handle she used to collect broken glass and scraps of food.

Wallis approached the girl called Hayley, his shoes sticking to the floor with every step, saw she was mopping up a pool of vomit and tried not to look at the lumpy mess while he spoke.

"Hi." Wallis could see from Hayley's face his was an unwelcome interruption. "Is Tracy around?"

"She's gone." The girl responded sullenly. "We'll be out of here soon as well, hopefully."

"Is there anyone who might be able to help?" Wallis explained how I'd had *an accident*, needed first aid or something, the smell of sick rising to his nostrils.

"I'll have a look." She disappeared into a storeroom, returning with bandages and ointment, Hayley staying stony-faced as Wallis thanked her profusely, turning away from him with a muttered *sure* to finish the clean up.

Back in our chalet Alice was making me sip the tea she'd made, its heat combining with the painkillers to numb my aching jaw. The girl had seen that discomfort in my face when I'd been speaking, so now she sat on the side of my bed and talked herself, filling the silence with anecdotes about her upbringing, the cultural clashes of her parents. Alice told me about her American father's foibles, the dislocated patriotism of the expatriate that led him to recreate Stateside celebrations on an ad hoc basis, everything from Thanksgiving to Halloween. He had a habit of putting on events in societies that didn't understand the traditions, seeking out amicable shopkeepers wherever they happened to live at the time, paying them extra to import the appropriate foodstuffs into Asia or Europe.

I listened and smiled at the appropriate times, wondering at Alice's ability to distract me and herself, how she could skirt around what had happened. Dale was still so close, just across the block, and he'd moved from a simple, pigheaded chauvinist, to a man capable of violence and rape. Nobody had arranged for him to be detained, we couldn't initiate any kind of arrest, and I found myself strangely bothered by the extent of his injuries. I didn't think I'd knocked Dale unconscious, but it took a lot to make a bull like him go down as he had, stunned and bloody. No doubt Packer deserved everything I'd thrown at him, but somebody still ought to patch him up, whatever his crimes. I wasn't content to just leave him there. The state I was in when we left the chalet I couldn't be sure, but if I remembered rightly Dale had been bleeding profusely from the head. It wasn't sensible to rely on the addled likes of Rob and Ejiro to revive him.

Wallis was back now, looking tired and troubled, said the nurse wasn't available and hadn't thought to ask when she'd be back, passing across those supplies he'd managed to solicit. Alice made me sit up, wrapping the bandage around my bruised middle and tending to my hand before I went to the bathroom, relieved to see my piss free from blood, coughing up phlegm and gingerly checking my teeth, none of which had been loosened by those crashing blows.

I felt awake but fragile, unable to sleep yet calm enough to discuss our next move, going to sit with Wallis and softly calling a reproachful Alice into the lounge.

"You should be resting." She told me.

"So should you." The fire alarm was still disabled so I lit a cigarette, not caring whether I breached the rules. "I can't hide from what's happened, we need to sort it out."

"You're in no state to be taking anything on." Alice scolded me.

My hand went to rub my jaw, withdrawing when the pain struck. "Who will then?" I exhaled smoke I couldn't really taste. "You know as well as I do, we need to make sure that guy's locked up."

Wallis looked at me seriously. "Do they have cells in a place like this?" In another circumstance I might have laughed out loud, but that would only have hurt more.

"Don't think there's much call for it in a family holiday camp." Alice was looking at me the way a doctor would, monitoring some errant patient who shouldn't be out of bed. "What about those bouncer guys? They could restrain him."

"You mean the security guards?" Wallis asked. "They're off-duty too."

"Besides, I don't trust men like that." I thought of that conversation I'd overheard in the pub, the possibility those burly individuals possessed criminal records. "It's only our word against Dale's. Catherine's in no fit state to tell anyone what happened, and I don't want to get into some big discussion over this." I took another drag, coughed. "Accusations will start flying around. They might even lock me up, I've assaulted someone too."

Wallis said, "We need to go to whoever's got the highest authority."

I thought of those army officers from the afternoon, they seemed a long way away.

Alice looked at my friend. "You mean Dobbs?"

I considered Norman. The last time I'd seen the supervisor he was borderline delirious. "I'm not sure how much help Dobbs would be right now." I explained to Alice how he had to be helped out of the party earlier.

"So we wake Dobbs up, get some coffee inside him. He's still the one in charge, this is no time to shirk that responsibility."

I remained sceptical, stubbing out my cigarette. "He won't have any idea what to do, no more than us."

"How do we know unless we try? You can't take this all on yourself Jay."

Wallis piped up, "One-one-seven."

"What's that mate?"

"Dobbs' chalet number." Wallis pushed at his spectacles. "You told me to remember it."

The lights were off in that ground floor chalet when we left shortly afterwards and I glanced across at the door I'd broken, wondering at the state of those inside. A yawning Wallis hadn't required much convincing to stay indoors and *hold the fort*, but Alice wasn't about to let me tackle Dobbs alone. The girl kept her pace slow to accommodate my sluggish lope as we crossed the complex. Even partially recovered from the blows I'd sustained, walking felt like an unusual activity, fraught with the potential for disaster, like picking your way through a minefield.

We headed for the perimeter road, a few working streetlights making up for the waning of that moon above. All the chalet blocks here were shrouded in darkness, no lights on anywhere I could see. Number 117 was in a block close to the adventure playground, opposite the pub, and by the time we located Dobbs' chalet I was moving more freely, intermittent pain running through my upper body but controlled by the strapping and aspirin, my mind focussed on finding Norman. It was unfortunate this man I'd overruled and disobeyed earlier now constituted our best chance, the most likely candidate for ameliorating the damage done by others. I didn't expect Dobbs to be particularly cooperative, even if we could wake him from that inevitable drunken stupor. Our only hope lay in conveying the gravity of recent events to our only remaining manager, perhaps he would have some take on what to do. Dobbs surely knew the workings of this camp better than anyone else left from the company and if he refused to talk to me there might be information among Norman's belongings, some clue that gave us an idea of what to do next. He just needed to let us in.

The signs were good, lights on in 117, the lounge curtains open to reveal a living area virtually unchanged from Dobbs' arrival on Thursday, the remote control for his TV on the table, a list of chalet contents underneath it, Norman's kitchen orderly and unused.

I knocked, whispering to Alice she should call out when there came no response, aware Dobbs was more likely to answer her request.

"Norman." She called, then louder. "Norman, are you there? We need your help!"

I banged again, nothing. "He's passed out."

"What do we do now?"

I tested the door, pushing my weight against it and feeling the lock give a little. Forcing my way in wasn't the ideal option but we didn't have a better plan. At least I could take sufficient care not to destroy the whole door this time.

"Jay!" Alice warned me.

"I'll say I was concerned for his well-being." I took a step back before barging at the chalet door, sensing it give a little more, the shock of impact reverberating through my body. But I wasn't about to give up now.

Moving to the edge of the balcony and gritting my teeth, I led with my shoulder and used the momentum to burst in, uttering a cry of pain as I did so. I felt more than a little sorry for myself, at everything I'd had to suffer through this trip so far. This thought was quickly wiped from my mind as I came to my senses, saw that my troubles were nothing compared to those of Dobbs. The man was flat on his back in the hallway, utterly lifeless, a knife protruding from his chest.

Chapter Eleven

He looked smaller somehow, diminished laying there, Dobbs was flat on his back with blood pooled around the wound, all soaked through his white shirt. Dobbs' arms hung at his side, and the expression on his face was strangely peaceful, eyes closed, mouth relaxed. There was none of that grimacing agony I would have expected in someone who'd suffered such a violent act.

There was no doubt in my mind he was dead, yet I remained standing there as Alice let out a gasp of shock followed by cries of denial; *oh no, oh no, oh no*. She moved to check for a pulse, put her cheek to his mouth when there was none, hoping to feel his breath on her face. But Dobbs had long since left this world.

"He's gone Alice." I said. That single stab from a pocket knife, the kind anyone might take out camping, had gone deep into his heart, a puncture wound draining all semblance of colour from this man, so that now he resembled a desiccated husk, even his hair was whiter.

Alice gave up her efforts and fell into my arms. I forgot the pain for a moment and supported this shaking girl, squeezing her tight, hard enough to block out the death and make her feel safe for a while. A miasma of thoughts were hurtling through my brain, pity for Dobbs, and the realisation I should have been less hard on him. I wondered what tragedies were occurring in Norman's life for him to take this way out, an improvised act of *hara-kiri*, that plunge of knife into his chest.

The girl held me and I clung on, feeling weaker by the second, her tears hot on my shoulder. The issue of what to do about Dale didn't seem so pressing now, here was a bigger problem. Our remaining authority figure for the weekend had been lost, that fear growing widespread among my colleagues could only get worse. No doubt the likes of Theresa had circulated yesterday's news, how we were cut off from the rest of this country, and now there was no officious manager to wave away their concerns. Our last organiser was here before us, a corpse on the floor, and we'd no way of contacting the authorities, couldn't call the emergency services and get his body removed. There was no one to take our statements or gather the relevant evidence for some future inquest, and because I'd forced the lock, this dead man wasn't even safely shut away anymore.

Feeling trapped and shaky, I persuaded Alice to relinquish her grip on me. The girl used a finger to dry her eyes, looked up at me entreatingly.

"We have to go." I told her.

"Go?" She glanced back at the corpse then turned away again. "We can't just leave him."

"There's nothing we can do before morning." Outside the calmness of night was interrupted by a hoot from some nocturnal bird. "I'm not tampering with a dead man. We have to leave everything the way it is, for the police." Whenever they might arrive.

Alice nodded. "It doesn't seem right somehow."

"It *isn't* right." I scanned the lounge and kitchen, everything there was disquietingly spotless. "But I'm not staying with him. We need to sleep on this. I'm worn out, and I hardly know what the hell's going on anymore. You look as tired as I feel."

It was true, her make up had run and I could see bags forming under Alice's eyes, the girl's skin sallow and lustreless in the artificial light. She took one last glance at Dobbs and shuddered.

"I'm staying in your chalet." She said.

Wallis was asleep when we got back to 364, curled up on the sofa bed. We tiptoed around his snoozing form, grateful to avoid questions relating to Dobbs. Once in my room Alice pushed the narrow beds together and we lay down in our clothes. I was too depleted, too cold and pained to think about changing into nightwear, so the girl rested her head on my covered chest. I felt her weight as I breathed, a smarting in parts of my torso as she clung on.

Eventually I adjusted to the ache and drifted off, came close to a loss of consciousness before being jerked awake again by images of Dobbs. Norman was in despair at everything his life had come to, overwhelmed by the situation he found himself in, unsheathing that knife he held in a trembling hand. This was a blade Dobbs had brought along to help with the team-building, one he carried to cut twine or carve wood. Now the man had a different purpose in mind.

Norman felt his chest, used a hand to locate the beat of his heart and marked the spot in his mind. Then came the climax to this brief ritual, the blade piercing his flesh up to the hilt, a soft cry as Dobbs' spirit took leave of his body, the empty shell collapsing backwards into that spreadeagled position where we found him.

I'd never seen a dead body before, past experience was limited to documentary footage or the relayed tribulations of relatives, I hadn't been there when my father expired. I found it both sickening and profound, that stillness and peace, the knowledge this person you knew as an individual, a unique breathing life form, would never again move or speak, never exhibit any of the mannerisms you associated with them. However much I might have disliked Dobbs, I couldn't help experiencing a sense of loss in amongst the shock, wondered if he had a wife and kids who would feel the bereavement that much more acutely, mourn the death of this man I'd treated as an irritation for so long.

After hours of thinking myself into some distorted type of guilt, increasingly circular and abstract mental processes looping back on themselves, I finally slipped off into sleep. I dreamt I was shut away in some kind of inescapable confinement, seized by insurgents and chained up in an oddly modern room reminiscent of a TV studio, forced at gunpoint to relay the message I was well and happy back to the outside world.

The scene ended with Alice shifting her weight. I briefly came back to the real world before falling back into unconsciousness again, the night wearing on as I fell through reveries, images of old friends and spiralling aircraft, snapping awake as the light of a newly-arrived day seeped in through the flimsy curtains.

I felt no better than I had before going to bed. In different circumstances I might have been jubilant at sleeping with a girl as beautiful and sexy as Alice, but all I could feel this Sunday was the rising thrum of a headache, pain through much of my upper body, great jolts of it whenever one of us moved.

Outside the bedroom door I heard Wallis' heavy footsteps, my chaletmate moving between lounge and bathroom.

"You awake Jay?" Alice asked, my view of the girl limited to that mass of ebony hair and the arms holding me.

"Uh-huh."

"I was thinking, you know, about Dobbs. About everything that's happened."

I waited for her to continue, my hand reaching out to stroke that smooth mane.

"Most of the time I can shut it out, you know? The horror of these last few years."

I thought of my tiny flat, weekends when I would only emerge to go to the gym, deliberately avoid those lurid headlines screaming off boards outside the local newsagents and 24-hour stores.

"I know what you mean," I said.

"You rationalise it to yourself, the chance of getting mixed up in some *attack* or whatever. It's tiny, right?"

"You're more likely to be hit by a bus."

"Sure, but I have this friend, Rae." From outside the room I heard Wallis padding around, a gurgling sound that emanated from the kitchen. "We used to work together. She's still in the office I left, right at the centre of town, where that car bomb went off last year."

"Which one was that?" There had been so many incidents, some foiled as others wreaked a unique kind of havoc. I avoided as much of the detail as I could, only reading about *actions* if they had a direct impact on my life. Thinking of it as the opposite of voyeurism, this approach seemed both sane and proportional, but my limited frame of reference became a disadvantage at times. "Was it the one with the limousine?"

"It was a really bad explosion. Lots of people were walking to work in the square. Eight dead I think."

"Eight? Yeah, I remember."

"So Rae's at her desk by the window, working hard like she always does, when there's this huge blast." Alice was up alongside me now, her face close to mine but averted, staring at the ceiling. "All those men and women outside her office. One minute they're hurrying along, checking their watches, wondering whether they'll make it to a meeting on time…."

"The next minute they're blown to bits."

"Because of where she is, Rae gets the full force of everything. Body parts hit the window by her desk, first one limb, then another. All these pieces of someone, a wave of blood sliding down the glass."

"God Alice."

"Rae doesn't know what to do. Should she go outside and help, or might there be more bombs? By the time she makes a decision the boss is at the door to stop her, because they don't want employees out there."

I ran a finger across Alice's temple. "Company policy."

"And over his shoulder she can see this woman with both her arms and legs gone, still alive and screaming for help, but you can see she won't be able to scream much longer. There's a pool of blood around her, around what's left of her, and its growing by the second."

I wondered if she was going to start crying again. "Alice."

"It's okay Jay." The girl's voice was shaky. She paused to compose herself. "They're locked down for the rest of the day, and Rae has to stay in there, that office I'd have been in with her if I was still at my old job. She's got no choice but to stare out at the carnage through her bloody window, praying the forensic teams get there soon so it can all be cleared away. So she won't have to spend more time staring at the blood, spread all over her building...."

I drew Alice close again. A seagull landed on the roof of our block, squawking repulsively.

"I thought that was it, the closest I was ever going to get to some kind of, well, some kind of atrocity." Alice felt so hot in my arms, almost feverish. "When Rae finally came to terms with it, when she could deal with the event well enough in her head to tell me what happened, it was only after counselling her boss arranged. She spent a long time talking it through and the psychologist tried to stop her feeling shame or guilt, but she did. Because so many people suffered far worse than Rae that day; those families who lost loved ones, all the people who went into hospital...."

"I can understand why she felt that way."

"But do you see Jay? I thought that was my brush with violence, that was my story. Except it wasn't mine, it was Rae's. Mine was on its way, still coming; I know that now. After what happened to Dale, then seeing Norman like that last night." Alice's eyes were fixed on me. "I was so complacent, but I didn't know the half of it, what was coming. Now I get my share of everything that's bad in the world."

Voices were raised somewhere across the complex, men shouting at each other this morning, words I couldn't pick out although the tone was gruff and serious.

"No one's *meant* to have horror in their life." I told Alice. "We're going to get back to normal, just you watch."

Alice made a sound, somewhere between a yawn and an expression of doubt, and moved to swing her legs off the bed. The girl left for the bathroom while I rose, easing myself up, aware of the damage to my body but coping, the pain present but dulled.

Wallis was staring out of the lounge window, still half asleep. I went to the kitchen intending to rinse out a glass.

"Water's off." He said as I turned the tap on and nothing came out, only the sound of a vacuum deep within the network of pipes, a pointless clatter and hiss.

"Damn."

"There's still a bit in the kettle."

I poured a few mouthfuls of water into an unwashed glass, pieces of limescale floating in the tepid liquid. Looking away as I sipped, I tried not to think about impurities.

"This is getting beyond a joke."

"Can't flush the toilet, can't have a wash." Wallis turned to me. "Do you think something's been put in it? Maybe they've contaminated the water."

There had been scare stories on the news, gossip around the office from employees more engaged with the world than me, talk of alleged plots to poison reservoirs and the like. The details were shady and arrests few, one result being increased surveillance anywhere that processed drinking water. Security was constantly being reviewed and upped, often arbitrarily it seemed to me, independent of intelligence received or the threat posed. The virus in the water story gripped our nation for a few days before being supplanted by other reports; the midair mixing of explosive chemicals, rockets fired from upper storey windows, a man with a bomb factory in his attic.

I remembered Alfred's words from yesterday evening, how sure he was we were being fooled with, that the loss of phone contact was down to forces within this camp. Perhaps Alfred believed the cessation of the water was a similar trick, the removal of one more modern convenience, power exerted obscurely to increase the pressure on our minds.

"I wouldn't jump to any conclusions mate." I told Wallis.

Alice reappeared, said she felt unclean without water, was going to perform what ablutions she could back in her own chalet, the question of how we were going to proceed forgotten for now. I checked the meter and saw that our electricity was running low, although there was still enough to last the day if we neglected to turn the radiators on. Wallis told me about Roger's failed attempt to buy more tokens last night and that made me think of Sid. Other people to check on, more factors to worry about.

We had some bread left so I spread margarine on a slice and ate at the table, the food forming a claggy ball in my mouth as I chewed, effort required to swallow each greasy bite. How I wished this was a normal Sunday morning, relaxed and easily wasted, posing none of my current concerns with other people, living or dead.

"Hey Wallis, anything on TV?"

"I can check." He moved to the set. "But if it's like earlier, I really don't want to watch."

Confused, I observed him press the buttons and access *Sunlit*'s in-house channel which was showing some kind of home video. The film was set in a mocked-up dungeon, a woman chained to the wall in a leather mask, and as I watched she urinated on a man with a moustache, vaguely Germanic in appearance. He looked as if he'd been recently flogged, ugly red marks prominent on the man's chest and back.

Wallis was already looking away from the screen. "Fuck no," I told him. "Turn it off."

Before I could properly process what we'd seen there came a knock at the door, Wallis craned his neck from the sofa to see who was out on the balcony.

"It's Pete."

I watched from my seat as Wallis opened the door to that man he'd been chatting with last night and I guessed he must have told Pete our chalet number then. In the light of day Pete was about half as large again as Wallis, both in height and girth, with the same style of spectacles and a similar bulge of flab hanging over his belt, had he worn a belt. Most of Pete was covered by an enormous grey sweatshirt, dotted with a number of darker stains. Beside him I caught glimpses of an even more obese man, light stubble covering his double chin.

"Hey Wallis, we were wondering if you had any food left."

My friend turned to the kitchen and I tried to let him know the answer without these visitors seeing my head shake. "I don't think so." He told them.

"It's just the shop's not open." Pete gestured in the direction of the camp's entrance. "I don't know if it's a Sunday thing or what, but you would think they'd arrange to be open today, what with us around."

I called over. "Have you tried asking in the dome?"

"Yeah, but we couldn't find anyone there either, everything's shut up. There's no one at the entrance and the barrier's down so we can't drive somewhere to eat." I wondered if there would have been anywhere to find before the roadblock. Maybe these men hadn't heard about the military presence.

"It's starting to really get me down." Pete told Wallis. "You don't know where Norman's staying do you?"

Suddenly I was on my feet, hurrying to the doorway even as Wallis said: "Dobbs? Yeah, he'd be the best person to…"

"He's, uh… he's not staying there any more." I interrupted.

Wallis stared up at me. "Isn't he?"

"Not this morning. Listen, I think we've got some food you can have, let me take a look." I pulled Wallis away by the arm, hissed at him under my breath. "Don't tell them about Dobbs' chalet, trust me on this."

"Um, okay."

Raiding the fridge, I made Wallis hold a bag into which I put our remaining eggs and some bread, the remnants of that sausage neither of us had particularly enjoyed, sending the grateful men on their way to create a breakfast that, while too meagre to fill their sizeable bellies, was certainly better than nothing.

"What was all that about?" Wallis asked after they had gone.

"There's a problem with Dobbs." A problem that could never be resolved, I hesitated to add. "Here, I kept the last of our chocolate."

"Cheers." Wallis broke off a piece and popped it in his mouth.

"You'll have to go with it for now." I told him seriously. "Don't tell anyone Dobbs' chalet number. He can't do anything for us now, we found that out last night."

"How come?"

"I'll explain later, I've got to go and sort it out now." I opened the door. "If anyone comes here, Alice or anyone, tell them I'll be back soon."

He agreed, perplexed. Better Wallis be that way than know our best hope of getting out of here was dead.

Once outside I tore down the stairs, emitting a brief groan as the movement inflamed yesterday's injuries. Striding between chalet blocks, the sky above me clouded up from the west and I tried not to appear panicked should anyone see me. I turned toward Dobbs' block, going up the metal steps unsteadily and having to halt at the top to catch my breath, bent over with both hands on my knees.

After a couple of seconds I scanned my surroundings and, content no one was in sight, pushed open that door I'd forced last night. Once inside, the first thing I did was draw the curtains, amazed we hadn't thought of that before. Then I pushed the sofa sideways across the doorway, just in case anyone took it upon themselves to try and get in.

Everything was how we'd left it, Dobbs there on the floor, a cyan tinge to his skin in the light coming from the bedroom. I wanted to get him out of sight and there was only one suitable place, a location that meant his body wouldn't be easily found, not unless someone conducted a thorough search of chalet 117.

Manoeuvring the single beds into the centre of the bedroom, I left a gap of about eighteen inches between the far mattress and wall. Then I put my hands under Dobbs' armpits and tried to drag him out of the hallway, wondering why a man would commit suicide in a corridor, so much premeditation in other aspects of this cataclysmic final act that the location felt incongruous. Surely Dobbs would have sat down somewhere to ready himself, gone through the preparations before slumping back, lifeless in a chair or on his bed.

I forced myself to stop mulling those aspects of the death that weren't sitting right, the position of Norman's body and the manner by which he'd taken his own life. Instead I concentrated on heaving his bloodstained form, Dobbs surprisingly heavy for one so skinny and repressed while alive. The rigor mortis didn't help, his joints had stiffened to the extent Dobbs was difficult to position once inside the bedroom. I basically had to lift his inflexible corpse into the corner, muscles tensing as I tried desperately to hold on, a cry of pain when I finally got Dobbs into a place where I could drop him against the wall.

The corpse landed on its side, knife knocked from the original position by a skirting board. I stood over Dobbs breathing heavily and stared at the askew blade. Here was another anomaly, had someone told me Norman would do himself in I would have been shocked and surprised certainly, but once I'd accepted that fact, the expectation would have been a very different cause of death. Maybe an overdose on prescription medication, a length of hose running from the car exhaust to window with the engine running. Something carefully worked out in advance with a high probability of success, a quiet and painless departure from this mortal coil, not a sudden bloody stab at himself. Dobbs could easily have missed the mark, inflicted agony rather than death, and Norman didn't strike me as brave enough to kill himself this way.

I rearranged the mattresses over the dead man to obscure him from view, blankets and sheets shifted so that no part of Dobbs' would be visible from the doorway. There was no use debating it, I had to assume Norman killed himself like this because he'd neither the pills nor the opportunity to do it any other way. My suspicions were disquieting but there were too many other concerns, like whether I'd broken any laws by tampering with this corpse, made myself a target for future criminal investigations. The most immediate problem was ensuring my colleagues remained ignorant of this death. I had to keep the fear and paranoia Dobbs' demise would unleash suppressed, retain some skein of normality for the group while we figured out what to do next.

On the bedside table there were a number of Dobbs' personal items, car keys and travel pass, a plastic folder with some papers in it I leafed through, finding the chalet list, a print out of who was staying where. I folded this up and put the piece of paper in my pocket, glancing at the other documents, an itinerary that said we were supposed to have gone go-karting and orienteering by now, another map of the complex and an email from someone called Sinclair Stenton who promised the company that their requirements would be accommodated. His agreement was a jumble of misspelt words and eccentric grammar, no signature at the end of this electronic message to let me know the man's role.

There came the noise of people then, the kind of urgent shouts you hear on the fringes of an emergency, and I realised I'd spent far too long in this chalet, pushing the sofa out of the way to leave Dobbs in his makeshift resting place.

Outside a few screams were intermingling with the yells and I sprinted back to the main road, seeing smoke rise from the other end of the holiday camp, so close it had to be a chalet block that was on fire.

Chapter Twelve

As I ran closer, following that acrid cloud of smoke blown eastwards over the rooftops, the burning smell became overwhelming. The blaze was to the back of camp, at the centre of that final row before the staff accommodation, and a group gathered at the block's base, watching smoke billow from the open windows of the top-right chalet.

Silvia noticed me arrive, the stocky woman flanked by Dave and a ginger-haired guy I had seen occasionally, working in her section.

All appeared strangely calm now. "Is everybody out?" I asked.

"Well, there's no sign of anyone trying to escape."

Dave turned to me, Suzie at his side, the tall girl wearing a baggy t-shirt that fell past her knees, like some kind of improvised nightshirt. "There wasn't anyone staying in the block but us, not that I know of." Dave gestured to the man with ginger hair. "Me and Adrian were in 619 when we smelt smoke. That's our chalet, there at the end."

The fumes were black and rising, no flames visible, but that last chalet was obviously close to being gutted, a mercy there was nowhere for the fire to spread. It would burn itself out without damaging the surrounding accommodation, although the smell permeated this whole area. Had the fire started in the centre of a block, or on the lower level, a dozen chalets could have gone up in flames by now.

I checked for *Sunlit* employees but found none, and if the staff weren't interested in this kind of emergency I supposed they must have left the premises altogether. Nearby Dave put an arm around Suzie's waist in a way that told me they had slept together last night. She accepted the touch but didn't reciprocate. What was he? Twenty years older than her? Twenty-five?

"Strange isn't it?" Silvia mused. "There was a fire on my street a few years back and I felt powerless then, but at least I could call the fire brigade."

"I know what you mean." I thought of Dale last night, how we failed to get Catherine treatment, were unable to call the police and tell them what had been done to her. "Now the water's off we can't even do that thing." Silvia looked at me questioningly. "You know, stand in a line, pass buckets of water along until we've put it out."

Silvia smiled. "I think that only happens in movies Jay." She looked round at everyone there, all of them watching passively. "Besides, I don't think anyone's bothered enough to do anything. It's not their responsibility."

I followed her gaze, the man called Adrian was emptying his sinuses into a handkerchief with some force as a couple of people drifted away, into the background. "You're probably right." I said. "Any idea how it started?"

"Not a clue." The smoke had eased to a plume now, the visible parts of that chalet dark and charred. "Faulty oven? Someone smoking in bed?"

It occurred to me I had information that might prove useful here, removing Dobbs' list from my back pocket.

"What's that?" Silvia asked, peering across.

"List of who's staying where."

"Great, how'd you get it?"

"Er, camp manager gave me a copy." I examined the piece of paper, hoping there weren't any clues on the sheet to give away my lie, no notes from Dobbs or handwritten annotations. Luckily the page hadn't been personalised and I saw that Dave was right, the sole occupants of this block were expected to be him and Adrian in 619. Unless someone had forced their way into the rooms where that fire started, or opted to stay there unexpectedly, no one should have been inside to turn on the oven or carelessly discard a lit cigarette. Besides, if someone had managed to escape the fumes, surely they would have been there at the front with us, coughing up an explanation of what had happened.

Which only left as possibilities an isolated instance of spontaneous combustion or sabotage. But who would commit arson on an empty chalet? Answers eluded me, I felt thirsty and sore and confused, the events failing to come together in ways that made sense.

A few others wandered over, all asking the same questions as me, Alfred stroking his beard and Anthea walking somewhat awkwardly, as if she'd injured her pelvis. Alice was with them, the girl approaching Suzie to confer with her while Wallis came across to me. I told him there had been an accident, this fire burning itself out with nothing more to be concerned about. Maybe I was trying to convince myself as much as him, and Wallis certainly didn't look persuaded, gazing up at the location of the blaze in silence.

Alice moved over to us. "So nobody knows what started it?"

"Not yet, no." I wondered whether experts needed special equipment to assess if such a conflagration had been started deliberately, or whether a person like me could detect suspicious circumstances, some trace of flammable accelerant lurking inside. Perhaps a kind of petrol or paraffin scent would be present underneath the powerful odour of smouldering furniture, were I to go in after the smoke abated. Alice came closer, took hold of my arm and brought me back to the moment. Her brow was wrinkled, face troubled. "What's wrong?" I asked.

"Natasha's not in our chalet and Suze hasn't seen her." The girl stared up at me dolefully. "I'm worried."

"She can't have gone far." Alice's expression told me this wasn't the answer I should have given. I thought of Dobbs then, less obviously depressed than Nat and subsequently dead by his own hand. "We'll find her." I asserted.

The list of chalet occupants was still in my hand, providing us with an invaluable guide, the means to check on everyone's well-being or otherwise. With Alice at my side, that girl's touch and voice, I reminded myself this was no day for lapsing into daydreams, a waste of time to stare at those smoky tendrils rising above our heads. We had to figure out ways of helping the people who needed it and get everyone out of here.

I told Silvia I'd be back when the fire was out, asking her to make a mental note of anything out of the ordinary before then as Wallis and Alice accompanied me back to that main road circling the complex. We arrived near the entrance, the barrier down and post unmanned, just as Pete had said, vehicles unable to leave or enter this site. The poky shop was all locked up too, its interior darkened and groceries visible through the window, only scant supplies lit up in the refrigerators.

Alice wandered through the exit, checking the control panel that rose and lowered that horizontal metal pole, buttons locked inside a metal box on the side of a wall. I followed the girl as she walked to the edge of the coastal route, looking left and right down the silence of the road, Wallis ambling behind.

"You okay?" I asked her.

"Yeah, thought I'd be hungry by now, but this experience is ruining my appetite." She tried to smile. "We're really trapped aren't we?"

I glanced at Wallis who turned away and fiddled with his spectacles, unable to disguise how forlorn he felt. My friend resembled a lifelong employee who has just been told his services are no longer required.

"Not for long." Gesturing across the road, I pointed to the beach, then east. "There are houses up that way, properties looking out to sea."

"Holiday homes."

"Probably, but chances are some of them will be occupied. We just need to find someone who'll let us use their phone."

"Aren't the lines still out?" Asked Wallis, cleaning a lens with the material of his top.

"That might just be in the camp." The road remained deserted, eerily quiet. "Even if they are, someone's bound to have internet access. If we can discover what's going on in the rest of the country, we might be able to form a plan and get the hell out of here. Sticking around, with everyone as they are, things are only going to get worse."

I hoped the responsibility I was about to hand my friend might give him new purpose. Help us certainly, but in the main I didn't want Wallis falling into the kind of funk that makes people give up on themselves. This ennui was fast spreading among people in the complex, endemic to the passive and hung-over.

"Are you going to be okay going down the beach?" Alice asked softly.

"Sure, of course." Wallis squared his shoulders. "I'll walk that way, see if I can find anyone."

"Okay mate, that'd be great. Don't go too far." I realised these were similar guidelines to those you'd give a child and tried to keep my tone free from condescension. "If you start to feel tired or whatever, come straight back. I'll see you at the chalet in a bit, alright?"

Wallis nodded, unnecessarily checking the thoroughfare for traffic as he gave Alice a little wave and set off in the direction of the shoreline. He looked more than ever like a mole that has taken human shape this morning, pulling the hood of his top up then disappearing off down the pathway.

Alice was standing closer now, black hair tied back from her face, reaching out to me as she approached. Thinking the girl wanted my embrace, I took her in my arms. The next thing I knew she'd stretched up to kiss me on the mouth. The feel of her lips on mine, imperfect but wonderfully soft, transported me away from our surroundings, left a warm glow in my chest just starting to emanate outwards when she pulled away, smiling and wiping at her mouth.

"What...?" I tried to finalise the question, failed.

"Whatever happens now, I wanted to have done that." Her eyes were on me, the fine structure of Alice's cheekbones, that petite nose and olive skin. I was unable to think of anything to say.

"So, where to next?" She asked, turning back to the camp.

A blast of wind hit my face. "Um, well, if we're looking for Nat it's difficult to know where to start." People might say a girl like Alice tasted sweet, but in this case it was literally true. I could still feel her body against mine.

We set off, passing that closed shop once more then winding round to the left, an artificial black cloud alongside us, hanging low over that charred chalet block and dispersing a little each time the breeze caught it. "We shouldn't just wander around aimlessly though." Alice noted. "You can't have that much energy, I know I don't."

"No, and I've been thinking about Catherine." I moved up beside the girl, showing her Dobbs' list of who was staying where. "Let's check on her and Cheryl, here they are." I pointed, "Chalet 226."

Wallis scrambled up those dunes we'd last climbed two days ago, although it felt like sometime the last century by now. My friend was relieved to be away from the smoke and fire, that confined pressure he'd started to feel inside the *Sunlit* complex, all those individuals with their strange agendas and odd ways, people like me who kept him in the dark, the only source of distraction those unsettling films on TV.

Up here, standing on the dunes surveying a beach empty of much except seaweed and pieces of driftwood, Wallis could almost believe the world was proceeding as usual. It wasn't much of a stretch to imagine a different motivation for his being here, some alternative reason that would make it entirely natural for Wallis to be part of this scene at the start of October, take a stroll and sample the sea air.

Reality intervened then. This wasn't some kind of planned morning constitutional, behind Wallis lay mainland England, a place where something bad was happening. His task was to find out the extent of this catastrophe, whether a bombing of the innocent or meteorite shower or poison in the water supply. If Wallis could discover what was going on, put in a distress call to alleviate our situation, then perhaps we could all go home.

Checking the coastline, Wallis slipped down that grass-spotted hill and saw I had been right, there was nothing for miles to the right, nothing but the coastline turning in on itself. His quest lay leftwards, out further east where the shore tapered into huts and other structures. That was where Wallis headed, passing boarded up cafes and ice cream stalls, services that catered for eager holidaymakers come summer but were currently unused and abandoned. He trudged across the wet sand, towards the bungalows that came into view, hoping one would prove occupied.

The first of these houses looked promising, sand from the shore tailing off in the walk-up to a paved area before its pleasantly sheltered veranda, providing relief from the wind beginning to whip up along the beach. A locked sliding door prevented Wallis from accessing the bungalow's bell, visible through the glass of that back entrance, and because he would have to go back to ring from the front, Wallis elected to rap at the window instead and call out his *hellos*. He saw wood and building materials and a number of tools out on the patio, a workbench with drill and a saw on the floor beside it, as if someone had taken a break from this DIY but would be returning any moment. Yet after several minutes of shouting there was no sign of anyone who might hear him so Wallis moved on, trying not to feel discouraged.

The rest of the bungalows were a mishmash of sizes and styles of architecture, some backing straight onto the beach, others with a path or gate barring the way. A few were boxy and slate-roofed, others hut-like in their construction, the only aspect in common a lack of inhabitants. These buildings must have belonged to people working elsewhere just as Wallis had first thought, affluent couples who only found the time to drive out here when the sun shone or they needed to perform maintenance, these properties too isolated for owners to worry about vandalism or break-ins during their long absences.

Hands weary after all the knocking and voice hoarse from being raised, Wallis strained to hear signs of life as he stood before each of these homes, looking lost and small at the edge of the beach. He sought out some sibilance from a radio or the crackle of a television, any activity or movement. All that came to his ears was the occasional caw of a seabird or, if he listened hard, the approaching ocean, distant waves hitting the shore as they drew in.

Growing sick of this futility, Wallis approached the thirteenth and final bungalow, aware the gradient was taking him higher, up to where the sand met the coast road a few hundred yards away. After that there was only the scattered accommodation of a caravan site, fenced off and secured this autumn, then nothing.

The last house was more modest than those others, Wallis thought its outer walls must have been painted their cornfield yellow some time ago, the colour was now fading and flaked after long exposure to the elements. There was a doorbell here so Wallis held the button down, hearing it ring through the interior, a noise that lasted longer than would normally be deemed polite, because he didn't expect anyone to be inside. In fact, a perverse thought occurred to Wallis then, a notion I'd deliberately sent my friend off on some wild goose chase just to get him out of the way, leaving Jay, his supposed ally, free to continue acting all secretively with Alice.

My friend stuffed numb hands into the front pocket of his top and rebuked himself for such pettiness, already halfway back to camp in his head, taken by surprise when an old man opened the door, greeting Wallis as if he was expected.

Back in the holiday camp we were having problems of our own rousing people.

"Cheryl, you in there?" I hammered at the door. "It's us." I turned to Alice. "You try."

The girl put her head against the door of chalet 226.

"We're just checking on you." She reassured the interior. "It's Jay and Alice, there's no one else here."

Eventually there came the sound of heavy objects being shifted, a few squeals of effort before Cheryl opened the door a crack, peering furtively at the outside before she let us inside.

In the lounge everything that had blocked the doorway was thrown into the centre of the room, chairs and a bedside table and even a mattress on its side. Catherine sat wrapped in a blanket, huddled on the sofa as if she'd just come out of anaesthetic after a major operation, a frightened animal with ghostly white skin. The room was cold and dark, its curtains drawn, and I pressed a light switch uselessly, realising the girls had used up their allocation of electricity keeping themselves warm.

Alice went to sit beside Catherine, stroked the girl's unkempt hair and made noises of reassurance while I watched Cheryl who remained in a state of some agitation. She was unable to stand still, pulling the sleeves of her cardigan over both hands and back again compulsively, moving around this room as much as she could while avoiding that junk-heap at its centre. The smell of rotting food was pervasive here, as if it oozed from the walls.

"How is she?" I asked, Alice continuing to coo platitudes over Catherine as she would a restless toddler.

"Not great, what'd you expect?" Cheryl went to place a hand on top of her friend's head. "She slept a few hours, then she woke up and started crying. We've been like this ever since."

"Do you need anything?" As soon as it came out I realised what a stupid thing that was to say.

"Water, heat, food. What have you got?" Cheryl looked different without any make up, young and unspoilt, innocent even, although she was suffering from a bout of severe rage. "What I really want is that fucker locked up."

"It'll happen." I didn't sound convincing. "We're going to get everyone out of here today. We'll take care of him then."

Cheryl made a *pah* sound and flounced into the kitchenette. Alice was looking Catherine in the eye, speaking softly but loud enough for all of us to hear. "You haven't cleaned yourself up babe have you?"

Cheryl snorted. "With what?"

"No." Catherine's voice was tremulous and distant, the girl on the edge of some strange state of being. "Why?"

"We have to take a swab." Alice sounded like some worldly older sister. "If you keep his DNA then we'll have proof."

Catherine shook her head faintly. "I just want to forget about it."

"What's the point anyway?" Cheryl's strident tone was starting to grate, her voice seeping through the thin walls. "They won't do anything. Loads of blokes have forced themselves on my friends, they never even got arrested."

Alice restrained herself, keeping patient. "Report this and it's the first step to stopping him doing it again."

"I don't want to think about it." Catherine whispered.

"How do we report it? We can't." Cheryl banged a cupboard door for emphasis. "What we should do is go back over there and sort him out properly, I know you fucked him up." She pointed at me. "But you didn't fuck him up *enough*."

"That's not a very good idea." I knew the Dale situation ought to be checked on, whatever his crimes, and I wondered if the only reason I hadn't looked in on his chalet today was cowardice, a reluctance to get embroiled in another violent altercation.

"You got any better ideas?" Cheryl was bitter and confrontational, furious with this world and the gender I represented. My presence here was ill judged, I saw that now. As the first example of maleness these girls had encountered since the rape, I was finding myself a focus for the anger in the air around Cheryl.

Alice must have seen it too, saying: "You go Jay, I'll stay a while."

The man wasn't just old but ancient, needed two sticks to walk, strange that his voice was so deep and strong.

"Hello!"

"Hello sir." Wallis often turned deferential around his elders. "I wonder if I might use your phone?"

The man, whose name turned out to be Emeric, looked Wallis up and down, apparently concluding he wasn't any kind of threat, that this wasn't some kind of nuisance call.

"Of course young man, do come in."

A dim hallway led into the bungalow, Emeric passing a bedroom on the left piled high with bric-a-brac, then a kitchen to his right. The man moved slowly, one stick in front of the other, while behind him Wallis asked if he could get a drink of water, elated to reach the sink and find Emeric's supply flowing freely. He drank for long seconds straight from the tap, then decided to fill a receptacle, take a supply back with him. Wallis cast around for some empty bottle or discarded flask, found nothing except pots and pans and plates covering the worktops, all coated with a thin layer of grease. Eventually he gave up on the idea.

Inside what the old man referred to as his *drawing room*, Emeric was surrounded by bookcases beside piles of newspapers, each several feet high. They filled most available sections of floor, while a grimy window looked out over fields to the north, that caravan park visible in the distance.

"I'll make some tea in a minute." Emeric said, unconvincingly, since it looked like he'd struggle to even stand up again.

"That's fine." His guest perched on a dusty armchair, noticing the nearest stack of papers was topped by an edition dated 13th September 1957. Wallis explained how we had got ourselves trapped in a holiday camp, telling the old man who he worked for and why they'd covered the expense of our weekend visit to the area, Emeric nodding occasionally in response. He was robust for a man his age, late eighties or older but full-bellied, a mound of grey hair on either side of his head, Emeric's wet mouth opening to reveal teeth that must have been false.

Wallis finished his account of events, expecting questions or at least some response from this old man, conjectures underpinned by the wisdom of his long experience. Instead there came only silence, as if Emeric expected his visitor to continue, even though Wallis's narrative had clearly ended. My friend began to wonder how much of his talk Emeric had caught, noticing no hearing aids attached to the pensioner's head. Perhaps he needed them.

"So, ah, would it be possible to use your phone?" Wallis asked, louder than before.

"Of course my boy, it's over there."

Wallis followed the frail wave to a round table covered by yellowing bills and circulars. Shifting aside some of these papers revealed an old-fashion dial telephone and, with a racing heart, Wallis realised he was close to summoning help, assistance that would release us all from the prison the *Sunlit Holiday Centre* had become.

He picked up the receiver, had already slotted a finger into the hole for zero before Wallis realised there was no dial tone.

"It's dead." Wallis told Emeric.

"Eh? What's that?"

Wallis enunciated more clearly. "The telephone isn't working."

"What? Oh yes, that." The old man stroked one of his walking sticks with a liver-spotted hand. "Had it disconnected back… when was it? Didn't seem to use it you see."

Inwardly Wallis gave a sigh. "Do you know of anyone else who might be able to help?"

"Archie comes round with my groceries every Wednesday."

"Okay." Wallis stared at the contents of the room, felt disappointed and melancholy, all this clutter was worthless to the world outside Emeric, would be thrown out and destroyed when he died. "Thanks anyway."

Without waiting for the old man to get up, Wallis hurried out the way he'd come in, finding the atmosphere of that bungalow oppressive suddenly, a recluse shut away from the world, waiting for his end. Wallis shouted a goodbye and secured the outer door, hit by a blast of wind and grit from the beach.

He carried on the short distance along and up, planning to turn at the road and walk west back to the complex, a way that would leave him less exposed. Soon Wallis was ascending, closing in on that deserted caravan park, seeing white boxes on blocks and rectangular trailers. That was when he caught a glimpse of a dark shape in the distance, an object both incongruous and alien dumped on the sand. Upping his pace to reach this silhouette, breaking into a breathless jog as he came closer, Wallis realised this was some*one* rather than something. The human form was clad in a dark coat, the details becoming clearer as he neared, that white, almost translucent skin of her hands, a mane of dark red hair, what did they call the colour?

Wallis was almost upon the girl before he realised it was someone he recognised, not some unfortunate stranger or drowned seafarer washed up by the tide. Natasha hadn't been touched by the ocean, and there was no way of telling how she'd ended up there, face down in the sand.

Chapter Thirteen

Wallis managed to turn her over before rushing from the scene to get me. We returned to find Natasha as he'd left her, the girl's breathing shallow, her pulse difficult to find but there, fluttering under the pressure of my fingers. Neither of us knew how long she'd been there, horribly exposed to the wind howling in off the coastline, that tide inching its way up the shore towards her, but we both understood it was time to get her away.

I tested Natasha's weight, realising she couldn't have been here overnight, the water would have come in this far, sea lapping over her body and claiming the girl for itself. She'd have been taken away by the tide in a few hours time if Wallis hadn't arrived. He looked shaken and I hoped my friend knew he had saved Natasha, this slender girl I lifted up gently, one arm gripping her torso and the other under the crook of her knees. I got Natasha off the beach and up to that footway alongside the road, pausing in a spot sheltered from the wind to gasp at my efforts.

That sedative she'd taken yesterday afternoon must have worn off sometime in the night, caused Natasha to wake early this morning and panic as she found herself alone. Suzie was sharing a bed with Dave across the camp, and Alice had slept down the block with me, but Nat wasn't to know that. Already nervy, and missing her boyfriend and family, all the anxiety returned as Natasha recalled those events at the checkpoint. The girl's fears could only have grown as she came to believe everyone had abandoned her.

Perhaps she threw on a coat, went out into the dawn and found no colleagues up at that hour, not after a night of partying. With no other signs of human life around the camp, the surroundings must have felt dreamlike and upsetting as she stumbled around on her own. Eventually Natasha would have left the complex. Maybe she thought about flagging down a car, someone who would take her back to civilization, human contact that proved she hadn't woken up on a deserted, post-apocalyptic planet, the last one alive in some disaster stricken world.

Eventually Nat realised there weren't going to be any vehicles passing, gave up and decided to try the beach instead, hoping to find signs of life there, some jogger or dog-walker. When the shore proved just as empty she started walking, determined to make it to a town or village, so delirious through hunger and fatigue the girl ended up picking a direction at random, over-estimating her body's ability to carry itself away. Half a mile later, having struggled with her lack of strength, suffering from exhaustion as well as the after-effects of that drug, Natasha's legs gave out. That was how she ended up there, drifting in and out of consciousness until Wallis happened by.

He helped support the girl now, taking hold of Natasha's legs while I maintained my grip on her upper body, cradling the girl with delicacy even as a voice in my head urged me to hurry. I didn't know how weak this girl had become, or if she was in immediate danger, but I understood we had to provide her with warmth and shelter quickly, baulked at the prospect of Natasha expiring here, dying in my arms.

We walked past the front of those bungalows Wallis had called to not so long ago, straining with the effort of each step, my friend in front of me, his arms wrapped around Natasha's legs. After leaving Alice with Catherine I'd gone back to our chalet feeling numb and useless, surplus to requirements and suddenly too tired to think. There were so many things I should have been doing, going back to that fire-gutted chalet or checking on the likes of Sid and Julie, but the most immediate concern pricking at my conscience related to those men across the block. I sucked on one of our remaining squares of chocolate, unable to bite without my jaw smarting, and reflected on the damage I'd done. Dale Packer was the worst kind of alpha male, privileged enough to think he could take whatever he wanted by force and get away with it. Underneath that professional exterior he maintained in the workplace I knew now Dale was a thug, someone who didn't suffer remorse from what he'd done, not in the least. But if I went on ignoring his presence over there, regarding Packer as someone else's problem, dismissing those injuries I'd inflicted, like some prizefighter justifying his career with hollow clichés, it made me as bad as Dale. That was the realization which finally took me back to chalet 327.

I walked past the stinking rubbish and glanced inside, seeing Dale laid out on the sofa, easing the smashed door open in a way that could have passed for a gust of wind. He was the only one in the lounge, a place reeking of sour bodies and something close to mouldy cheese. The blood around Dale's forehead had dried now, forming a kind of crimson tiara above his closed eyes and Packer made a strange sound, somewhere between a splutter and the snort of a randy pig. It took me a few moments to work out he was snoring.

There must have been some credit left on the electricity meter because their television was on with the volume muted. On the screen a prisoner was whipped by a masked man in a jailer's get-up, the picture grainy and monochrome, as if this footage had been filmed on an antiquated video camera. There was no sign of Ejiro in the chalet but I found Rob in the bedroom, passed out fully clothed, his face buried in a pillow, only unwashed hair and one fuzzy sideburn visible. Back in the lounge I sat down at the table and wondered what I should do next, knowing it would be unwise to try and clean Dale's wound myself, even if I'd the means to do so. Equally I didn't want to ask anyone else to come in here, attend to this man who was too out of it to take care of himself amongst the filth and stench.

Once I was sure I wouldn't rouse the snoring man I reached behind to open the fridge, found a few unopened cans of beer and little else. In the midst of the paper and wrappers on the table was a transparent bag of marijuana, a packet of white pills, and the remnants of some cocaine wraps. On the TV images flickered, that manacled man burning his prisoner with a hot poker now, steam rising from the flesh, a mouth screaming in agony. This looked like some kind of snuff film, although I had never believed the stories, hearsay that claimed circles of men passed these videos amongst each other in secret, obtaining some kind of illicit thrill from the suffering of others. The pain of that man in the film looked real enough, that glowing poker placed on his tongue now, causing him to have some kind of fit. I wondered if this was an obscure art house flick, deliberately filmed to resemble an illegal act, one imagined sequence from a seedy dungeon in some obscure country.

That was when I heard Wallis, calling my name out across the grassy rectangle that separated the blocks, almost tripping over a table leg as I rushed out, trying to get to him before the shouts woke those men inside.

Wallis babbled and gesticulated to little avail as I followed him to the beach although I got the gist, understanding about that girl he'd found and what we had to do. We were back near the entrance now, resting at the side of the road, me supporting Natasha while Wallis got his breath back. Then we lifted her again, negotiating the narrow path by the barrier, past a group of men who peered into the closed shop. Pete and some of the techies were conferring, overweight men who discussed how they might get at those supplies they saw inside, too caught up in this desire and the temptations behind the window to take much notice of us. One turned our way and saw us carrying the unconscious girl but he said nothing, preferring not to get involved.

It was a struggle, getting Natasha's dead weight up the metal steps, her limbs and hair falling everywhere. I wanted the girl in our chalet while we still had enough electricity to turn a radiator on and get her up against it, warm Natasha right through. Wrapping her in blankets once inside, I despatched Wallis to find Alice who happened to be along the balcony, Suzie coming across with her to fuss over Natasha, the girl laid out on our sofa, pale and lost but alive.

Concerned as I was, it quickly became apparent there was nothing more for me to do as the girls took over nursing their chaletmate. It was then I had an idea about how to help everyone else, leaving Wallis to fill them in on events before going back outside, coming down the stairs at pace. That was when I heard the sound of glass breaking near the camp's entrance, understanding immediately what it meant.

The splintering noise continued as I strode towards the shop and sure enough that group of men had broken through the large window, one of the fattest kicking away the shards of glass that remained, low down on the window frame.

They had got hold of a crowbar from somewhere, broken the pane to begin their raid and were squeezing inside now, passing sideways through that hole where the glass used to be, stepping over the fragments that littered the floor. There were five of them, bellies immense and breathing rapid, surprisingly quick as I followed the last through, watching them grab at the food, those cakes and biscuits and crisps on the shelves. Standing in front of the broken window to block the exit, I had to yell to make myself heard above the looting.

"Wait! Stop for a minute!"

The men paused in their stealing, groceries piled high in cradling arms, turning to look at me uncomprehendingly, as if I was speaking a foreign language.

"Look, I know you're hungry, everyone is, but we need to be organised about this." The suggestion didn't seem to make them happy. "There's enough food for everyone if we distribute it properly. Some people in the camp need it more than us."

I moved behind the counter, beneath the locked cash register was a pile of carrier bags I grabbed, then went to my pocket, bringing out the list of people staying in the *Sunlit* complex.

"There are nineteen chalets to feed according to this." I thought of Dobbs and revised my estimate. "Eighteen, I mean. We can bag up food for each of them. The rest is yours."

There was grumbling from a couple of the men dressed in huge fisherman's jumpers, a pair who wanted to take a pile of everything they craved, meat pasties and sugary snacks, do nothing but indulge themselves until they were sated. Fortunately Pete and the others understood my logic and the majority won the day. These were basically placid men, IT professionals who had passed through life without even considering criminal acts until today. They worked sedentary jobs and were content to treat themselves to food and alcohol and do what was expected, accustomed to obeying orders as long as they came from the appropriate authority. None of these men were natural rebels, and the sudden madness of their vandalism was only inspired by the overpowering appetites ruling their days, hunger that rendered them unable to think straight and the motivation for this larceny. It was the same irrational passion which kept them eating, even though they knew it was bad for them, when every expert and doctor and close family member told these men that gluttony was a killer. Here were addicts desperate for a fix, brains intent on satisfying a craving as they broke in, and it took my intervention to bring them back to civilized ways. I wasn't particularly entitled to tell anyone how to behave right now, but those who'd seen me overrule Dobbs yesterday knew I wasn't to be trifled with.

Pete helped me bag up the groceries, a mixture of almost-fresh milk and bottled carbonates, basic foodstuffs that wouldn't require preparation, because it seemed most chalets would have run out of electricity by now. Soon we had a score of plastic bags on the shop-floor, all containing cereal and snacks and essentials, one each for men I invited to gather anything else they wanted from the shelves and freezer, one saying there might be enough power on his meter to operate the oven for a while, perhaps cook some pizza and chips. He led the others back to his accommodation in an upbeat mood, ready to prepare a veritable banquet, the scarcity and rationing of this morning long forgotten.

I left Pete guarding the remaining groceries, packed some cans of soup and extra bottled water into my allocation and went to 364 where Alice was mopping Natasha's face with a cloth she'd moistened with water from the freezer compartment. On seeing the provisions I brought with me Suzie became elated and boisterous, stealing the bag to warm up some soup for Natasha, that girl who was awake now but made no sense, sounding delirious whenever she spoke, Alice shushing her as she tried to cool the fever.

Wallis looked like a spare part here, sitting at the table to watch proceedings, detached from all this feminine nurturing. I told my friend I had an important task for him and he accompanied me back to the shop. Once there Pete opted not to leave, talking with Wallis as they kept an eye on the premises together, content to perch on the counter and snack while I began distributing food among the inhabited chalets.

Starting from the back of the camp, I walked past that charred shell of an upper level chalet, wondering again what had caused the fire. The wind was subsiding a little, although it still whistled along the balcony as I knocked at Dave's door.

"You the new Dobbs?" Dave asked when he saw me, hair matted and mouth grinning. Getting laid last night had improved his mood no end, Dave looked younger today.

I tried to form a smile but mention of Dobbs had led to a variety of unsettling thoughts. "We managed to find some supplies."

"Airdrop was it?" He opened the door. "Want to come in?"

"I've other deliveries to make but I could use your bathroom."

"Number ones only." Dave led me inside where I greeted Adrian, in the lounge reading last week's newspaper. I'd expected to find more disarray, another all-male mess, but these quarters were refreshingly ordered, rubbish in the bin, belongings tidy.

"We've no water to flush with." Adrian confirmed.

"It's the same everywhere." I moved to the bathroom where the situation was much worse. The stink of dried urine pervaded this room, piss glistening on the toilet bowl's rim. After relieving myself I tested the light switch but nothing happened. They were out of electricity here too.

"Now then Jay," Dave said as I returned. "When do you think we're getting out of here?"

I told them tomorrow, gave the men the story behind yesterday's aborted trip into the outside world, how I hoped the situation would change by Monday, staff back to operate the barrier and let us out. Although what the *Sunlit* employees would make of the fact we'd looted their shop I didn't know, quickly changing the subject.

"Any more thoughts on the fire?"

Adrian blew his nose extravagantly. I put him in his late twenties, about six foot and slim, the kind of genetic heritage that doesn't stop at orange hair, permeates the skin with freckles, makes even eyelashes appear ginger.

Dave turned to him, "Didn't you hear someone out on the veranda before it started?"

Adrian nodded. "One person, he had really heavy footsteps. I was on the sofa and I wish I'd got up to look but at the time I couldn't be bothered."

"Might be a good thing you didn't." So it sounded like a big man. Here was a suspect but still no motive.

"I didn't remember it until after the fire. You don't think someone walking about is strange."

"Not in a camp this size."

"Then I thought about it and there was no reason for him to be out there." Adrian rubbed his forehead. "We're the only ones staying in this block and he wasn't coming to see us."

"Right." I moved to the door. "Look, I've got to get going. There are hungry people out there." Dave saluted me, a gesture not obviously ironic. "If you think of anything else or see something strange, let me know, alright?"

They agreed and I walked along the balcony, towards the smell of burnt furnishings and smoke which grew stronger as I approached the end chalet. Glancing inside, I found a scene of devastation. Number 629 now contained nothing but the charred and twisted remains of furniture, a pile of ashes in the centre of the room like the site of a bonfire. The walls were blackened or burnt white, and a layer of embers covered the partially melted radiators, this conflagration having spread into the damaged kitchenette and similarly gutted bedroom but no further, the walls between chalets enough to keep the blaze localised.

There was no smell of fuel and the close stink of recent flames was difficult to endure for long. I knew I was getting distracted, standing there hypnotised by these incinerated ruins, what was left of the beds and chairs, unable to discern from the melted plastic of the smoke alarm whether it had been disconnected, or simply failed to work. Time was passing and I needed to get back to distributing supplies, feeling again like a local hero who feeds the impoverished because the authorities won't, although my neighbourhood was this holiday camp, not some poor ghetto slum.

Absorbed by these visions of chivalry, I retrieved two bags of groceries from the shop, Wallis and Pete deep in conversation, talk of fantasy movies they were looking forward to seeing back in the world. I went to Silvia's chalet first, enjoying her gratitude and telling the woman of my suspicions, how this morning's blaze might have been started deliberately. Then I asked if she had managed to get any sleep last night, to which Silvia replied Lindsay must have stayed in James' chalet, because her part of the block had been wonderfully peaceful.

Next up was Anthea, and I found Ejiro inside her accommodation along with a couple of other youngish men who looked worse for wear, not even close to recovering from the previous night's activities. They said nothing as the woman dressed in black accepted a delivery from me, Ejiro not even looking my way. Perhaps he didn't want to see that bruise on my jaw, the stiffness in my upper body.

Then it was back for more. I managed three bags this time, remaining focussed on my gallant fantasy, to feed everyone here and make our final day in camp bearable. Alfred responded to my knocks with congratulations on this work. I barely had time to hear him before moving on again, spending long minutes convincing Cheryl it was best if she allowed me a brief period of access, hearing her repeat the rigmarole of shifting that barricade, opening the door a crack at last.

I began reciting my Good Samaritan spiel but Cheryl wasn't interested, snatched the bag from my hand with a muttered *thanks*. Behind her, I saw Catherine coming back from the bathroom. The girl definitely looked better, understood where we were and what I was doing. Unfortunately she regarded me with the same hostility and suspicion I saw in Cheryl, deflating my pride and making me realise food alone couldn't resolve the tensions between people stuck here. The resentment of these girls wasn't so easily quelled.

Resolving to dally no longer, I put hubristic thoughts from my mind and just got on with it, hitting a snag almost immediately when I found no one in the chalet my list said Theresa was supposed to be occupying. Thinking back, I recalled the scene in reception, how Theresa had badgered that girl at the desk to let her stay with Julie. Cursing myself for not thinking straight, and having to walk further because of my confusion, I pressed on towards chalet 467. This block was close to the first aid point which had been functioning earlier in the weekend and I checked for signs of life on my way past. The hut was all shut up now, securely locked and unlikely to be as easy to break into as a chalet. In fact, it looked easier to knock through the cabin wall than kick down its reinforced door, and there was no guarantee I would find anything useful if I did smash my way in.

There was no answer when I banged on Julie Newman's chalet. I stood there for a while, wondering what to do, dark clouds approaching overhead, their texture promising another downpour. These women could hardly be anywhere else, the communal areas of the camp weren't open and neither of them could drive, not that they'd have been able to get off the site if they could. I considered the possibility they might have been invited somewhere else, but nobody except Alfred was friendly enough with Theresa to entice the women away, and there had been no one in the bearded man's chalet when I visited, less than half an hour ago.

Perplexed, I checked the window and saw that the curtains were drawn tight, put my ear to the door and listened hard, hearing only a couple of distant bangs from somewhere inland that sounded like army exercises, two seagulls bickering nearby. Finally a soft snuffling came to my ears, a sound I couldn't quite place, definitely human and emanating from within.

"Theresa? Julie?" I called. "Open up, it's important!"

No response, and nothing when I yelled again, asking the person inside if they were hungry or thirsty. I decided to leave the bag on the ground outside, shouting for them to come out and collect the supplies before leaving. I headed back toward Wallis and Pete then, still bothered by the unwillingness of those women to come to their door.

Halfway back to the shop I realised what that unfamiliar sound had meant, somebody was weeping in there. I knew I ought to find out the cause but realised any investigation might make a bad situation worse, terrify Theresa and Julie as I forced my way in when all that was wrong amounted to homesickness or disproportionate anxiety or some kind of mild medical ailment. Changing direction then, I returned to Alfred who was happy to help, made knowing remarks about where I'd obtained the food while we walked back, as if robbing the shop was somehow akin to stealing office stationery in the grand scheme of criminality.

"Can you hear her?" I whispered when we were outside 467, watching Alfred listen with his head cocked, beard angled towards me.

"Yes, yes. I believe that's Theresa in there crying." Alfred moved his face to the pane from where the sound rose, speaking into the window. "Theresa? It's Alfred. Could you come to the door please?"

The weeping stopped and then there was silence. I watched rain begin to fall behind, the walkway overhead preventing us from getting soaked. I was about to ask Alfred whether we should think about forcing our way in when I heard the sound of movement, a slow shuffle that resulted in the door coming unlatched.

"Ah, there you are!" Was how Alfred greeted her, as if Theresa were some happy-go-lucky child he'd briefly lost sight of at a fairground. "Would you mind if Jay and I came in?"

She let us into the lounge, that interior intensely gloomy, the only light from a tiny kitchen window illuminating dust motes in the air. Plates and cups were piled in the sink, waiting to be cleaned by water that might never arrive. Alfred sat next to Theresa on the sofa, the woman wavering like a flag in the wind as he placed an arm around her, uttered reassurances and attempted to make her be still. Theresa leant forwards, both shoulders folded into her body, holding a balled up wad of toilet paper she used to absorb the tears running down her face.

"Come on old girl, you're fine now." Alfred promised. "What is it? You can tell me."

There were two bedrooms in the chalet, one with a few clothes on the bed and the other neat as a hotel room. I wondered where Julie was. In the lounge Alfred didn't seem to be getting any sense out of Theresa, just more tears and halting, irregular breaths. Heading into the bathroom I got an answer when my entry was blocked. Pushing my way through the narrow space between door and wall, I saw what was preventing my access. Julie had slumped there on the hard floor, must have slipped on a pool of water near the shower and fallen, cracked her head and been left dead in an instant.

Chapter Fourteen

I didn't even try and find a pulse, Julie wasn't breathing. Her limbs were splayed out at unnatural angles and a flannel nightie covered much of the woman's fallen body, mousy hair mussed but framing an expression I wouldn't soon forget, some intermingling of astonishment and terror. In death Julie was compelling in ways she'd never been while alive, for the first time the woman demanded my attention, caused me to put the toilet seat down and watch over her, knuckles pushed into my cheeks.

The uneven bathroom floor had no mat to absorb puddles, water that must have spilled from behind the shabby curtain yesterday or early this morning, back when the supply was still on. Slippery and dangerous, particularly for a barefoot inhabitant still drowsy from sleep and left unsteady by the sedative she'd taken, that shock of the cold on the soles of Julie's feet caused the woman to lose her footing and tumble headlong to the floor, her skull dashed and neck broken, death instantaneous.

First Dobbs, now this. The weight of these people gone from the world pressed down upon me, a centrifugal force dissipating my resolve, leaving me powerless and uncertain. I'd suffered the responsibility of saving Natasha, tried to put right what Dale had done as best I could, come out the other side briefly optimistic and determined to feed my colleagues, keep them all safe until we returned to the city, get everyone back to their loved ones. Now the sight of Julie there, the victim of a tragic accident, it made me realise how naïve I'd been. None of these people were within my control and I couldn't prevent bad things happening to them. All my efforts were futile, pointless. I knew how Dobbs felt then, unable to talk himself into carrying on. Norman's escape route, that knife through his own heart, might have been incomprehensible to me at the time, but I was coming to understand.

A grey head, Alfred's azure eyes and unmistakeable facial hair appearing in the doorway. He took in the deceased woman and me sat there, staring at her corpse, my face empty of anything.

"Damn it." He said. "So that's what's poleaxed the old girl." Turning his attention to me then. "How are you bearing up son?"

"It's too much Alfred, I don't know what to do."

"There's nothing you can do now. Leave this to me."

I felt like unburdening myself, telling everything to this man with the ability to remain calm in the face of tragedy, self-control that must have served Alfred well through his years of military service. He could share in the toll, learn that Julie wasn't the first dead body I'd seen this weekend. The horrors were piling up, along with my knowledge no one could stop them. I'd unwittingly put myself at the centre of this accelerating devastation in a way that helped no one, a new Jay at odds with the persona I'd adopted for much of my life, jumping in like a man of action without considering the impact on my own mind and body. I hadn't thought about the implications, whether I was capable of overcoming everything this trip had in store. Now it felt like I'd overestimated my own strength, needed to divide and share this load if I was going to carry on.

But I didn't say anything to Alfred, instead following him back to where Theresa whimpered, witnessing the scale and depth of her grief. Theresa Barnes had lost her best friend and there was a son waiting in London who no longer had a mother. He would be anticipating Julie's return right now, trusting she was fine, that the company had taken care of her. My faculties clicked back into place. Everything I'd been through felt miniscule compared to the grief of these people. I would manage whatever lay in store for me here; there was no alternative.

"I'll see if I can get her to eat something." Alfred told me, collecting the bag of consumables I'd delivered. "You should go back to your chalet and do the same Jay. You look as if you need to."

I tried to think how long it was since I'd last eaten. "You sure you'll be alright?"

"Positive, there's nothing more you can do here." He opened a bottle of water and went back to Theresa, telling her to *drink this*. It was an order, not a request, and the hunched woman obeyed.

"You'll find me if you need me? If anything else happens?"

"Of course." After she'd swallowed a few mouthfuls, Alfred removed the bottle from Theresa's lips. "Now go and pull yourself together, for God's sake. You'll do no good if you carry on racing around and end up collapsing."

Outside I slammed the door without meaning to, came out onto the grass to be hit by the kind of rain that feels light at first, like a cobweb you can brush off, but within minutes your outer garments are soaked. I zigzagged between chalet blocks, the bad weather bringing dusk in before its time, dark clouds making the day seem as if it were ending hours early.

Back in 364 the girls remained in my lounge, Suzie talking softly to Natasha on the sofa, the pair putting aside their differences when confronted with this emergency. Nat took in everything the taller girl said, nodding and muttering between shivers, their heads almost touching.

Alice was in the kitchen tidying and when she saw me the girl ceased whatever automatic chores she'd found to occupy her time, came over to give me another negative appraisal, say I didn't look so good. I took her hand and led Alice into the bedroom, sat on the mattress and told her what had happened to Julie Newman, feeling everything in my head, all that had gone on today, slowly becoming more manageable, even as I ruined Alice's mood, made her smiles morph into alarm then sadness.

"Alfred's staying there." I explained. "It was horrible, seeing her like that. It made me wonder how much more…."

Alice interrupted, pressing a finger to my lips. "You can't think like that." She admonished. "Whenever things would get bad, back when I was young, my dad used to say, 'there are only problems and solutions'."

"Practical man."

"Nat's lucid, we've made her better, at least for now. If we can get her to a hospital she should be fine."

"She looked so tiny out there." I thought of Natasha lying on the beach, battered by the elements. "We need to get her checked for exposure, pneumonia, all that…"

Alice's eyes burrowed into me. "We've got food inside her, we've got her warm, that's thanks to you." Her hand fluttered to my cropped hair, moving down to stroke my cheek. "You look terrible Jay."

"Thanks."

"Come on, I think there's some soup left."

"Alice…" I drew her to me then, long and chaste and tight, and when our embrace ended I felt ready for whatever the world might throw at me.

She went back out and I sat at the table to be served tomato soup I ate with white bread, the creamy broth stimulating my appetite as I became engrossed by the food, devouring it hungrily. When I looked up from the empty bowl I saw the other girls conversing, rain coming down behind them. Natasha regarded me the way a pet watches television, distanced from understanding somehow, while Suzie's attitude to my presence was faint distaste, her antipathy rising as I reached for my cigarettes and lit one, feeling truly relaxed for the first time all day.

The tall girl cleared her throat loudly and rose. "Come on Nat." She cried, much louder than necessary. "Let's go back to our chalet, you might be able to breathe in there."

I held my tongue until they were gone, enjoying every inhalation while Suzie helped a swaddled Natasha out of the door and back to 368. Alice came and sat at the table with me then, smiling sadly.

"She's worried about second-hand smoke at a time like this." I waved the cigarette before me like a sparkler. "We carried that girl back here from the beach. Suzie thinks I'm going to deliberately harm her now?"

Alice observed my outrage with measured calm. "She knows. There's something about Suze that's always got to be hostile with someone. Nat's not fair game anymore, so she's moved on to you."

"Why? Why does she need to have a go?"

"That's just the way she is." The girl's voice was soothing, it melted away my offence. I wish I could have shown her equanimity, Alice's acceptance of the flawed.

"I saved Natasha's life." I asserted, sounding more than a little petty.

"She knows."

I exhaled. "Well, that's not entirely true. It was Wallis too." I thought of him, out there on the shoreline. "Mainly Wallis, if I'm honest."

"Where *is* Wallis?" Alice glanced around the chalet, as if expecting to find him there, hidden among the grey furniture and beige carpeting like some drab chameleon.

"Still at the shop." I looked at my watch, how long had I left him there? An hour, two hours? "Damn, I'd better go get him."

I left my cigarette burning on a saucer, heard Alice telling me to wear a coat as I dashed out.

Pete and Wallis were still there, faithfully guarding the groceries that remained but understandably a little bored. Even for two men with a borderline obsessive knowledge of popular culture, topics of conversation will eventually dry up. Wallis sat against the counter, bouncing a multicoloured rubber ball on the shop floor as Pete examined the racks of utensils and handicrafts, like he'd suddenly developed a fascination with sewing kits.

I wiped the rain from my face and apologised to both of them, said I was feeling unwell, had gone to lie down for a while, a flimsy excuse I wasn't sure if Wallis believed. There were half a dozen carrier bags left so I returned my attention to the list, found a pen under the cash register to circle the remaining chalets, those places I hadn't yet visited. There was Derek and Sandy in 680, a couple of other occupied blocks toward the centre of the site, Roger and Sid last, with or without James.

The men agreed to take a couple of bags each, finish their errands quickly, and that was when I saw Roger through the broken shop window, striding purposefully towards the car park. Deciding to take this opportunity and save myself some time, I grabbed his groceries and followed.

The shop and everything still in it was abandoned now, all those goods we were happy to leave for whoever might be passing. I carried a bag in each hand, kept up a brisk trot through the mist of rain, feeling the jolt of my feet hitting the tarmac with every stride. I needn't have bothered hurrying, Roger had stopped at his car to open the boot, bending over with his upper body inside, rummaging around for something.

"Hi Roger!" I yelled, causing him to reappear from the trunk. "I've got some stuff for you and Sid!"

"Cheers." The black patches around Roger's eyes were bigger than the last time I'd seen him, while his usually tidy clothes were rumpled and rain-drenched, the zip of his trousers half undone.

"Uh, no problem." I stood there, getting wetter as Roger delved into the dark boot of his car. "Shall I take it across to your chalet?"

He emerged holding an old hammer. "I'm going back now." Roger said, locking the vehicle.

I walked with him, wanting to see for myself how Sid was coping without his medication, faintly concerned at what this man with the determined walk and unreadable expression was going to do with the tool he wielded absently. Trying to make small talk a couple of times as we negotiated the blocks, I asked about Roger's well-being without getting a reply. Either he was ignoring me, or genuinely hadn't heard. The rivulet of a wrinkle on the side of Roger's face twitching faintly every time I spoke.

Roger unlocked the door of chalet 676, this accommodation not far from the northern edge of the complex. Inside the place was crepuscular and murky, the legacy of twilight outside and an absence of power. The only lights came from two green dots, the fire alarm and some other device, high up on the opposite wall.

He retrieved a torch from somewhere within and turned it on, lighting up the furniture which had apparently been arranged at random. I cleared a space beside the kitchen sink for their supplies while Roger called out to Sid who answered with a bout of choking, phlegmy and harsh. I took some water in to him and found Sid in bed having failed to rise today, the very picture of a housebound invalid. Roger kept the room partially illuminated as I encouraged Sid to sit up, put a hand in the centre of his back to support the man as he drank, noticing the mug he'd been spitting in on a bedside table, trying not to dwell on its viscous contents.

From somewhere nearby there came a faint panting that gradually grew in intensity and pitch, until it became clear the sound originated from the next room. Soon the noise became impossible to ignore, and I looked up at Roger as Sid continued to sip from the bottle.

"James and Lindsay." Roger said, keeping the light centred on that wall beside me. "They're treating this trip like a dirty weekend."

From the next room a female voice began to squeal, either from pleasure or discomfort, I couldn't tell. Sid shifted his weight to lean over the side of the bed, hawking spit into the mug.

"Did James ever find his laptop?" I asked, trying to deflect attention from the increasingly frantic copulation happening nearby.

"Hasn't mentioned it, too distracted I think." The noise next door was becoming more frenzied, that male voice uttering ferocious grunts. "They're at it day and night, I can't believe he keeps going that long naturally." There was disgust in Roger's voice. His attention switched to that man I was supporting. "You still with us Sidney?"

Sid nodded weakly and I left the bottle of water within his reach, heard the bed next door moving in time with those cries, wondering how the pair could find it in themselves to ignore the larger circumstances, indulge their new-found infatuation when all around them people were deteriorating, dying like animals.

Perhaps there was a positive aspect to this, at least James' passion for the young temp kept the lid on any disagreements with these two other men, a contrast to Friday afternoon when he only cared about accusing them of laptop theft, the first threat of violence I'd dealt with this weekend. Roger disappeared from the room now, leaving me in the darkness next to Sid. I thought about the other instance when I'd seen a laptop recently, in that staff chalet where employees filmed themselves having sex. I'd been so distracted by the unpleasant sight, so caught up in my unwitting voyeurism, I hadn't realised that might be the same computer, stolen from this chalet when no one was around by someone with a spare key, that kid Neil or another member of staff.

There was no proof it was the same machine of course, I'd have to show the laptop to James to be sure, and I suspected it would have been spirited away by now. I'd look pretty foolish if my suspicions were wrong, breaking into Neil's chalet to discover it belonged to him, had been acquired honestly, bought by parents or saved for over long weeks working at *Sunlit*. But if that *was* James' machine I'd seen through the window, as the obese girl prepared to straddle that acne-speckled teenager, it would certainly tie in with the presence of other electrical goods in Neil's chalet, meant everything had been taken from visitors like us, people staying here in the complex.

The thought left me more than uneasy, less the theft itself and more the notion camp workers saw guests the same way a parasite sees its host, to be exploited in the most fundamental way. If there was no sanctity around the possessions we had brought with us here it wasn't much of a stretch to suggest that those with control over events had no respect for individuals either. That led me to the belief they were willing to tamper with our existences, manipulate visitors' minds and increase the discomfort of our bodies, actions far from hospitable and stretching into the sphere of illegality. Had they turned off the water supply and knocked out the phones? Abandoned us here with no means of escape?

My ruminations were interrupted by the sound of sudden destruction from the lounge, objects smashing against each other with force, the clang of metal and shattering glass. I left the bedroom and almost walked into a wall before successfully feeling my way along the corridor. Roger was in the kitchen, partially obscured by an open cupboard, his torch on the worktop, its light picking him out as he swung the hammer.

"Roger!" I yelled. "Be careful!"

The man was panting, stepped back to take another swing at the meter, a shard of glass flying towards him as the hammer made its impact, narrowly missing Roger's face. "I don't care!" He shouted back. "I'm not having another night like this!"

James emerged from the bedroom and I caught a glimpse of Lindsay sprawled behind him before he closed the door. It was difficult to make out much through the gloom, but she appeared to be naked and sprawled at an unnatural angle, restrained in such a way her body had to remain still. Lindsay's lover was red-faced after his recent exertions, had thrown on a t-shirt and too-short jogging bottoms to regard this vandalism quizzically. Roger stayed intent on his task, bringing the head of his hammer against the exposed dials. It rebounded off the electricity meter with a *clang* and slipped from his grasp, hitting the wall behind Roger before falling to the floor.

"What's going on?" James asked fuzzily as I moved to collect the hammer, Roger gasping before me. There was nothing wrong with his course of action, particularly in light of my recent understandings, but Roger was going about it the wrong way, unfocussed and flailing, in danger of damaging himself rather than the meter.

"Let me try." I said, ushering Roger out of the nook to give me the space to take over.

"Is this wise?" James asked tentatively.

"Shut up." Roger told him, and before James could respond I aimed for the workings of that metal box. I tried to avoid the casing and smash the machinery instead, take out that slot where tokens were inserted, putting all my anger at what had been done to us into the swings, causing plenty of damage but with little overall effect, raining blow after blow down on the unsuspecting meter.

Just as I was feeling the results of my efforts, arms aching and torso pained from earlier injuries, one particularly forceful thwack caused some setting or other to fall into place. The lights came on, temporarily dazzling us, and I dropped the hammer with an extravagant moan. Sound arrived too, from the TV that must have been left on. While I recovered in the kitchenette, staring at the mess I'd made of the cupboard, the other men seemed to forget their differences, moving nearer to the television screen.

"Jay...." Roger called, calmer now, his voice apprehensive. "You might want to come and look at this."

I went over to the set, black and white footage shot from a high angle playing on it, images of men and women in living quarters much like these, the same sofa bed and furniture, an identical layout to the surrounding rooms. We watched these individuals, most in their thirties or forties, play some kind of drinking game on a floor strewn with newspapers. One was passed out, flat on her back beside the main group. I didn't recognise any of these people, they certainly weren't from our company, but the situation felt eerily familiar, perhaps because we knew it so well.

"What's going on?"

James stared intently at the image. "They were being filmed."

"But who *are* they?" Roger demanded, mystified and emotional. "Why are they showing this?"

I'd been right. "Someone's fucking with us." I said.

On the television a woman downed a shot of something dark and everyone cheered, a portly man making some kind of weak joke as he moved a hand up to caress her knee. James went closer, his body partially obscuring the set, tall enough to reach up beyond the TV on its wall bracket, grasp that box resting on top.

"What if this isn't receiving?" He pulled at the oblong box we'd assumed was some kind of digital receiver. It came off the mounting and James put his fingers in that hole near the front where a green light was flickering, able to pull the casing apart. "What if it's transmitting instead?"

Inside that black shell, removed from its position above a television showing previous inhabitants laughing and drinking, was a tiny camera. James held it up for us to see. A high-tech device, like those used in CCTV across this closely observed country, this was a means of sending images from the chalet to who-knew-where, and was filming our every move.

Chapter Fifteen

"Deactivate it!" I ordered James, sounding like some desperate official addressing a bomb disposal expert.

He wrenched at the cables, the man's ungainly fingers trying to disconnect the power. My hand moved over the lens of the device, feeling the camera pan sideways with a shudder as I prevented it capturing any more footage, like a bodyguard blocking out press photos.

After long seconds the construction came apart, that tiny pinpoint of light which had shown it was active disappearing, pieces of the camera dropping from James' fumbling hands, as if this were some kind of living threat. There came a crunch as I crushed the device under my shoe, the three of us standing there, staring at its remains in silence, as if we'd been struck dumb.

A muffled voice came from one of the bedrooms. Outside the rain grew heavier, hitting surfaces and blowing against the windowpane.

"What the hell?" Roger muttered at last.

On the television the group in the chalet had reduced to three, a woman passed out on the floor while the portly man stretched to kiss and grope a younger girl. I moved to turn the set off and unplugged it from the wall, resisting an urge to smash the screen in with Roger's hammer.

"What now Jay?" James asked, as if I were in charge. I decided not to disappoint him.

"Get this place ready to accommodate people." I stabbed a thumb in the direction of the nearest bedroom. "Untie Lindsay and get her decent, as decent as you can."

"Okay."

I turned my attention to Roger. "This is the only chalet with unlimited electricity, that means anyone who needs warmth or hot food should come here. I'm going to make sure they do."

Roger nodded, James look pensive. "What are you going to do?" He asked.

"I don't know yet, but what *you're* going to do is make this place a kind of emergency shelter. I want you and Lindsay acting as Red Cross workers when the others arrive, looking after anyone who gets here." I met his eye, James' bland features seemed to have slackened somehow. "You're going to put lusts aside and concentrate on helping people, alright?"

"Alright."

Roger watched James go into the bedroom. "Do you have any idea what's going on around here Jay?"

"I will have." I sounded determined. "Just get the radiators on, heat up some soup for Sid, tidy this chalet and make it as roomy as possible." I took in the messy lounge. "You're going to need to fit a lot of people in here."

Back in 364 Wallis was napping on the sofa, the sudden and plentiful supplies of the afternoon having taken their toll. The power had finally run out while I was away, meant that green speck above the TV was more obvious. I moved through the dark now, draping a tea towel over the camera that filmed our lounge, waking Wallis gently, a hand resting on his shoulder blade. He listened as I described Roger's chalet being converted into a well-lit refuge, the urgency of getting our sick colleagues over there as soon as possible.

He nodded drowsily and sat up. I passed Wallis his coat and our map of the site, asked him to brave the rain and go to Theresa's chalet. There he should find Alfred, tell the bearded man about chalet 676, how he and Theresa would be better off in that outpost of heat and light towards the back of the camp. Thinking of Julie then, dead in the bathroom, I told Wallis not to go inside, just explain the situation then leave. Once I'd packed him off, I went down the balcony of our block.

The girls were gathered around candles in the lounge when I arrived to tell them the same thing, about a cosy refuge not two minutes walk away where they ought to go immediately, if only for the sake of Natasha's health. Suzie helped the pale girl up and they set off while I watched that green dot above their television. Beckoning Alice close to me, I whispered it might be a good idea if she told Cheryl and Catherine, convincing them to relocate too. Despite the male presence in that power-burning chalet, they'd be better off there. Suzie could always form a buffer between those girls and the likes of James.

Alice agreed, asking me if she should stay with them to ensure everyone got along. I shook my head, told her to come back for a while and be with me. People would have to cooperate with each other for once, they weren't children. Besides, I needed her here when she was done, there were issues to discuss.

Taking a couple of those miniature candles the girls had brought here, either for emergencies or more obscure feminine reasons, I went back to 364 and lit them, watching the shadows flicker on the wall as I smoked a cigarette.

I sat there for a while, thinking at the table, feeling my clothes dry as clouds of smoke lingered in the candlelight. When I was down to the butt I went over to the towel hanging atop the TV. Removing it, I took down the CCTV contraption, keeping the box faced away from me, disturbed by the thought of persons unknown spying on my actions. I dismantled the device then, much as James had earlier but with a calm, methodical manner this time, setting the pieces of apparatus down on the table, a neat row of wires and tiny speakers, the lens and plastic casing. Then I draped a dishcloth over the equipment, leaving only an outline of shapes, feeling like a magician about to smash some audience member's watch. I remembered Roger's hammer, that tool could have come in useful but I'd left it in his chalet. I was just thinking about getting it and maybe the torch too, when Alice knocked on the door.

"Jay?" She called. I let the girl in, getting her my almost-clean towel from the bedroom to dry her face and hair. Alice sat on one of those hard chairs opposite me and we talked across the pieces of camera, obscured between us.

"How'd it go?"

"Not great." Alice smoothed a fishhook of hair away from her forehead. "Suzie and Nat were easy enough but Cheryl took some persuading. Catherine's better, although she seems to have caught Cheryl's anger. I don't know where those girls get the energy to be so pissed off."

"It's understandable."

"They've been through a lot, sure. I just think there are better uses of time and effort right now than plotting some kind of hazy revenge against Dale."

"You tell them that?"

"God no, they wouldn't have taken any notice if I did." She sighed. "I finally got them to 676 though. There's like, ten people in that chalet now. I saw Lindsay for the first time in ages."

"It's only been a day."

"Yeah, I guess." Alice fixed me with her gaze. "She's got bruises and bite marks all over her you know. It looked like some of her hair had been pulled out. I saw this red patch on Lindsay's head she was trying to hide. I wanted to ask about it but there wasn't any privacy…"

"Alfred and Theresa there?"

"Alfred was helping out, Theresa looked terrible. She wasn't talking much either, first time ever." Alice massaged the side of her neck with a hand. "They let her have the sofa and put Nat in a bedroom. I had a word with Suze about sticking close to Catherine, I think the men were making her nervy."

"Sounds complicated."

"It wasn't that bad." The girl leaned forward, her elbows on the table. "Alfred was organising everything, I saw Wallis."

"Where is he?"

"He was going back to the shop. See if he could salvage more food for everyone, now they had a way to cook it."

"He's a good lad."

The girl moved her fingers to stroke my arm. "What about us Jay? Are we going back to that place you've made? There's not much room."

"Maybe you should." My hand held hers, the girl's touch pulsing through me. "I'm going to put an end to all this."

She squeezed my fingers. "Then I'm helping you."

I found a smile. "Thought you might say that." My other hand moved to the tea towel before us, pulled it away. "The first thing we need to do is find out who's responsible for this."

Alice stared at the components. "What is it?"

"CCTV."

I started by telling Alice about Roger taking a hammer to their electricity meter, progressing through everything that had happened. How we'd realised everyone was being filmed, that footage of past occupants broadcast on the internal channel, no doubt showing more exploits from past visitors, even now.

"But why?"

"To monitor us, for somebody's sick pleasure, who knows?"

Alice fiddled with the camera parts, running her fingers over the lens. "Then why play film like that if they don't want us to know what's going on?"

"Maybe they thought no one would get the power back on. Maybe whoever's doing this has become complacent. I don't know."

The girl looked puzzled, put the piece of glass down. All this second-guessing was getting us nowhere.

"What I do know is that this doesn't have anything to do with our safety." I pointed to the outside world. "Whatever's happening out there, whatever that army outpost was protecting us from, it provided somebody the ideal opportunity to toy with us, play around with our lives for their own amusement."

"But who are they?"

"Think about it Alice, who has the power to wire these chalets on a closed circuit?"

"Only the camp higher-ups I guess."

"Like the owner."

"Sure, okay. But who is the owner? How do we find him?"

I remembered the name on that email in Dobbs' chalet, Sinclair something, the badly written message promising his *Sunlit* holiday camp could provide everything our company needed for its team-building weekend. He had to be the key, the individual in charge. Maybe this faceless man was sitting there now, watching film from those chalets where the CCTV hadn't been disconnected, events transmitted to his base, wherever that was. It couldn't be far, this part of the world was too isolated, didn't offer the likes of control facilities or modern studios. There were hardly any buildings of note around here, and someone like that wouldn't want to be far from the action, preferred to remain where he could keep a close view on everything.

"We should go to the dome." I told Alice. "The answer's there."

Easier said than done. When we got to the main building I found the front entrance locked, as was that side door by the pub. Even the fire exits were secured, this structure impossible to break into without making enough noise to alert those inside, and I'd only do harm to myself if I tried to force entry. Alice and I ended up standing outside the *Splash Zone*, rain falling on our heads, looking at each other expectantly, as if waiting for divine intervention. I was aware of the potential for more CCTV filming this complex, kept checking the walls along the building's side, expecting to see that telltale green light on a mounted device, the camera changing positions, angling itself to follow us.

Alice brought me back to the reality of the situation then, staring over my shoulder as she spoke. "What are those blocks over there?"

"That's the luxury accommodation." I remembered the security guard I'd seen enter an apartment two nights ago. "Probably empty but we might as well check."

We approached from the front, near the tennis courts. There were ten blocks arranged in two E shapes containing chalets one to ninety-six, the grass moist and slippery underfoot as we circled the accommodation, hearing an avian coo from somewhere nearby. The lights were off in these chalets and my sleeve grew increasingly sodden, wiping the rain away from my face. When the road at the back became visible, lampposts lighting the camp's edge, I caught Alice's attention.

"That's the…"

"Ssh!" She pointed to the block on our left where a downstairs chalet was illuminated. I moved to get a better view and saw that pig-eyed security guard I last encountered escorting Dobbs from the party on Saturday evening. He was cooking something in the kitchen, facing away from us, and I was careful to remain out of sight, hugging the shadows.

"Will he have a key to the dome?" Alice whispered.

"I think so."

We sheltered under the upper balcony, observing this squat man who resembled a kind of fat goblin. He shovelled food onto a plate then collapsed down to watch television. Moving closer, I realised he was enjoying some kind of prime-time panel show, the set positioned to his left. He chuckled intermittently at the jokes, this programme of a type we'd been denied all weekend, told the aerials were out, that such entertainment was impossible. His picture was perfect and I could see the guard spitting bits of chicken on his clothes as he laughed. Alice pulled at my arm then, afraid I was getting too close.

"It's okay." I told her, confident I could take the man out if it came down to it, although I preferred not to test this theory, he might have been carrying a knife or some other weapon. Luckily the slob was far too engrossed in his meal and the bantering contestants to notice me peering in the window above his head.

I approached from the side, telling Alice to stay out of sight as I took in the chalet, that man gobbling his dinner on the sofa while I checked the interior.

There was nothing in the lounge or kitchen to draw my attention, although the door to the bedroom was open and the light on there. I had to squint to see what appeared to be some personal effects on his bedside table, a wallet and what looked like a bunch of keys.

Disappearing from view just as the security guard struggled up from his seat, I ushered Alice away from the chalet to a sheltered area under some stairs.

"Did you see anything?"

"What we need is inside but I can't get it while he's there."

Alice chewed her finger. "I could do my damsel in distress act."

"What?"

"You know, pretend to be lost. Ask him to come and help a girl get her bearings." Alice fluttered her eyelashes like a dizzy bimbo, I couldn't help but grin.

"You'll have to get him well away from this area so he doesn't see me." She nodded. "And give me a few minutes to force the door."

"No problem, I'll bet he hasn't had any female attention in a while."

"Not from someone like you." I kissed her lightly, my lips touching the top of a glistening ear. "I'm going to stay here. You approach from the other side and call for help or something."

"I'll meet you at the front of the dome afterwards." She touched my face. "Hurry."

The girl disappeared, skirting the blocks as I positioned myself behind one of the industrial rubbish bins, able to see along the pathway leading past the man's chalet. I revealed only a sliver of my face, was nearly impossible to see in the darkness of the area, and relaxed for a moment then, leaning on the wet plastic of a waste receptacle, feeling my joints throb and the blood pound through my head.

Her call came in the air, a distant and questioning *hello?*, as if some foolish visitor had stumbled into the area and lost track of her whereabouts. The cry was repeated as Alice came closer, until the guard must have been able to hear her, in spite of the televised clamour.

Sure enough, when Alice got to the middle of the three blocks that framed her presence his door opened.

"What you doing here?" He demanded.

Alice came closer, opening her coat once she was under the veranda, the better to reveal her body shape. When she spoke again the girl's voice had grown husky. "Hey you. I'm Alice." She gave a breathy giggle. "I must have got lost."

"Steve." Inclining my head, I saw them shake hands.

"Could you show me how to get back to my chalet *Steve*? I've lost my map and it feels like I've been wandering around for *years*."

"Dome's just over there." He pointed. "There's a sign at the front, it shows all the blocks."

"Could you take me there?" Alice simpered. "I'm afraid I won't be able to find it."

"Give me a minute." He disappeared inside and I moved out of view, waiting for his door to open then close again. These sounds were followed by inane patter as Alice asked the guard what he did, telling Steve she was a PA at our company, how the weekend hadn't gone quite as planned, but she'd kind of enjoyed it anyway. Perhaps the babble was kept up for my benefit, or maybe Alice wanted to annoy this man, get Steve so irritated he wouldn't try and escort her back to whichever chalet number she gave.

When Alice's voice had faded into the distance I moved out from under the metal steps and went to the chalet, trying to nudge the door open with my weight. There was precious little give, soon I was having to take a run up, worried this was taking far too long as I barged against the wood, my shoulder taking the brunt, feeling bruised and tender as it struck again and again.

After my tenth desperate charge the door finally gave and I burst inside, greeted by minor celebrities chortling at their own jokes on the TV and the remains of Steve's greasy meal abandoned by my feet. In the bedroom I grabbed his bunch of keys, opening the guard's wallet to find five twenty-pound notes I also took. I checked the violence done on my way out, seeing I'd splintered the lock and cracked a door panel.

Steve would soon know his keys were gone but still I fiddled with the lock, trying to push the metal back into place and provisionally latching it, managing to leave the place close to the way I'd found it, at least until you tried the door.

Glancing around furtively, I rushed back to the road. I was assuming Steve would take the quickest route back to his accommodation so I avoided his path by going the long way. Hunched up in my coat, my feet splashed through puddles as I circumvented the camp and approached the dome hesitantly. I stayed close to the edge of the chalet blocks in case Steve was still there and when nobody was visible at the front of the building I closed in, looking round and up, trying to work out whether any cameras were filming the front of the dome. That was when Alice appeared from the shadows.

"Get them?"

"Yep."

It took me a while to find the right key, there were about twenty on the bunch of varying shapes and sizes, but once I got us inside and locked the double doors behind me I felt safer, which wasn't particularly rational. We had no idea what lay in store for us after all.

"Where to?" Alice asked, serious now. I raised a finger to the ceiling then strode up the stairs, another key opening the door of that main hall, my eyes trying to adjust to the lack of light in that first-floor hallway. Inside the bar was dimly lit, enabling us to make our way to the other end of the space, nerves jangling as we passed the dance floor, that curtain-covered stage on our left.

Near the DJ booth was the door marked *Private*.

"I didn't know this was here." Alice said as I went through the stolen keys again.

One of them turned. "Got it."

Then we were through, up another stairway towards the dome's top level, a passageway with several doors, one directly to the left and two others where the corridor ended. This section of building smelt of chemicals and bleach, like a hospital but with a competing odour underneath, something musty and ancient. I felt myself about to sneeze, pausing to hold my nostrils together until the urge passed, Alice watching me with concern. She knew the slightest noise would reveal our whereabouts to any people here, those who might have been in the nearby rooms.

Trying not to sniff, I put an ear to that door on our left, hearing nothing but my own breathing. When I eased down on the handle, it gave and we crept inside, into a darkened room divided in two by a partition. In the first section there was a television on a desk beside a video recorder, shelves containing hundreds of tapes nearby, all labelled with dates and some kind of capitalised code, cartridges called things like FGT-11/05 or SX3-07/09. I could just about make out the notations in the light from the TV, a screen that showed three men I didn't recognise brawling in a chalet. The lack of a soundtrack gave the footage an unreal air, one man with a shaved head and an angry expression rugby tackling another guy, a third failing to break up the altercation.

This must have been the office where the programming for *Sunlit*'s internal channel was scheduled. Another look at the row of tapes revealed that some were labelled coherently. They included a 'Promotionel Film' and 'Ads 2001', although the vast bulk remained undecipherable. I wondered if there was footage of me in there somewhere.

On the screen the one with the shaved head punched another man in the face repeatedly, breaking his nose and making blood appear, bubbles of black against his light skin. Alice had seen enough, slid the partition aside and I followed her through. We found ourselves in a cramped back room, barely enough space for the swivel chair a controller would sit in to pour over that bank of screens before him. Nine separate monitors were arranged in a square, transmitting live images from places around the camp. A control panel gave observers the means to zoom and pan within the operable CCTV units, allowed a watcher to switch between chalets on a whim, and there were headphones for listening in on conversations, faders and dials to control the audio reception.

"Jesus." Alice muttered as we took in the scale of the operation. Two of the screens before me were blank. Perhaps they'd been receiving footage from the cameras James and I had taken apart. The other seven monitors showed locations and individuals unnervingly familiar.

On the top-centre screen Dale lowered his nose to snort something from the chalet's cluttered table, dried blood still on his forehead.

Below Sandy tidied Derek's lounge, the man coming up behind and squeezing his mistress through her dressing gown, crotch gyrating into the woman's middle-aged body.

Dave and Adrian sat talking in their chalet, faces beyond bored, two men waiting for something to happen.

Three of the overweight guys who had broken into the shop earlier were eating again, stuffing peanuts into their mouths, some falling to the carpet when they missed.

There was no movement whatsoever on the next screen, the chalet so tidy it looked as if it were unoccupied. I moved my face closer to the image, saw a dark stain on the carpet running past the bedrooms. I recognised the location then, it was the chalet where Dobbs had been staying.

A woman whose skin looked deeply tanned faced away from the camera and wept. From the shape of her body I could tell it was Silvia. The cause of her sadness wasn't immediately obvious, maybe everything had just become too much.

I looked again at the shot of Dobbs' accommodation. If it was being filmed all the time, they would have a record of me tampering with his body.

The last screen showed Anthea, naked and on her knees, being taken from behind by Ejiro. He pounded vigorously while another man, only visible from the waist down, forced his cock into Anthea's throat.

As I watched the rhythmic movements a third male came into shot, masturbating before he took over from Ejiro, pummelling Anthea who looked glaze-eyed and absent in some way. I began to grow queasy then, was about to turn and leave when a sudden movement on the top screen drew my attention.

Two girls arrived in Dale's chalet, standing either side of the drugged man who regarded them woozily, before endeavouring to get up. Catherine pushed him back down into the chair while Cheryl swung the hammer she held, striking Dale on the back of his head. He slumped forward and Cheryl continued her assault, shattering Packer's skull with half a dozen blows before passing the weapon to her friend. Catherine battered the dying rapist with even more ferocity, until the blood and brains oozed from his head to splatter the table, the girls regarding their handiwork with grim satisfaction.

I pointed to the attack, this murder happening before our eyes. "Christ Alice," I said. "Have you seen this?"

No reply, and it was then I became aware she was no longer present at my side. It was possible Alice had been gone a while. I turned to see where the girl was and felt a sudden pain in my arm. Tracy stood where Alice had been, the camp manager brandishing a syringe. I was about to rebuke this woman, demand to know what was going on and why she'd injected me like that, but I lost all sense of balance, my legs gave way and darkness engulfed me.

Chapter Sixteen

I woke up not knowing how long I'd been out, although it felt like a while. Coming into consciousness with a start, I expected to awaken from the nightmare and return to my regular life. The position of my body told me otherwise. I was tied to a chair and could feel cold floor under my bare feet. Recollections flooded to the forefront of my brain, overriding whatever bad things had been happening in my dreams, a palimpsest of memory telling me this reality was worse.

My body was bound tightly at the wrists and ankles, a gag made from old cloth wound round my head and into my mouth, soaked with saliva and tasting like a dirty sack. I opened my eyes, unable to see anything in the darkened room but sensing the walls pressing in. This place was confined as a cell, the stink of disinfectant stronger in here. Long minutes passed as I acclimatised, my surroundings bare and windowless and a single door before me, the only speck of light a green dot, visible if I twisted my neck as much as the position would allow. My eyes rolled up in their sockets to see this pinprick and its purpose became clear, I was being filmed.

I remembered Alice then, horrified at whatever had been done to her, knowing I had to find the girl. Beginning to flex and move my hands, I tried to get free but the ropes were too tight. All I succeeded in doing was rubbing my wrists sore, grimacing under the gag as my bonds failed to loosen.

A shaft of light appeared through the gloom, caused me to shut my eyes for a moment and evade this painful brightness. Tracy Ashborne had to duck as she came inside, the woman dressed in some kind of dark, shapeless smock and carrying a leather attaché case which was placed on the floor. She stood looking at me for long moments, hands on her hips, a medical professional assessing my demeanour.

"How are we feeling today?"

I tried to hit back at her faux-concerned manner, demanding to know where they'd taken Alice, an expletive-filled tirade. All that came out was a muffled drone.

Tracy regarded me thoughtfully, her features square and unattractive. "I don't think this is the right time to give you your voice back, not yet."

She knelt down and opened her case, the woman's face no more than a couple of feet from mine, searching through the contents as she spoke.

"If you're wondering about the girl, she's with Mr. Stenton. I'm sure they're having an interesting time." I lifted my knees as much as I could, stamped both feet down repeatedly, making an angry thudding sound.

"Now, now. You'd better keep your cool Jay. It would be so easy for me to administer another sedative, but Mr. Stenton wants all your faculties available."

The woman dug out a succession of objects I couldn't quite see.

"I've been working with Mr. Stenton for many years." She mused, standing once more. "A long time. He has such an original way about him. Yet so few bother to look beneath the surface."

The items in her hand were candles, long and yellow, the kind a mother positions in the icing of her child's birthday cake.

"He used to come to my hospital regularly because of his condition, that's where we met." She lit one of the candles and held it between her fingers, cast a glimmer of light over the two of us. "I was his favourite nurse. I suppose he must have seen something in me, something in the way I acted. Nobody had paid much attention to me before, particularly men." She blew out the candle. "Mr Stenton made me a proposition. If I worked exclusively for him I could earn a great deal of money. Far more than I would ever make in the NHS."

Tracy bent down again. "I wasn't sure at first, it was a big step. But I was young, I had no responsibilities, no husband, no friends, no family to speak of. There was nobody to talk me out of it so I thought; why not? Let's give it a try, you only live once."

My toes were eased apart, objects inserted into the gaps between them.

Tracy said, "I had my reservations at first, most definitely. Some of Mr. Stenton's more *extreme* ideas took a little getting used to. But he explained everything to me clearly, extremely clearly, and I came to understand."

The woman pushed candles between the toes of my right foot then rose to stomach level, arms resting across my knees and face looking up at me, close enough I could see black hairs protruding from her nostrils.

"I think you might have noticed this before." Tracy moved an arm out from under the smock to show me her scar, just as horrific and raw as the first time I'd caught a glimpse, back in her office. The damaged area extended most of the way to her elbow, this wound brown and scaly and uneven in places, it would clearly never heal.

"Sulphuric acid does that." She noted, tucking the arm away again and bending back out of view. "Eats all the way to the bone if you let it. After *that* I understood."

I heard the flick of a lighter, felt heat near the arches of my feet. Tracy rose, her hands around the back of my head to untie the gag and whisper in my ear, positioning herself in such a way the talk wouldn't be captured by that camera, filming above.

"It gives me no pleasure Jay." I heard her say. "I was trained to cure people, not harm them." The cloth fell away from my mouth. "But Mr. Stenton likes the noise, it gives him a kind of gratification. If I were you I'd yell and scream, pretend you're in a lot of pain. That way I won't have to take this to the next level."

Tracy threw the gag to one side, pushed herself up from my lap and backed away in one fluid movement. I coughed and spat on the floor, running my tongue over mouth and teeth. Down below I could feel the flames closing in on my flesh, and when the first drop of wax hit my skin I had to suppress an urge to cry out, the pain hitting me in a wave. Whoever this sick fuck Stenton was, I wasn't going to give him the satisfaction of hearing me scream, and I certainly didn't want Alice to know I was suffering, assuming she could hear me.

I bit my lip as the wax continued to drip, determined to master this pain. My face reddened and I felt like some weightlifter, a man who can't hold the barbells above his head much longer. This performance was upsetting the woman before me, that hypocrite who didn't want to think of herself as a torturer.

"Where's Alice?" I managed to blurt out, even as my flesh burned. "What have you done with her?"

Tracy grabbed her case from the ground and I saw the woman clearly then, her expression lit up by the flames. I realised how scared she was of this Stenton, Tracy's inability to gain the right reaction endangered her. She feared the self-restraint I was exerting with every ounce of my being. Despite those sizzling drips falling on my feet, I felt like I had some measure of control for the first time.

This sense of ascendancy didn't last long. The door flew open behind Tracy, allowing that goblin-like security guard to enter. Alice was over one of his shoulders, her jeans unbuckled and top on back-to-front, as if a drunk had dressed her in the dark.

I watched, horrified, as Tracy took another chair and the security guard deposited Alice onto it, the pair of them having to hold this flopping girl up, reposition their captive in order to bind her. From what I could see of Alice, unconscious beside me, she wasn't obviously injured, but I didn't know how they'd rendered her insensible, what those hastily applied clothes might be hiding. The thought of harm done to her terrified me, and I understood then how close we'd become, this girl with black hair half-obscuring her face, a body that threatened to slip onto the floor, that flaccidity causing Steve to push Alice's torso firmly and sit her up. However I ended this, I knew a failure to rescue this girl would mean I never forgave myself.

Gritting my teeth against the burning below, prepared to make my voice sound threatening as I condemned the abuse, I was cut short by the sound of another speaker in the room.

"Ah, Jay."

He was leaning before me to blow out those candles between my toes. Now Sinclair Stenton rose to his full height, under five feet at a guess, and it became clear this was the man I'd seen the night of the party, lurching across the hall with his spastic gait. Up close Stenton was even more hideous, glabrous and ill-proportioned, a swollen head above that skinny body, fierce green eyes and a weak, spittle-specked mouth. His face ended below the bottom lip with no jaw to speak of, just a nub of flesh, lumpy and tumorous, that tapered into the blemishes on his neck.

Stenton wore a frayed suit that might have been made to measure many years ago, had little interest in the goings-on nearby, those employees struggling to tie Alice up a foot away. Instead Stenton looked me up and down, like some businessman inspecting a line of prostitutes before making his decision. There were pains throughout my body, from aching head to blistered feet, but they fell away when I looked this man in his eye, became transfixed by the resentment and violence blazing there.

"You're depraved." I blurted, trying to work up enough fluid to spit in his face, saliva that wouldn't come.

"Whatever you say Jay." His voice was high-pitched, less effeminate than shrill. "Forgive me if I behave as if your opinion counts for nothing."

He glanced over at Tracy and the security guard, the pair continuing their attempts to bind Alice at the wrists and ankles.

"Come on." Stenton urged them, shepherding his underlings

towards the exit. "I need to be alone with Jay."

Tracy ducked out, followed by that fat man who had to angle himself sideways to get through the door. I gazed at Stenton, the owner of this camp, a man who had gradually upped the suffering of my colleagues all weekend. He stood before me, legs bowed, misshapen face alive with power, believing the logical conclusion to events was upon him, this trap Alice and I had fallen into, a place where he could inflict the hurt directly. We were Stenton's hostages, held together in hostile territory dominated by warring factions, except there was no government pressing for our release, no loved ones out in the world upping pressure on our captors. The spindly freak hadn't taken us for political reasons; this was all some kind of perverted power trip.

Waiting for Stenton to speak, I regarded him with all the contempt I could muster. He sucked dank air in over his gums, Stenton's mouth almost toothless, produced a staccato noise somewhere in the back of his throat, a *kkkkkk*. At last I realised he was laughing.

"Ironic Jay, isn't it?" He grinned. "Out of everyone they sent here, you were doing the best. You just had to take it that little bit too far."

"What are you talking about?"

"I'm just letting you know about the rest of them, all those people out there." He raised a hand close to my face, flapping wizened fingers as if performing a benediction. "They didn't do terribly well. I can't say I've much faith in them surviving a real emergency, but perhaps your employer will see it differently."

"They know about this?"

He'd chosen not to hear me. "Mr. Dobbs, for instance. Now there's a perfect example of a man who will cave in when faced with unexpected responsibility. Very sad."

"Norman." I saw him again, a vision of Dobbs, animated and patronising, then his lifeless corpse. A certainty gripped me, an understanding I hadn't allowed myself to possess until now.

"You murdered him." I spat.

"Come now Jay, do I look as if I'm capable of killing anyone?" From this distance I could see the lumps on him, protrusions beneath the hairless skin of Stenton's temples and the side of his neck. "Steve, on the other hand, can be very useful. Loyal too, like a dog."

He moved across the space in an unsteady motion, this captor's version of pacing a room. I wondered if Steve had lit that fire burning out chalet 629 too. It felt plausible in the light of those other crimes. Another violent act, designed to increase fear around the camp. I managed to hide our dead supervisor from everyone, but arson wasn't so easy to conceal.

"We've got footage of you Jay, in there with Mr. Dobbs, and film can be doctored to incriminate you further. There's no lack of witnesses to attest the two of you didn't exactly see eye to eye…"

As loudly as I could I said. "What do you want from me?"

Near the edge of my vision I thought I saw a flicker of movement from Alice. Stenton ceased his shuffling. "You can start by listening Jay. Listen, and perhaps understand."

I forced myself to concentrate on him, keeping my eyes away from the girl beside me, wanting Stenton to direct his attention my way. There was evidently some need for exculpation here, a secular madman's version of the confessional, his prisoner replacing the priest in this closed room. Or perhaps Stenton was simply savouring his hold over me, having a brawny man in the palm of his hand. Owning the camp gave Stenton a chance to indulge his evil genius fantasies, and this was the scene where I heard his back story, whether I wanted to or not.

"Do you know what neurofibromatosis is Jay?"

I shook my head.

"I won't go into specifics, you're probably to stupid to grasp the details." He made that noise again, the throaty *kkkkkk*. "Suffice it to say, neurofibromatosis is a medical condition I suffer from, and it's the reason I appear to you the way I do. This malady is something I've always had and it's incurable."

A pause that lasted an eternity. Images of this man as a child came into my head while Stenton considered his next words. A boy forever in and out of clinics or surgeries, the other kids laughing at him whenever he made it into school. The young Sinclair must have hated that powerlessness, feeling inferior to classmates who didn't possess a fraction of his intelligence but could still participate in physical education, run cross-country or enjoy the sports day. Those other children weren't watched as intently by the teachers; adults who believed the young Stenton might suddenly collapse or expire. He would have nurtured the feelings of alienation that came back then, resenting those fates that left dumber boys to waste their robust health on unmemorable lives.

"Very early on I realised this country, this world, was full of fools." He continued at last. "Some of them would try to sympathise with me, say they *knew how it must feel.*" Stenton's face was a rictus of loathing. "Idiots. None of them had the slightest idea about my experiences, the days when my body felt like a dumping ground for sickness. Each time I found a new lump I wondered if this was it, the one that would kill me."

The man seemed to catch himself then, came back to the moment, leaving his memories behind. "They were never malignant of course, so I went on living, and things changed over time."

Stenton bent over awkwardly, bringing his face close to mine, a face lurid in its ugliness. "Perhaps you had a similar epiphany Jay, whenever you realised the freedom money could bring, enough of it enables a man to do anything." His breath smelt rotten, like decomposition. "When I inherited this place, that's when my life began in earnest. Now I have the kind of place I deserve, this camp has become my fortress." The fury returned to his eyes then, Stenton's tone of voice moving from wistful to its default angry whine. "And *you* thought you could break in here and bring down everything I've achieved." The back of his hand hit me in the face, not powerfully, but hard enough to destroy any sympathy he might have evoked. "Fools."

I allowed my head to be knocked to the side, took the opportunity to glance at Alice. I couldn't see for sure, but it looked like her eyes were open.

"What I've arranged for you here, this is just a little game." My gaze was back on Stenton now. "No more of a challenge than the city you face every day, hardly more perilous than that world out there." He gestured. "Less dangerous, I would say. Here people have only to face what's inside themselves, whatever the worst of human nature can do." Stenton smiled. "We don't have terrorists or suicide bombers at *Sunlit* Jay, you ought to be grateful. But even without such threats, you people have really outdone yourselves."

I wanted to punch that smug face. "So what is going on out there Stenton?" I cajoled.

"The usual Jay, nothing to worry about." He sounded uninterested all of a sudden. "You ought to be more concerned with what's happening in here. I haven't decided yet what I'm going to do with you and the young lady."

"Wait a minute, hang on." Something in his words nagged at me. "You called this 'a game'."

"Did I? Well, that's what it is."

"My employer would see all this…"

"You're rambling Jay."

"No, no...." Should I believe it? "You mean the company knows what you're doing here?"

"*Knows* about it?" He laughed, harshly. "They *condone* it Jay. My word you're slow, what a big, lumbering dimwit."

His insults bounced off me. "They arranged for this to happen?"

"You would have me as a lone conspirator in this?" Stenton was acting offended. "*Of course* your employers knew what they were putting you through, that's the whole crux of the matter."

All at once a wave of agony engulfed me. "But, why?" I struggled to get out.

"You'd have to ask them." Stenton sucked at his bottom lip, the moisture there gleaming. "Unfortunately you're not going to get the chance." He paused, thinking. "I could perambulate a few of my own theories if you wish."

I coughed, hard and long. My mouth and throat were so dry, brain unable to accept we were pawns in some life or death scheme, concocted by our employers.

"Anything wrong Jay? You look pale. I'd offer you some water if I cared enough..." That *kkkkkk* again. "I digress. You asked why a corporation such as yours would bring its staff here and put them through all this. I suspect they do it in response to the current climate. With death and destruction everywhere, your employers see this as an opportunity to test their workforce, find out who is best able to cope with this new world you find yourselves in."

He was shuffling back and forth again, I had a compulsion to wrestle Stenton to the ground, make him be still, but my bonds weren't getting any looser, no matter how much I struggled.

"Something like this, it's a good way of finding out who to keep on board." Stenton continued. "After all, firms invest huge sums of money in you people over the course of a lifetime. They need to find out who is substandard, who isn't up to the challenge."

The man was enjoying these ruminations, lurching back and forth in front of me.

"Then there's the question of natural wastage. A great deal of money can be saved by reducing staff numbers. If an accident befalls one of you there's not the nuisance of redundancy. I understand the sums involved when firing someone can be quite large. No doubt the downsizing achieved this weekend has been to your employers' satisfaction, what with the aforementioned Mr. Dobbs, and poor Julie of course..."

That was when I lost it, wrenching at the chair like a madman, as if enough effort could bend the metal and let me attack this man, take Stenton out with whatever I had in reserve, bite his scrawny body or butt that bulb-shaped head, screaming all the while.

"Oh dear." Stenton backed off, trying not to look afraid as he was confronted with the bout of madness. "You really must exert stricter control over yourself Jay. No wonder you've found yourself in such difficulty, a civilised man knows when to leave well enough alone."

I was beyond words, yelling obscenities at this murderer before me, wanting to get at him and leave nothing, rip the man apart.

Sinclair opened the door and called outside. Within seconds the guard was beside Tracy on the edge of the room, the pair watching me bellow and threaten.

"Should I give him another injection?" Tracy asked, concern in her voice.

"No, no." Stenton was already on his way out, pushing past them. "It amuses me to see him like this. He'll shout himself out in time, and when he does we'll return to put an end to this folderol..."

Steve followed him out, asking Stenton what needed to be done. Tracy gave me one last glance before allowing herself to be led away too. Then we were in the dark, just me and Alice, that green speck above us. My cries of frustration sounded even more futile now, reverberating off the walls and coming back to my own ears, serving little purpose except to remind me that I wasn't holding it together.

Eventually I went quiet, remaining still for long seconds until the soreness in my vocal cords abated, unable to think of anything but the vicious rage gripping my viscera, nothing until a voice whispered from nearby.

"Jay." I looked over, caught myself staring at Alice and remembered that camera above us, turning away then. Black hair covered the girl's face, obscuring her lips as they moved. I lowered my head, hoping Stenton and the others wouldn't see me as I spoke, too absorbed in settling on their next move to observe us.

"Alice, you okay?"

"Yes. Can you shuffle closer?"

"I'll try."

Putting my damaged feet down flat and biting my lip, I managed to lift myself and the chair, moving both ever so slightly rightwards, a squeaking noise rising from the floor as, millimetre by millimetre, I approached the girl beside me. I prayed anyone watching would see my shaky form and think it another angry fit.

"What did he do to you?" I got out, between heavy breaths.

"Nothing, they just took my clothes off. Stenton made me stand there in the nude while he looked."

"All he did was *look at you?*"

"For ages, I'm okay Jay." She remained motionless. "Just get over here."

I redoubled my efforts, the scraping of metal setting my teeth on edge as I gradually slid across the floor. At last, when I was no more than a few inches away, I felt Alice's hands on my wrists, the girl reaching out to the back of my chair.

"You're free?" I was astonished.

"Played possum. They were in a hurry and didn't tie me up too well." Her fingers felt the coarse rope binding me, tried to work it loose. "Damn, I can't get any purchase. It's too tight."

"This is dangerous." I spoke into my chest again. "You shouldn't take the risk."

"We have to." Alice jiggled at the knot behind me, head facing the other way. "You heard what Stenton said, they've no qualms about killing us."

"We're on our own aren't we?"

It would have been difficult enough to untie me had Alice been able to see what she was doing, but attempting this blind wasn't getting the girl far at all. I knew that from her cursing since I was unable to feel much, the circulation below my wrists had been restricted for so long, both hands were entirely numb.

"Can't do it." She muttered, frustrated.

"Don't worry." I told her. "Get yourself free, I'll watch the door."

I waited for Stenton's return, positioning myself to obscure Alice as best I could, although if anyone had been watching they would have quickly discerned what she was doing. Alice bent over, endeavoured to untie the binding around her ankles as I kept my eyes on the entranceway. I was unable to see how far she'd got before a crack of light appeared, made me whisper at the girl to stop.

The sound of Alice rearranging herself, aping that position they'd left her in, then the door was opened. The security guard entered first, standing to the side with his arms folded like a bouncer. Stenton swayed in after him, a sick smile on his pale face.

"Well Jay, I'm sorry to say this is where we part company." Stenton wasn't getting too close, he didn't want a repeat of my screaming. "After due consideration, and taking into account the opinions of my staff…" He glanced behind at Tracy who emerged from the darkness holding her attaché case. With her dark smock and solemn expression, the woman looked like some kind of religious penitent. "We've decided to make this quick and painless, a nice shot of pethedine and you'll sleep forever."

"I'm going to kill you." I promised him, struggling against my bindings. Alice had definitely loosened the rope around my wrists, I could feel that now.

"I think not Jay." He watched Tracy draw fluid into a syringe. "Medical science doesn't have the power to raise the dead. In fact, I'd be surprised if your bodies were ever found."

He turned to the former nurse who placed the vial back in her bag, the syringe that contained a lethal dose held between her teeth. "The girl first. I want to watch his reaction."

She nodded, stepping round her diminutive employer who seemed almost gleeful now, crazed with anticipation. I pulled harder at my bonds, several fingers were out but I couldn't quite wrench my hand away. Tracy was quickly upon Alice, rolling up the sleeve of her top for a place to inject, bending over the girl to push that needle into her skin, drawing blood there.

Alice's movement was sudden and unexpected, a powerful right hook that landed on Tracy's cheekbone and sent the woman sprawling in the guard's direction. My right hand came free and I worked on the left one. Stenton took a step back, his expression changing from excited to fearful. Steve pushed Tracy aside and the stunned woman slid to the floor. The security guard made for Alice who stood, readying herself for his assault.

"Get back!" I yelled, pushing Alice away so that she stumbled against the back wall, diving between her and the onrushing man.

Steve hit me with a grunt, took us both crashing down, the chair still tied to my ankles, impeding me as we grappled. Stenton must have abandoned the scene then, scurrying out while Tracy tried to stand. I lost all sense of my surroundings, seeing only that assailant looming over me, trying to grip his neck as Steve punched me in the stomach. Unable to stand, I felt the accumulation of injuries leach whatever strength I had left.

Somewhere far away there came a *thwack* and a scream of pain. I was trying to get enough momentum to roll us over, but Steve was too heavy for me. His porcine features contorted with effort as the guard grabbed my head with both hands, smashed it to the floor with a *crack* that reverberated through my cranium.

The pain cut out everything else. I could feel Steve about to repeat the action, dash my brains out. Staring into the face of this man who was going to kill me, I watched his eyes glaze over with a look of incomprehension, the guard's body instantly going limp.

I lay there gasping, that man on top of me a dead weight, the back of my head nastily bruised, working up the energy to ask what had happened.

He was rolled off me and Alice released my legs from the chair at last, helping me to stand. That was when I saw the syringe protruding from the back of Steve's neck. Over in the corner Tracy had begun to cry.

"You alright?" Alice asked. Her face was hard, the power of life and death rising in this girl.

"Just about." I looked over at the wretched woman, failing to make herself small below us, thought of her boss and his crimes. "I will be when this is over."

With unsteady hands I embraced Alice, watching Tracy over her shoulder all the while. When we separated I gestured to the pieces of rope, discarded around Steve's body.

"Tie her up." Alice nodded. "I'm going after Stenton."

Out in the corridor I saw the door opposite had been left ajar, went through into a brightly-lit office, scrubbed so white the glare stung me at first. There was a laboratory feel to the extensive space, desks and filing cabinets and a set of steps going up. When I got to the top I found a hatch that was also open and I knew then I'd been right to come this way. Panicked and in a hurry, Stenton had taken the nearest escape route without thinking to cover his tracks.

I pulled myself up, hit by the rain coming down heavily, shutting the hatch behind me. This exit was a kind of extreme fire escape bringing me out beside the roof of the dome, a pathway round its circumference and a flag blown by the wind above me. A ledge rose to my waist and over it I could see across the whole complex, the roofs of chalet blocks and lights beside roads.

My bloody feet hurt with every step and the pain in my head was piercing. Still I could feel the anger roil, spurring me on as I loped along the walkway, knowing I would gain on Stenton even with my injuries, catch that cripple who wanted me dead, a man who had killed many times before.

The rain fell and cleansed me, felt good as it hit my skin. I flexed my fingers as the sensation returned, picturing Stenton, conceited and murderous, a man who believed he was entitled to exploit others, snuffing out their existences as it suited him, getting his own back on the world of men because of what nature had done, because he had the money and wherewithal to do it. My fury hardened then, became a corporeal thing, extrinsic and growing. I let out a cry and shouted his name to the night sky, knowing Stenton would hear me.

Silence then, only drops of water hitting the dome, a faint echo of footsteps coming to a halt behind me. I swivelled round and there he was, even smaller out here, the rain glinting on his bulbous head, hands up against my approach, as if that would stop me.

"I'm not the one you want Jay." Stenton pleaded.

"Maybe not." I grabbed the back of his suit jacket, my other hand circling an emaciated leg, lifting the man above my head as he screamed for me to stop. "But you'll do."

He was even lighter than I imagined, nothing compared to the wrath pulling my strings, anger that gave me the strength to hold Stenton up there for long seconds, offer this mistake of a man to the heavens, asking some deity to confirm I was right to extinguish his will, a personality more warped than his flesh could ever be.

Then it became too much, the man struggling and howling in my grip. I pitched Stenton over the side, heard his shrill cry taper off as the man fell five storeys to earth. And perhaps I was too detached, oblivious and distracted, but I don't remember a sound when he hit the ground, just a noiseless relief overwhelming me.

Chapter Seventeen

I stood there in the rain a long time, the shabby, semi-lit camp, and Stenton's broken body below, unable to move in the wake of what I'd done. Later I would rationalise it, telling myself repeatedly the owner of this place would have continued his murderous ways had I not acted. Stenton had no qualms about ending the lives of myself and Alice, so why should I regret his death? I was no different to a soldier, some grim-faced man on the battlefield who does what he must and cannot be allowed to regret the results, not when the world comes down to kill or be killed.

But just then, as my rage subsided and I was able to think clearly once more, the enormity of my deed, this revenge, it didn't seem so heroic. That deformed man hiding up here no longer posed a threat, not to me. In my anger I'd been drawn into the kind of savagery I had spent my whole life trying to avoid. We could have left after escaping from our bonds and forgotten all about Sinclair Stenton. That way I wouldn't be standing there, staring down into the gloom at his resting place, the man's blood on my hands.

"Jay?"

Her voice came from around the walkway. I pushed down at the swell of remorse inside me, telling myself the world was better off without Stenton in it, that this girl and others needed me to be strong, for a while at least.

Alice climbed through the hatch and came into view, looking up at the peak of the dome, at the flag with its cartoon animals flickering in the wind. That was when I appeared to her, drenched and hobbling.

"I heard something."

"You're getting wet." I said. "Go back in."

Inside the windowless room I found Tracy, all tied up and lying on her front. She was no more than a foot away from the security guard, a man who had been drained of life by her overdose of pethidine.

"What are you going to do with me?" The woman struggled to turn her head, observing my reappearance with scared eyes.

"Nothing." I told her, reaching down to search Steve's pockets, trying not to touch the dead man's skin as I sought out the bunch of keys he'd taken from me. "This is how they'll find you. *If* they find you."

Tracy's inability to move or stand reminded me of some lost sea creature, washed up and helpless on a beach. "You can't leave me here!" She cried, lifting her face from the floor to speak. "Not with him."

I studied Steve's shoes, they were clearly too small for me. "Can we not?"

"Listen to me Jay." She was pleading now. "I've got supplies, I can fix you up if you'll let me. Just get these ropes off and we can…."

Her voice was already so much background noise, zoning out entirely when I glanced over at Alice. The girl stood there, blank-faced and silent, prettier than ever. I signalled to her that it was time to go.

We left Tracy calling after us and went down, back into the hall. Alice asked if I was okay to walk and I said I was. Not far to go now.

I unlocked the double doors and then we were back outside, steering clear of the area that contained Stenton's body. Giving Alice my chalet key, I made sure she still had hers, told the girl to go over and pack our stuff.

"How are we getting out?"

"Leave that to me." I felt in my back pocket with rope-burnt fingers, the site map was still there. "Meet me by the shop in ten minutes." Alice hesitated, as if she didn't trust me to get anywhere by myself. "Go!"

Dobbs' chalet was just the way I'd left it, his car keys there on the bedside table. I grabbed them, noted the vehicle logo on Norman's key fob, then went into the bedroom. His body was in the same position too, partially concealed by the side of a bed.

"I'm sorry Norman." I told him.

The shoes on his feet were about my size. I thought about the water and mud and hard concrete I'd limped across to get here, that risk of treading on something abrasive between the chalet and car park. Apologizing to Dobbs again, I sat on the bed and untied his shoelaces, slipping my sore feet into Norman's loafers. I shuddered as the pressure sent more pain through my nervous system, somehow managing to stay silent.

Keen to get away, I struggled back outside, hoping this was the last time I would ever see the interior of a chalet. I'd experienced enough of this identikit confinement, pulling the door shut as I left.

Gripping the handrail in case I lost my footing in the unfamiliar footwear, I descended the metal steps, taking the path back to that exit road where Alice waited for me before the broken shop window, sheltered by the eaves with a suitcase and my rucksack on the ground beside her.

Alice was glad to see me, even after such a short time, listened as I told her what we were going to do. She agreed and we stood there for a moment, staring out at the rain-battered accommodation, a spasm of conscience hitting me, for everyone we were about to leave behind, the lost and the sick and the dead. I thought of Wallis in a chalet with the others, knew they would look after each other in there. Soon the guilt passed, Wallis was better off not coming with us, I didn't really know what we were doing, leaving like this, and a leap into the unknown would be achieved more easily with two. Going back to rescue one man couldn't be done, not without alerting everyone else, people who would want to come along more than Wallis. I felt bad about abandoning my friend without a word, it wasn't the first time I'd done it over this weekend, but I knew he wouldn't hold it against me, not when Wallis understood everything I'd been through.

Alice snapped me out of my trance, picking up her suitcase and telling me to get moving. We circled the parked vehicles of my colleagues, found a model that matched the logo on Dobbs' key fob, a purple family saloon. I stored our luggage in the boot, passing the car keys to Alice who got in the driver's side and started up the engine, manoeuvring the vehicle away while I trudged towards the exit.

At the barrier I crouched down to see. The rain was coming down in sheets now, restricting my vision as I went through the keys, praying the one that would give me access to the controls lurked somewhere on this bunch. Alice had the saloon idling close by and I must have been through most of the keys before I found the one that fitted, opening the metal box with its switches and buttons inside, electing to eschew subtlety, pressing them all in turn until I got the right result.

The metal pole moved upwards agonisingly slowly, becoming diagonal then vertical as I staggered to the car's passenger side, opening the door to slump inside, Alice accelerating out onto the coast road, warm air coming through the vents to dry me off.

She took the roads slowly, knew our route from the time we'd driven it in the minibus, slowed to check the signs when she wasn't sure. The car's headlights were on full beam, to illuminate our surroundings through the rain and because there were no other motorists to dazzle. As the adrenalin rush of escape evaporated I became aware of how much I'd been through, every part of my body contributing some kind of discomfort, from that dull, pulsing headache to the flayed skin of my toes. I tried not to think about the damage, checking the dashboard to see we had a third of a tank of petrol left and the time was just after five in the morning. Exploring further, I retrieved a map from the glove compartment, fiddled with that furry giraffe behind the windscreen, a toy that reminded me this vehicle once belonged to a human being, someone with feelings and quirks and loved ones, a man who had died needlessly.

Alice steered into the turnings of isolated country roads with stalwart concentration. The girl was clearly suffering from the same affliction as me, I could see it in her eyes, forced to cope with all the weight and horror that comes with someone dying at your hands. I wondered if either of us would ever come to terms with what had happened, ending the lives of that camp owner and his security guard, or if we were forever caught in some horrible web of memory, one that brought an aura of shame and contrition with us wherever we went. Worse, might we forget those deaths we'd caused, go on with our lives as if nothing had happened, a part of our humanity lost forever?

The car headed inland now, closing in on that place where the roadblock prevented our progress last time. I leaned forward in my seat, trying to anticipate the encampment through the downpour, and Alice must have been thinking the same thing because she slowed us down, keeping progress at fifteen miles an hour as we peered out into the night.

"It was here." She claimed, while traversing a particularly desolate part of road, fields and darkness on both sides.

I wasn't so sure, but as the minutes wore on with no sign of soldiers, I came round to Alice's way of thinking. When we approached a major junction I'd never seen from this direction I conceded she was right, the military must have packed up and gone.

We drove on, out of the county, onto wide roads and through villages, the inhabitants just beginning to rouse themselves from sleep. The rain eased off and a hazy sun struggled to rise. Alice flicked our fog lights off as we came upon other vehicles, tractors passing the other way and a delivery van visible in our wing mirrors, stuck behind and impatient to overtake.

For the first time in days I envisaged the wider world, my flat and its waiting bed, the sound of my parents' voices and Grace. I wondered how she was, what my ex would say when I told her about this weekend, soon deciding I didn't actually care for her opinions any more, might never again see that girl who had left me for another. Glancing across at Alice then, the one who had supplanted Grace in my affections, I realised something good had come out of this ordeal, in spite of everything.

A garage came up on our left and Alice asked if we should pull in, the fuel gauge low and neither of us sure if we would make it back to London on the remaining petrol. I found some of those banknotes stolen from the security guard's wallet, soggy and stuck together but still legal tender, and while Alice filled up I browsed the shop, greeting the middle-aged man behind the counter enthusiastically. This assistant eyed me with suspicion and I must have cut a bedraggled figure, limping around the aisles like I'd been hit by a car, studying the sandwiches and drinks before moving to the magazine display.

Usually I would have thought twice about going anywhere near the newspapers laid out there, but today was different. Questions remained that needed answering. I bought a tabloid and a broadsheet, scanning the latter back in the car while we ate. Alice flicked through the red top and we quoted news stories out loud to each other between mouthfuls, details of a chemical leak on the outskirts of the capital, an outbreak of some new virus among cattle that resulted in exclusion zones around the country, the culling of livestock by farmers. There were floods in South America, escalating tensions between several nuclear empowered nations, more terrorist suspects detained indefinitely across the UK for reasons unclear, but nothing to explain our experiences.

These newspaper stories were akin to the reports on any other Monday, the articles not too different from those despatches I read the last time I found a paper on the bus or tube. They didn't mention specific incidents, that shockwave we'd felt on the beach or the blocking of roads by the army, so maybe there was simply too much to convey. Perhaps the media had already moved on from whatever shocking events grabbed the weekend headlines, trying not to over-estimate the attention span of its readership.

I found I didn't much care anymore, reinvigorated by the food and drink, leaning over to stroke Alice's hair and kiss her on the cheek before the car started up again and we got moving, out into the thickening traffic.

Epilogue

Later Wallis would tell me what happened next inside the *Sunlit Holiday Centre*, how Monday began with a rap on the door of chalet 676, the noise waking those men who were sleeping in the lounge. Outside paramedics in their signature uniforms waited alongside a couple of men in suits, men Wallis assumed were from the company because they were telling everyone else what to do.

The occupants were given half an hour to find their possessions and pack them up, putting everyone into their cars or the communal minibus by noon, no guarantees any personal items left in the complex would be returned to them. Stretchers were brought out and Wallis saw Sid carried to one of the waiting ambulances just inside the entrance, a place where I'd struggled to raise the barrier no more than a few hours before. Nat and Theresa were helped into the emergency vehicles too, given oxygen and placed on drips where necessary.

My friend didn't linger to watch, Wallis hurrying back to what had been our chalet, seeing my stuff gone and understanding I must have left some time during the night. Wallis didn't have time to think about why as he rushed around, throwing clothes and toiletries into his backpack before scurrying off again.

On his way to the car park Wallis passed two paramedics carrying a body under a sheet. From his description of the shape, the way two men were struggling to keep the bulky corpse on their stretcher, I guessed it must have been Dale. Wallis took in the scene as he approached the minibus, no police on the site, just representatives of our employer ushering people to their cars, uninterested in preventing the survivors from seeing the dead bodies being loaded up and taken away.

He was directed to the bus where several of those who had come down with us waited, Anthea, James and Lindsay joined inside by Catherine and Cheryl, the latter staring at her hands. I wondered if Cheryl was trying to come to terms with what they'd done, Wallis unaware these young girls were killers. If he'd known my friend would have been uneasy in their presence to say the least, had he seen what I watched on a monitor in the dome. Instead he observed the girls' anger had evaporated this morning, that murderous rage having been vented as they sat there before Wallis with faces full of trepidation, like defendants who have been found guilty and are now waiting to be sentenced.

Everybody was avoiding each other's eyes in there so Wallis turned to look out the window, seeing Pete and a couple of the overweight men struggling to climb into their cars, Derek getting a lift back with Sandy, Suzie in the back of Dave's electric car, Silvia looking upset as she unlocked her vehicle. He saw a succession of beaten down faces, all tired and mournful, the bus passengers remaining in oppressive silence until one of the suited men got in the front, turned the ignition key and took them back to the company building in central London. The capable and healthy were told, in no uncertain terms, they would be expected to return to that workplace the following day, spend Tuesday in the office as usual.

Not me, I called in sick for the rest of that week, bandaged my feet and talked to Alice on the phone, sleeping for ten hours at a time as the weekend's events appeared again in my nightmares, rising from my subconscious in ever more horrific permutations. A surprising number of people did go back to our workplace straight away according to Wallis, found the supervisors, Giles Fairbrass and John and Nigel and Malcolm, back at their posts and acting as if nothing had happened, each of them impervious to questioning. Meanwhile Dobbs' desk had been cleared, all trace of the fifth supervisor removed forever.

Those colleagues who'd fucked and fought and abused one another must have left all that behind them somehow, returned to the professional reality, displaying their customary politeness in smoking areas or around the water dispenser. They were eager to gossip about some aspects of what had gone on, who had done what to who, but seemed unable to grasp the enormity of events, treating the deaths as more fodder for small talk, incorporated into time-wasting discussions along with celebrities and reality TV, who had gone home with that new temp after last night's visit to the pub. My colleagues didn't know it, but their lack of outrage was simply a reiteration of that lifelong pledge they'd taken to the company. Either that or, like Wallis, they had no other ideas about what else to do, returning to work out of habit, staying at their desks with heads down and minds on the screen, keeping themselves to themselves.

Alice and I went back briefly, handing in our resignations to different people and staggering the announcements so as not to arouse suspicion. I told my superiors I'd been offered a better position in a rival organisation while Alice explained she was moving back to America. Both lies of course, but after many evenings of long reflection and slow sex we'd become so paranoid about the corporation's methods, how far its power stretched, that it felt safest to misdirect them, keep our former employers off the scent for as long as we could.

Whenever inquiring didn't feel risky or intrusive I asked around, talked Wallis into making discreet investigations, finding that those worst affected by our team-building weekend had been paid off or blackmailed into keeping quiet. Theresa Barnes never went back to work, not even to collect the pharmaceuticals and spare clothing she had stored in her desk drawers. The company offered her early retirement, Theresa took it, and nobody ever saw her again. The absence of that irritating woman from the workplace wasn't much of a loss to them, although I believe Alfred kept in touch with her for a while. The occasional phone call, until Theresa's mental state deteriorated so badly she couldn't remember who he was anymore.

The families of Dobbs and Julie were easily silenced, frightened people used to doing what the powers-that-be advised. I managed to speak to a couple of the relatives who said company representatives had turned up on their doorsteps accompanied by uniformed officers, all extremely convincing as they took the families through those *tragic accidents* that had befallen their loved ones. The bereaved quickly saw that going to the media with any concerns they might have could only cause more sadness in the long run, as well as negating the generous compensation this company was willing to pay the next of kin.

Only Dale's parents turned down the approach, unwilling to meekly acquiesce, demanding a post-mortem be held instead, desperate to determine what had happened to their only son. That was when a gimlet-eyed man took Dale's father aside, ran a film clip that showing Dale as he carried Catherine into his chalet on that Saturday night, zooming in as the man forced himself on that unconscious girl, just before I intervened. Not the clearest of pictures, but sharp enough to make his point.

That left Dale's father to deal with his hysterical wife, try to bring her round to his new way of thinking without going into the motives behind this change of heart. It was a concealment of the truth she would never forgive him for, but at least it meant the image of Dale as her beloved golden boy remained intact. At least, that was what Dale's father told himself and he didn't invite any other opinions, I was the only one he ever shared the whole truth with.

That was how my former employers ironed out their problems after our return, with ruthless efficiency. Sid took long-term sick leave, while Catherine and Cheryl kept silent. Perhaps they'd been told footage of their violent act existed too, I didn't know. As for everyone else, they had mortgages to pay and children to provide for and while some were less than happy about everything they'd been subjected to, in the end it was easier to suppress irritation and curiosity, not rock the boat by complaining. Progressing with lives and careers was the pragmatic approach, never mentioning the events of that weekend unless they were in the presence of those who had experienced it too. Because good jobs were rare, and most of these people could never land a position with such excellent prospects anywhere else.

The company's representatives must have stepped in on the coast too, enlisting local police to suppress the facts of what had happened. Shortly after our return I found a news story on the internet saying the *Sunlit* camp was to be shut after almost sixty years. A regional reporter blamed the increased holiday options for working class families, that proliferation of cheap flights and budget vacations abroad. His angle was the job losses and impact on the local community, the piece didn't mention Sinclair Stenton. There was nothing on his penchant for voyeurism and violent death.

I trawl the web more and more these days, for suppressed information and news outside the mainstream, an increased level of engagement partially inspired by Alice. Her hunger to understand the world proved contagious as we became lovers, although I like to think it partly because of what the company did to me. They paid a lunatic to test us, to find out who would survive, and I often recalled Stenton's hints, that other corporations acted similarly. Neither of us looked for work after resigning, instead Alice and I found ourselves in the anti-corporate movement, now that we knew first-hand how capitalism discarded those who didn't meet its standards, that mercilessness in the pursuit of profit.

Some of the newspapers denounce us as terrorists, mainly the ones that are part of some larger conglomerate themselves. They write about the need for tougher sentences, more stringent laws to prevent the disruption we cause, even though our action never goes beyond the peaceable and the protests are always non-violent. That isn't to say we've never been affected by brutality, although it's invariably brought to bear against us, both by the authorities and the hired muscle of industry. The only act of vengeance I've ever committed remains the killing of Sinclair Stenton, and his face still appears to me every day, usually when I'm least expecting it.

One thing that surprised me was how easily I adjusted to the underground lifestyle. It helps having a beautiful girl in there too, Alice who currently sleeps at my side, curled up and dreaming, her swollen belly evidence of our child, coming into the world any day now. Alice's pregnancy finally gave me the time to set this story down, during the weeks I've spent nursing and watching over her. Our leader in the movement, Richard, always told me I should document what we'd been through, every time I was asked why we had left behind the conventionality and routine of the past.

Back then I would agree with Richard, but I'd always been too busy to find the time. There were demonstrations to organise and contacts to make, trips around the country for networking with like-minded souls. I was always preoccupied until that day Alice needed my full attention, when a virus struck in the middle stages of her pregnancy. Suddenly there was no putting it off any longer, I asked for a typewriter and enough supplies to get me through the writing process, then sat down to record what happened over that weekend last autumn. When she was well enough, Alice helped me remember, and I went back to those passages she saw differently, got my girlfriend's perspective to go with the impressions of Wallis. Alice added a suitable phrase here or a word there, until she was content I'd got as close to the truth as it was possible to come.

Seeing it here, set out in front of me now, I realise it *was* important to get the facts down. With our country the way it is, all those threats the public faces every day whether real or spurious, the smaller tragedies often get overlooked, forgotten in our everyday litany of foiled attacks and homegrown bombings. Richard has contacts in the media, sympathetic people who know he only deals in the truth, so maybe my story will be heard. I think it needs to be. People died over that weekend, and I don't want them to be forgotten. The world ought to know what happened, I truly believe that. Perhaps one day soon it will.